CW00504726

'You're rather a maddening fellow, Dobie
to be such a harmless chap and in reality y
harmless as a king cobra in a lucky dip. 1
going to have to deal with you accordingly

Sent into exile by those of his friends
still reeling from his exploits in *The St*
Professor Dobie arrives on the isle of
Cyprus) prepared to induct his students i
of Higher Mathematics. But the local g
or two in store for him . . .

Aided and abetted at long range by his
tic) companion Dr Kate Coyle and baf
effusions of a zonked-out young compar
a murder charge, Dobie – with his custo
aplomb – investigates the Amphitryon
intermingling of myth, reality and app
manner of political and sexual shen
divergent thinker if ever there was o

Fortunately they don't come any
Professor D and his wayward dither
a memorable final confrontation ir
legend is at last stripped away –
highly contemporary and unusual

THE MASK OF ZEUS

Desmond Cory

MACMILLAN
LONDON

First published 1992 by
MACMILLAN LONDON LIMITED
Cavaye Place London SW10 9PG
and Basingstoke

Associated companies in Auckland, Delhi, Dublin,
Gaborone, Hamburg, Harare, Hong Kong, Johannesburg,
Kuala Lumpur, Lagos, Manzini, Melbourne, Mexico City, Nairobi, New
York, Singapore and Tokyo

ISBN 0-333-57555-5

A CIP catalogue record for this book is available from the British
Library

Typeset by Pan Macmillan Limited
Printed in Great Britain by
Billing and Sons Ltd, Worcester

FOR RICHARD
who likes Cyprus

This is the sadness of the sea –
waves like words, all broken –

William Carlos Williams

Prologue

THE MASK OF ZEUS

by Adrian Seymour

The moonlit nights were best, when without turning on the electric lights he could move quietly from room to room, everywhere in the house, upstairs, downstairs . . . Well, not quite everywhere, but everywhere he chose, which was what mattered, the important thing, that at night choice should become action in this way, become movement of feet and hands and eyes instead of lines of words on white paper. Of course, being what he was he had no need to move feet or hands or eyes; he moved because he chose to, quietly, from room to room, acquainting himself with the appearance of this house, of this world, in the darkness, becoming an intimate of the night.

Appearances were what he had to get used to. To the fact that eyes that see can themselves be seen. For this reason he chose to move at night, when all or most other eyes were closed, though he found the darkness strange in itself, he being compound of sunlight and of giddying aether like some mysterious mutant in an SF story; from the wide window of the sitting-room he could look through those alien golden-brown pupils at those other mindless living-boxes with their lines of glass windows meaninglessly blank as the lines of print in an open book, though glittering sometimes with reflected moonlight, with light that came from outside, not from inside. Inside the boxes there was nothing. Only people. People, asleep.

Awake, they could make light by pressing a switch. They could make little rectangles of radiance, curtained off yet glowing in the stillness, behind which they too moved. Not as he *moved but as shadows; they were the victims of darkness and soon they would surrender to it. They would sleep. Inexplicable compulsion. Yet they had no choice but to sleep. He had given them none.*

As he had given no choice to the stars that pricked out their eternal patterns in the blue-black velvet sky behind and above the buildings, over the shadowy trees. They made light, too, as they wheeled across the horizon in their great circle; light, but not the true light. The real *light. Their patterns could be changed, and would be. When the* real *word was said, the word that was to the words in books as his own light was to those other lights . . . Not even said. Not even thought. But willed . . .*

Then the stars would stop. And change their names. And appearances would be otherwise. Destiny would be fulfilled. His own as well, though he himself had chosen it. The gods, the other gods, were after all there amongst the stars: Mars, Venus, Mercury, Pluto, though set on other courses; that, at least, was a way of looking at it. A poet's way, perhaps. I see the stars at bloody wars/In the wounded welkin weeping. *All lies, of course, and yet, and yet . . .*

He looked down at the sheet of paper on the typewriter roller. His fingers, poised above the keys, showed a strange reluctance to move, to make the needed addition, and in the end he took them away. Something had gone wrong already and he knew it. Morn the star of horn. Star the horn of morn. Or, if it came to that, QWERTYUIOPASDFGHJKLZXCVBNM *straight across the board, it all came to the same in the end. Stuck.*

Impotent.

Knowing, as always, that all he needed was there. Letters, spaces, punctuation marks; it was only a matter of putting them in the right order. The same with words, with paragraphs. A matter of knowing what. That had to be the trouble. The page he'd written, was it the beginning of something, as he'd thought? Or the end of something? Or neither? Until you knew that, it made no sense. Or not the right kind of sense. He didn't have to read through what he'd written again; he never did. The writing might pass, for a first draft. That wasn't it. Word was following word across the page in the customary manner. But . . .

He stared for a long while at the wall in front of his desk and some three feet from his nose; a blank wall, except for a handout calendar that hadn't been sellotaped there quite straight. He was back in the cage. A caged tiger. There should a plaque on the door of his room saying Tigris tigris; *what the hand dare seize the fire indeed. Not much of a tiger, ever, if you faced the facts. But at least a published and publishable tiger. A young man of flair, of promise. A young man to watch.*

Well, that's what people do. To tigers. They watch them go up and down up and down up and down up and down; there's not much else that a tiger's good for when it's in a cage. Facing a blank wall. And a calendar.

He heard the car drive up and park outside and a minute or so later the front door key turn in the lock, the door open and close. The zoo-keeper was back. It was feeding time, maybe. But the quick tap of heels on the tiled floor didn't lead to the kitchen. They led to the door of his room, where they paused. He waited for the door to open. Eventually, it did.

'Hullo,' he said.

He went on looking at the calendar. A hillside, tall spiky trees — cypresses, maybe — and a row of stone columns modelled out of icing sugar. Italy, he rather thought. Or some other place where he'd never been. Beside the desk there was a chair where she could sit down, if she moved a jumble of opened books out of the way. She did so.

'Where've you been?'

'Just down to the village.'

She looked tired. Her face was a little pinched, if that was the word, though also flushed from the heat of the summer night. On the heels of her shoes, smears of mud. Noticing them, she twisted one foot and rubbed the shoe gently against the edge of the brown patterned rug.

'So what's the latest gossip?'

'I don't think there is any.'

'Ah.' It was a pity he could never think of the right things to say. The implications of that question weren't, after all . . . Exactly. Very flattering. 'I've got something down at last,' he said.

'Oh, good.'

'Well, no. Not good. I'm afraid not.'

'Still, it's something. Isn't it?'

'I thought when I started that it might be. But then one always thinks that. Or one wouldn't start.'

She closed her eyes for a moment. 'I suppose not.'

'Tired?'

'A little.'

A little tired. He wondered what that meant. Surely you were tired or else you weren't? . . . Staring all this while at the blank wall in front of him. Perhaps if you weren't in a cage it would be different. But then she wasn't really a zoo-keeper. She was a caged animal, too, in a different way. You get tired, pacing up and down.

She said, in the end, 'May I read it?'

He pulled the paper from the roller and handed it to her. She opened her handbag, took out her reading-glasses, put them on. Then started to read. It was all very casual and yet very formal, like part of a well-practised ceremony. That was what it was. An established marital ceremony aimed at the relief of impotence. In other words, a going-through of motions. Still, it was important, in a way. Especially when motions are all you have left. Up and down, up and down, the patten moving steadily while the typewriter ticks . . .

'Science fiction? That's a new idea.'

'It's not that really. At least I don't think so. Maybe it's not fiction at all.'

10

'Well, but it might . . . Mmmmmm . . . ' Her head, bent over the paper, showed an escaped tuft of dark curling hair at the nape of her neck. The reading-glasses didn't diminish her obviously spectacular beauty, though sometimes they made her seem demure. Which she wasn't. Beauty, though, is sometimes a matter of unobvious things, like little undisciplined wisps of hair, the half-furtive rub of a shoe against the edge of a carpet. Often when you look for it somewhere, it's somewhere else. She took off her glasses. 'What's the matter with it?'

'Whatever it is I want is some place else. That's all.'

'Story of everyone's life.'

'Is it? Maybe. What do you think?'

'I'll admit I don't quite see where it's headed.'

'Nor do I.'

'It is the beginning?'

'I think so.'

'Well . . . Mostly I like it.'

'Good.'

'Though it's maybe a little pretentious.'

'You think so?'

'I mean . . . "intimate of the night" . . . That sort of thing.'

'It's a Robert Frost echo.'

'Oh.'

'No, you're right. It's lousy.'

'I don't think that.'

'You know, if I ever have to get a book out and look something up, I know it's got stuck, I know it's hopeless, for some reason I just can't . . . '

He stopped. She put the paper on the desk, put her glasses away in their case. Small neat movements of small neat fingers. 'Have you had anything to eat?'

'No. Not hungry. It doesn't matter.'

It really didn't.

He slid another sheet of paper into the roller after she had gone. Motions are important. Going through the motions. While she doth horn the star of morn And the next the something farrier, shit, how did it go? He reached towards the pile *of opened books, checking the movement as the door closed behind her. I know more than Apollo. I know it's hopeless. He stared towards the wall.*

But now his own planet was slowly rising. A prick of light, what else? in the distant south. Lifting itself above the horizon as the door clicked shut, in the same immense instant of astronomical time; an instant foreordained; a moment among countless millions of such moments, yet – because foreordained – determinable. Of such moments was his own calendar composed; written not on perforated pages but across the heavens and in starry signs, moments foreordained, predeterminable, and yet . . . he chose them. He chose them as at this particular moment he chose to be made a man, to be made a man, in the likeness of Adrian Seymour, that pretentious fart Adrian Seymour . . . Pretentious? What nonsense. He didn't choose to pretend to be. He was.

The strengthening moonlight commenced to outline his face as he stood at the window. A man's face. Adrian Seymour's face. Narrow, thinly bearded. The eyes no longer a glimmer of gold but a dull, uncomprehending blue and with lids that moved constantly, blinking, blinking. The mouth a mere slit, a sharp line of petulance. It moved; it smiled; everything was movement: mouth and feet and hands and eyes, all in constant motion, all in endless and meaningless quest. Where was the great inner stillness of Olympus? What could human beings understand of it, being twitched here, jerked there, in this weird puppet play they called life? And where was . . . ?

Ah, well. It didn't matter. It really didn't. What mattered was the action. The happening. The face, the hands, the feet, only means to an end. A means of brief escape from that stillness of total foreknowledge, the full recall of things that hadn't yet taken place . . . Yet, they said. And, not yet. A word that implied expectancy. Anticipation. Excitement. Of such things as these, he knew nothing, precisely because he knew everything. Only mouth and eyes and hands and limbs could resolve that paradox, resolve it in action. Arousal. What's to be a god but to enjoy? Yes, but how to enjoy, other than through abnegation? Through the forgetfulness of all that he knew?

A swan, now. Rising from the water in an angry white whirl of glittering feathers. Or a milk-white bull, great shoulders steering the bladed horns through arcs of vibrant power. Creatures obedient to the urge of a clearly sensed purpose, simple yet irresistible. Tonight the same purpose, expressed through another, a far more stimulating agent. A man. This man. Tonight I will enjoy Amphitryon's wife. The action simple, inevitable, ordained.

He sat carefully down in the chair and laughed, making no sound. Amphitryon, indeed. That field-marshal of words, that starer at walls. I am not he. I am still I, though appearances may deceive.

I am great Jupiter. And my words are thunder.

'Why do you keep looking at your hands?'

'Must have caught one of my fingers between the keys.'

'Oh. Does it hurt?'

'Not really.'

She sat down on the chair and crossed her knees. He wondered why she'd come back.

'You ought to eat something. If you're going to work late.'

He shook his head. He felt a little giddy. 'It's pretty late already. Did you eat something? . . . Down at the village?'

'Eat? . . . No.'

Better not insist. When her lips pressed together like that . . . She was nervous. He didn't wonder why. She often was. She started to pick up the books she'd moved from the chair and to leaf quickly through them, one by one. 'Hey, look at this.'

Nervous tonight, yes. But when he turned his head she was smiling. Reflectively, almost secretly. 'Where'd this come from?'

13

What she had in her hand was an old theatre programme, the covers yellowed but not too badly, the papers crumpled but not too much. 'Oh, I was just looking through some of the old Cardiff stuff . . . ' Scraping the bottom of the barrel, you might say. The past is past. John Dryden, Amphitryon. *Produced by Adrian Seymour. Big big deal.*

Nothing there to be proud of, anyway. Gimmicks, in the usual undergraduate way, substituting for talent; all the actors dressed in white or black or in combinations thereof, Alcmena making her entrance behind a bloody great hairy borzoi on a leash., A white borzoi, of course.

She was looking now at the signatures of the cast scrawled over the back page of the cover, her own at the top. 'You remember that dog?'

'I should say so.'

'What was the tyke's name?'

'His name? Shuffle.'

'Shuffle, that *was it. Should have got his pawprint.'*

'You should, yes. The star of the show. A born upstager.'

She put the paper back on the desk, still smiling to herself. 'You know something else I remember?'

'What?'

'I remember thinking you were a bastard in those days. A real conceited bastard.'

'While I, on the other hand, admired you very much.'

'I know. That's what got to me in the end. I was swept off my feet.'

Though it wasn't exactly admiration that he'd felt. You admired ability, a talent – not the simple projection outwards of youthful grace and beauty. You need more than that to be an actress, to resist more or less successfully the brutal buffetings of the roles one plays, of those countless occasions on stage when one doesn't pretend but is. *Not that she'd ever seriously intended to be an actress. Her talent was for mathematics and always had been. Ah, but she'd been admired, that was the point, admired and envied and, naturally, lusted after. It wasn't something that made things now any easier.*

14

*Looking at her again, he saw that she wasn't far off tears.
Not in itself an unpleasant condition; her eyes had been damp
when, standing straight-backed in her allegedly Grecian tunic
of virginal white, he'd seen her take the spotlight for her
curtain call; damp, and shining all the more alluringly
in the sharply focused brilliance. As indeed they shone in
that photograph on the wall in the sitting-room. Allure was
the key word. You needed allure, to play Alcmena. While
Jupiter—*
'It's no good going back to look for ideas. You said so
yourself.'
'I think I was looking for excuses.'
'You can't have it both ways. I won't let you.'
*What was she looking for? Now as then? A light, perhaps,
for her eyes to shine in? Something like that?* 'What do you
mean?'
'I mean you can use the one thing as an excuse for the
other, I don't mind that or at least I . . . But if you go on
making excuses for not getting anything done then it's all a
bit much, just . . . too much of a bore.'
'All I said was that I thought the two things might be
connected.'
'Getting it down and getting it up. If anything I'd say they
were opposites.'
'Only if you want to play with words.'
'You're accusing me of that?'
'Look, whatever the problem is, we're not going to solve
it by talking about it. I thought we were agreed on that.'
'It's your problem, sonny boy. Not mine.'
'It's like . . . when the lights go out.'
'What?'
*Put out the light and then put out the light. But not a
power failure, no. A loss of desire, rather, or maybe a loss
of will. In the Elizabethan sense, maybe; oh yes, they'd seen
the connection.* 'It doesn't matter,' he said. *They'd talked so
many times and yet they hadn't. Caged. Looking at each other
through the bars. Regret? Yes, of course there was regret.*

15

But that wasn't enough. The regret was for the light that had been extinguished already, not for the quiet darkness that was to come.

'All right.' She stood up. 'If you don't want to talk, then you'd better work.'

'It's not that I don't want to talk . . . '

He picked up the programme, stared at it gloomily. Programme notes. Written by himself, of course. When? He couldn't remember. Not by him, then. By Adrian Seymour. Some other fellow with the same name.

Jupiter takes on the form of Amphitryon in order to lie with Amphitryon's wife, Alcmena; from this union is to be born Hercules, greatest of mortal heroes. Similarly from this unlikely material does Dryden, in the footsteps of Molière, fashion a brilliantly amusing satirical comedy, not without profound political implications. We who have seen in modern Europe a resurgence of the law of tyranny . . .

The usual semi-journalistic rubbish. Why hadn't he burnt it with all those other papers? A dark wisp of smoke, that was all it was. Ashes at the bottom of the dustbin.

'I'm tired. I'm going to bed.'

He nodded. Staring at the wall.

His gold-brown eyes watched her as she undressed. He saw no grace in her awkward movements, read no awareness in her of the coming ritual; she was going to bed, just like she'd said. Yet even in the unthinking movements of a human routine a god can take pleasure; without routine, no revelation, no glory in the revealed godhead. In the heat of these summer nights she slept naked, with the window wide open, but first she would take her usual shower and emerge from the tiny bathroom fastening the sash of a towelling bathrobe around her waist. Uneasily, she sat down on the bed and turned her head to look out of the window, staring out into the moon-shadowed darkness as he had done; her bedroom, too, was small, the window a bare three feet from the side of the stripped-down bed, and in the absence of any night breeze it was warm and close; there were tiny drops of moisture at her temples and in the shallow clefts of her collar-bones where they slid under the soft white towelling. Her head was tilted to one side like that of a wary antelope, and as he watched in silence she took a cigarette from the packet on the night table and struck a match to light it, the sharp sputter of the flame illuminating more sharply the line of her brows and the lowered eyes lying deep in their hollowed sockets.

Political implications. Journalistic rubbish. All burnt, all black and twisted ashes, hers as well as his. She pulls the bathrobe down from her shoulders, lies back on the bed and is motionless, except for the movement of the arm and hand that carries the burning cigarette up to her lips and then lowers it again. A wisp of smoke. What of those other bodies, black and twisted? The law of tyranny? No point in asking such questions. Leave them to the journalists. Alcmena abides no question. No argument asserts my will. Tonight I choose to survey her unknowing nakedness as the falcon in the treetop observes its unknowing prey scuttling through the grasses, and even when she turns her head again on the pillow to stare directly at me, her dark eyes wide open and perplexed, I choose not to reveal myself, though already she feels the sensual warmth reaching out for her, enveloping her like the still heat of the night, disturbing her; she looks out of the window again, then towards the closed door, before raising the cigarette to her mouth again. Smoking in bed. A bad habit.

'There's someone in the house.'
  'What?'
  'I said there's someone got into the house.'
  'Oh, come on.'
  'Well . . . Please have a look round. Please.'
  'But how could anyone have—'

17

'Please.'

'Oh, all right.'

She sat down in the chair and rubbed her bare arms. She wasn't cold, though. Not cold at all. She was making a fool of herself, she realised that. She heard his footsteps moving to and fro. After a while, he came back.

'No?'

'No. What made you think there might be?' He plumped himself down at his desk again, blowing out his cheeks. 'Did you hear something?'

'I just had a feeling I was . . . ' She hesitated. 'Being watched. Being looked at. It got me worried.'

'Where? In your bedroom?'

'Yes.'

'That isn't possible.'

'All the same . . . '

'You're nervous.'

'Yes.'

'It's pretty hot tonight.'

Nervous. Yes. But he probably meant neurotic. And why not? If she was, it was all his fault. Though she felt irritated at herself as much as at him. Not that the cause of the mood mattered very much. The events of that evening would in themselves account for it, if you wanted to . . . 'It's not that.'

'Sorry?'

'I mean it's hot but that's not why I'm nervous.'

'Oh.'

He looked down at his typewriter, at the ranks of black keys glittering in the lamplight. He spent hours on end looking down at the typewriter. Or gazing at the wall. Never at her.

'There's something I want to talk to you about. Or rather tell you.'

'All right.' His tone, exactly as before. 'Tell me, then.'

'I got myself laid this evening. After you'd gone.'

'Do you have to put it that way?'

'OK.' He could tell that she was angry. Perhaps that was

18

natural. 'Phrase it any way you like. It's not a matter of how I put it, it's a matter of where someone else has been putting it, if you'd like to get around to thinking about that.'

'It's not a thing I much like thinking about.'

'I'm afraid you just have to make the effort.'

'Well, when did this . . . ?'

'I told *you.* Right after you left. And then again on the way back here. Since you ask.'

He looked at the typewriter. At the eight pages of paper in the wire tray. He knew there were eight pages but he counted them again anyway. In the end he said, 'You know, it's really a bit too . . . On top of the other thing . . . '

'I'd been seeing him before. As you should have guessed.'

What she wanted, he thought, was for him to ask questions. But he didn't intend to. 'I don't see how you can put that particular ball in my court and expect me to play it. You know I don't want a divorce. I'm against divorce.'

'As a matter of principle.'

'That's right.'

'A pretty convenient principle.'

'I don't think so.'

'I do. All *your* principles are convenient. They save you having to face up to facts.' She shrugged. 'I shouldn't blame you. He's just the same.'

. . . got myself laid. *It wasn't her usual habit to be crude. Verbally crude, anyway. That day's events had changed her somehow. Words aren't actions but they echo actions, reflect them like mirrors.* 'Some facts are easier to face than others.'

'It should be easier for you now that you know what they are.'

'Is that why you've . . . told me about it?'

'Of course. Why else?'

He picked at his fingernail. 'The trouble is it isn't a matter of what you know.'

'But of what you feel?'

'Well . . . That ought to come into it.'

19

'Certainly it should. And what you feel is nothing very much.'

'Oh, hell, you've got to give me a chance. I mean a chance to . . . get to grips with it, with this and the other business. I need more time . . . '

She lay down on the bed again, waiting for him. He watched her as he stood by the wide-open window, the star-hung sky behind him. Gradually he let his brooding presence still the movement of those stars, let the past and future merge with the present, the imperceptible become the infinite. Slowly, he took on imperfection. She had lit yet another cigarette, was blowing smoke whorls towards the ceiling. An amateurish puffer. Nerves on edge.

Imperfection there, too, of course. How could it be otherwise? She was human. She argued, quarrelled with her husband; already today she had committed adultery, as they called it. Now she was feeling excitement, triumph, guilt, all manner of incomprehensible emotions, raising her head to exhale another thin tendril of smoke, the angled light of the bedside lamp catching the tautened contour of her throat, whiter than snow, smooth as monumental alabaster, and watching her he could at the same time see himself taking shape in the long mirror, head and broad bared shoulders being formed in the dusky lamplight, human, human too. Bone, flesh and blood. Imperfection, yes, but with new possibilities inherent, a future predictable yet still to be built waiting for him there on the bed. What am I making? he thought, staring at the watching mirror-face, darkly, obscurely shadowed; or rather, what is to be made? He could hear as he moved forwards the slow, purposeless tick of the clock on the bedside table; clocks of course would go on though time had stopped; clocks were outside his province. Advancing, he saw himself from another angle, the great brown body vibrant with unearthly power and crouched down like a warrior's; behind it in the mirror the turned-down bed, the smooth arm and curved fingers that held the spark of the cigarette-glow,

20

the long pearly line of the uplifted neck. And the round clock face. Put out the light, he thought, hide the clock face from view. Lest she suspect. He reached out, pressed the switch. A sudden darkness came. 'Oh, my God . . . !'

'Yes,' he said.

'Is that you?'

'Of course it's me.'

'You gave me a fright. I didn't see you come in.'

'Often the way of it.'

'What?'

'Never mind.'

Leaning over her, over the bed, he tried to match his movements to those of his image in the mirror before remembering that it wasn't necessary; her huge dark eyes would shine in the lamplight but couldn't see in the dark and besides (he remembered now) he only did that when trimming his beard, the scissors clicking away between clumsy fingers, eyes half anxiously observing . . . Absurd, to need a mirror to check on reality, when reality was . . . was . . . but he didn't know what reality was, not any more. He had taken on imperfection. The clock tapped gently in the stillness and the typewriter answered it downstairs with a sharp irregular rattle, softened by distance.

'He's spaced out again,' the woman said.

'He's what?' He didn't understand.

'Up on cloud eleven. I tried to talk to him but I don't think he really understood.'

What was there to understand? The moonlight dappling the sheets, outlining the long naked body. He reached down for the pillow. Reach me a torch then, let me guide myself down the darker and darker stairs to the other room where the typewriter taps; words words words in spasmodic bursts criss-crossing the metal heartbeat of the clock, tick tick tick. Her hand, too, reaching out and moving across to press the cigarette stub into the centre of the ashtray. 'What are you . . . ?' The dark eyes staring up at him as he covered them with the plump white pillow and pressed down upon

21

them with all his weight. No cry, no sound at all, only the thin fingers jerking and plucking desperately at the sheet as the roller spun and the quick black keys rapped out a single space sign:

\#

and still he sat stooped over the desk, the words spraying swiftly out over the paper in long orgasmic surges, his head lowered in ultimate indifference to the stuttering ripple of sound, the roller sliding back and forth, as out of the words a pattern took shape, a pattern of figures glimpsed as in a darkened mirror, a blue and black mosaic of interlocked shapes . . . The end as clearly in sight as had been the beginning, becoming actuality as the last lines thrust their way past the narrow channel of the keyboard and out on to the paper, black on a trembling whiteness, and he sat back and lifted his hands from the machine and stared for a while, only for a while, at what he had done. As time returned.

And he thought, Well, that's it. It's finished, and placed one finger back on the keyboard to add the final touch.

\#

1

It wasn't true that after the death of his wife Professor Dobie went completely to pieces. Some of his friends, however, were deeply concerned.

Among them, the rector of his university.

'Something must be done,' the Rector said, 'about that bloody man Dobie. Something, I mean, quite definite must be decided.'

'Quite so,' Professor Traynor said. 'However, I'm glad you said *definite*. Not *drastic*.'

Despite the impetuousness of his tone of utterance the Rector was, as Traynor well knew, not in essence a decisive individual. It was simply his habit to address all the problems attendant upon the day-to-day running of a large university – the regrettable moral behaviour of the students, the even more regrettable laxity in the discipline exercised by members of the staff, the state of the drains, the abundance of windblown scrap paper in the carpark – in just this way; something had to be done about them. By somebody else. After a full and democratic discussion, naturally.

Traynor sat back in his chair with a painful wheezing noise, emitted not by him but by the foam-rubber cushion directly beneath him; all the armchairs in the Rector's office could be relied upon to produce these strange farting sounds at unexpected moments, usually to their occupants' extreme embarrassment. Not to Traynor's, however. As Chairman of the Mathematics Department he was a seasoned armchair-sitter and wheeze-provoker. 'He certainly seems,' Traynor said, 'to be temporarily not quite up to the mark.'

'There's something . . .'

' . . . *zombie*-like . . .'

' . . . about his conduct these days . . . '

'Not, of course, that that would normally excite remark in the circles he frequents. Or be accounted in any way out of the ordinary. Dr Hayling, for instance . . . '

'Indeed. The original Nightmare on Elm Street in outward guise. Dobie's not quite as bad as *that*. The difficulty lies rather in the special circumstances.'

'He's become something of a celebrity, you might say.'

'And in a most unfortunate way. It's this combination of the characteristic qualities of Boris Karloff and of Jason Donovan that I find disturbing. *Deeply* disturbing.'

Traynor nodded sagely, though both of the names just cited by the Rector were totally unfamiliar to him. He was cognisant, however, of the event which the Rector clearly had in mind and which had occured only a few days previously. Professor Dobie, according to reports, emerging distraitly from the Senior Staff Room, had then been seized upon by a group of screaming female teenagers and borne forcibly down to the floor, where sundry intimate items of his apparel had been removed (without his consent) and his person subjected to various other unmentionable and unsolicited indignities. The perpetrators of this outrage had not, in fact, been members of the university, but this had not been properly established in the subsequent lurid reports of the incident appearing in the (deservedly) popular press and the Rector had therefore had to deal with numerous irate enquiries emanating from members of the Senate – who after all should have known that full term hadn't even started yet.

Nor was this all. Far from it.

'Some modus operandi,' the Rector said, 'must be found for suspending him from his teaching duties. Temporarily, of course. Until this present quite extraordinary—'

'Unfortunately he can't be truthfully said to be performing

24

them inadequately, since he hasn't actually begun lecturing yet.'

'In times of war,' the Rector said, 'truth is the first casualty. And this is war, let's be in no doubt on that score. With *your* department in the front line.'

Traynor elicited another agonised *ppf'fffff* from the cushion as he leaned forwards to reach for his sherry glass. Some earlier brief exposure to the ethos of a Cambridge common room had induced the Rector somehow to suppose the imbibing of sherry to be an essential concomitant to all civilised and intelligent discourse, such as the one in which he and Traynor were at that moment indulging, the actual quality of the plonk provided being so secondary a consideration as to be deemed irrelevant. This accounted for the strangely withered appearance of the potted plant beside Traynor's armchair (*Dryophilus academicus*) which was constantly receiving surreptitious libations from those many of the Rector's visitors whose throats were not lined with asbestos.

'You speak,' Traynor said, disposing of the vitriolic liquid with a neat and well-practised jerk of the wrist, 'metaphorically, I hope.'

'Do *you* think he murdered his wife?'

'Dobie?'

'Yes.'

'Dobie's wife?'

'Yes. *And* that other one. Mrs Whatname.'

'Oh, well. Why would he do that?' An experienced academic, Traynor evaded the question with dexterity. 'Nice little thing, I always thought.'

'I've had the Chief Constable's personal assurance that the police regard the case as closed. *Both* cases, that is. But that in itself is hardly . . . What I'd really like to know is how he did it.'

'Me, too.'

'Or more exactly how he managed to get away with it.'

'Yes. But then there's this opposing school of thought, as

25

you might say, which holds that he was in fact responsible for bringing the murderer to book.'

'But no one's been brought to book that I'm aware of.'

'Just so. Which adds fuel to the fire of those who maintain the contrary contention.'

'Well,' the Rector said, after a pause during which he regarded Traynor's empty sherry glass with a certain suspicion. 'Something's got to be done, don't you agree?'

Now that the matter had been democratically discussed and a safe return effected to square one, Traynor felt able to put forward a suggestion. Or more exactly, a proposition. 'When all's said and done, Dobie is a distinguished scholar. Probably the most distinguished scholar in the department. Whether he may or may not, as the case may be, have murdered his wife is, strictly from the academic viewpoint, irrelevant. He has, however, unquestionably been overworking.'

'He has?' The Rector was shocked. Such accusations had rarely been levelled against members of his academic staff.

'No doubt about it.'

'But this is still the summer vacation.'

'That, in fact, is the period when most of the staff pursue their research interests, free from all unmannerly interruption by the student body.'

'Yum,' the Rector said. He might, he thought, be unwise to press the point further. 'And what exactly is the nature of Dobie's research?'

'I understand him to be probing the ultimate secrets of the universe.'

'Ah.' The Rector sighed wistfully. 'An intellectually taxing pursuit, I shouldn't wonder. Possibly productive of brain fever and similar undesirable spin-offs.'

'Indeed.'

'Also of regrettable anti-social tendencies.'

'Very probably.'

'Perhaps we might offer him a sabbatical.'

'No.'

'No?'

26

'No. He wouldn't accept it.'

'Shit,' the Rector remarked.

'I was thinking rather in terms of a Visiting Professorship.'

'You mean . . . somewhere outside the UK?' The Rector brightened visibly. 'Maybe Fiji? Kuala Lumpur? Ulan Bator?'

'Let's say somewhere sufficiently far removed from his present sphere of operations—'

'Ah, but would any of those places be far *enough*?'

'It's debatable. But in any case, none of them represents an immediate possibility. Whereas Cyprus—'

'Cyprus?'

'North Cyprus, to be exact. My old friend Bernard Berry is at present heading the Department of Mathematics in the University of Salamis. And North Cyprus, I might point out incidentally, is a country which doesn't exist.'

'Doesn't *exist*? My dear fellow—'

'It has no official recognition and hence no diplomatic representation elsewhere. For the same reason, other countries have no embassies there, either. In such circumstances, Dobie can hardly prove to be a serious embarrassment to the Foreign Office or to anyone else. Nor could he be held responsible for starting up a war or an internal revolution, a possibility which would otherwise have to be very seriously borne in mind.'

The Rector picked up a pen and made quite a lengthy entry into his notebook. 'And this friend of yours—'

'Professor Berry has very recently contacted me and asked me to recommend an appointee for a Visiting Professorship of Mathematics and as a matter of extreme urgency. I'd be pleased, with your permission, to nominate Dobie for the post.'

'That would really be an admirable solution to the problem. When you say urgent . . . ?'

'Immediately. Forthwith. I understand that the vacancy has arisen as a result of the previous incumbent's sudden and unexpected demise.'

The Rector was now showing every sign of an unwonted

27

enthusiasm for the project, as outlined. 'Better and better. One might say ideal. No doubt there are any number of hideous and debilitating local diseases—'

'Well, no. I think it's a fairly healthy place, as far as that goes. Berry didn't expound that point in any detail but I was led to believe the poor young lady met with some kind of violent death. A car accident, maybe . . . I'm not at all sure. Most unfortunate, if so, but it's an ill wind—'

'A *lady*, you say?'

'Yes. A most promising—'

'And a . . . violent death? T'ck t'ck t'ck. Still, it does seem to be the sort of place where Dobie should find himself in his element, so to speak. And you think the appointment is one that he might accept?'

'I'll certainly bring my powers of persuasion to bear. Such as they are.'

'Then I've every confidence that we've found the solution to our little dilemma,' the Rector said. 'You're a very persuasive fellow, Bill. Now I wonder if I can tempt you to a little more sherry?'

In fact the Rector, for once, wasn't making a fuss about nothing or a mountain – to use one of his own preferred expressions – out of a molehill. Dobie *was* feeling pretty much under the weather these days. Traumatised, maybe.

He had his reasons.

Jenny's death and its attendant unpleasant circumstances had naturally provoked in him a violent nervous reaction. At first this reaction had been conveniently dulled by shock and by his subsequent sustained efforts to unravel those unpleasant circumstances, or in other words to find out who had murdered her. Although this effort had in one sense been crowned with complete success it had also, from another viewpoint, to be seen as a failure, since Jenny's murderer had never – as the Rector had rightly observed – been brought to book but had died instead of a broken neck, having been pitched full tilt down a steep staircase by (as the police

28

maintained but couldn't satisfactorily prove) Professor Dobie himself.

'Letter for you, Dobie.'

'Ugh,' Dobie said.

Well, he was never at his best before breakfast.

The whole Strange Attractor affair had created a miasma of seething rumour which, in conjunction with the near-libellous outpourings of the tabloid press, had in turn converted Dobie into a semi-mythical figure around which the serried ranks of Rome and Tuscany (his supporters and detractors respectively had engaged in furious, if exclusively verbal, combat. Dobie himself, meantime, instead of straddling the bridge Horatius-like and belligerently shaking the computer print-outs that only he could wield, had retired to a cosy cubby-hole provided by his good friend Kate Coyle where he had worked himself almost to a standstill checking out a series of programmed formulae originating from his American colleagues at MIT and from which, as Traynor had hinted, some kind of unified field theory might eventually be derived . . . maybe in ten or fifteen years' time but not, as Dobie's frenzied work-style appeared to indicate, within the ten-week space of a summer vacation.

If his colleagues were worried about him, so was Kate . . .

He opened the letter and read it while she was frying the eggs and bacon.

Dear Professor Dobie,

I am delighted to be able to offer you the post of Visiting Professor at the University of Salamis for the coming semester.

Your teaching abilities have been most warmly commended by my old friend and colleague Professor Traynor, but of course your work in the field of Gaussian paradox stands as a sufficient recommendation in itself. We would indeed be greatly honoured if you should agree to join us.

29

I may add that your skill as a supervisor has been also praised by your predecessor in the post, Mrs Derya Seymour (whom perhaps you will remember as Ms Derya Tüner).

Your teaching commitments here would not be particularly onerous. I would be most happy to have you conduct our fourth-year course in Finite Element Method, which will certainly pose no problems to you, and the relevant seminars and study groups. The medium of instruction here, of course, is English.

You will find details of salary, accommodation, etc., on the attached sheet furnished by the university administration. Please contact me directly if you require any further information. I hope very much you will be able to join us before the commencement of term in early September.

Yours most sincerely,

Bernard Berry
Chairman
Dept. of Mathematics

'Ugh,' Dobie said again. He knew a bug-letter when he saw one. He passed the letter over to Kate and got going on the eggs and bacon while she read through it attentively.

'Well, I'd call that a very charming letter.'

'Ugh.'

'Oh, don't be so *grumpy*.'

'Ugh. Ugh.' Dobie was not this time expressing his sentiments but merely had his mouth full of buttered toast. 'Wock,' he said, finally clearing the obstruction, 'do you think?'

'I think you should go.'

'Oh. You do,' Dobie said, 'do you?' He ruminated while chewing further cud.

'You need a nice long break,' Kate said firmly. 'You know you do. You said so yourself when Bill Traynor asked you about it.'

'He didn't ask me about it. He broached the subject. That's all.'

30

'Whatever.'

'And I told him this wasn't exactly what I had in mind.'

'Why not?'

'I'm not much of a one for holidays. Sun oil and beaches and all that sort of thing.'

'It's not supposed to be a holiday. It's a *job*.'

'I've got a job. And so have you. And you can't get away right now. Can you?'

'No, I can't. But—'

'There you are, then.'

Dobie glowered crossly at his coffee cup. Kate had a job all right. She was a GP and, in cases of emergency, a police pathologist. No way she could get away at the start of the sniffle season. Doctoring is of course an admirable profession but not one that invariably makes for a satisfying marital relationship. The hours are too long and the work too tiring. Not, of course, that Dobie and Kate were married. They weren't. Or not, at least, to each other. Dobie *had* been married, certainly, but wasn't disposed to repeat the experience. Once bitten, twice shy is one of the oldest and most frequently tested of all mathematical precepts. As for Kate . . .

Oh, well. Skip it.

In fact Dobie was extremely fond of Kate and had in the recent past and on appropriate occasions afforded her signal instances of his favour, this on the whole to their mutual satisfaction. On what occasions, you ask? Well, there, you might say (or the Rector might have said) was the rub. It was true that of late he'd been working much too hard and had been subjected to a great deal of nervous strain, as are most figures of universal celebrity. Whether this was the sufficient cause of this lamentable lack of, er, um, sexual ardour on his part or merely an excuse for it he didn't know. He was a mathematician, damn it, not a psychiatrist. It seemed to be rather a pity, though, since it had all started off so well.

'You need a break,' Kate said again. There was certainly nothing in Kate's external aspect to account for Dobie's indifference; most of his colleagues considered her quite

31

a dish and would have wished to get so lucky. He had, after all, the certainty of immediate medical attention should over-exertion on her mattress lead to a myocardial infarction, a prospect which otherwise invariably does very little to fortify the over-forties. 'From *me*, as much as from anything else. And that's the truth of the matter.'

'No, it isn't.'

'Yes, it is.'

'No, it isn't.'

'Yes, it is. You've gone and got me all mixed up in your mind with what happened to Jenny and with what happened afterwards and you've got to disconnect me from all that somehow and forget all about it. If you go away for a spell that'll maybe do the trick.'

Kate wasn't a psychiatrist, either. There were times when Dobie felt like reminding her of the fact, but he restrained himself from doing so now; as yet they hadn't quarrelled over breakfast and this didn't seem to be the right moment to begin. 'What happened afterwards,' he said, 'was very nice indeed and you know it was.'

'Yes, but it all happened too soon and too quickly and that's why you're feeling guilty about it.'

'I do not so.'

'Yes, you do.'

'No, I don't.'

'Yes, you do. And so you should. After all, you practically raped me.'

'I most certainly did not.'

'Well, if you didn't then you should have and then maybe *I* wouldn't feel guilty about it. It was just typical male lack of consideration.'

'*Do* you feel guilty?'

'Yes. Well . . . Sort of responsible.'

'But that's silly.'

'I know. Maybe I need a nice long break, too.'

'If you're serious,' Dobie said mutinously, 'I could always move back to my old flat. It looks as though we won't be able to sell it, anyway, with interest rates up where they are. I can't think why the Chancellor of the Exchequer—'

'*That* might be a good job for you, too. They could certainly use a mathematician or two at the Treasury. But sad to say you haven't been offered the post. *This* one you have.'

'I wouldn't want to be a Tory Chancellor, anyway,' Dobie said, even more mutinously than before. 'Not, of course, that they're going to get in again. After this poll tax business—'

'Yes, they will.'

'Oh no, they won't.'

'Look,' Kate said sweetly, 'be a Visiting Professor instead. There's a dear.'

'Well, I'll think about it,' Dobie said.

A former student of yours, Dobie thought.

Curious.

Of course he remembered Derya Tüner well enough, not only for her outstanding mathematical abilities but for certain other and more obviously outstanding qualities. He even remembered the guy she'd apparently gone and married. Adrian, that was the name. Adrian Seymour. A somewhat bumptious young git. 'Derya Tüner, now,' he said diffidently.

'You'll remember *her*, surely. You were her supervisor.'

'Oh, of course. Certainly. Yes. But. However.'

Traynor, who was very familiar with Dobie's rather peculiar methods of verbal communication, sighed deeply. 'Derya Tüner, when she was studying here. Though she usually spelled it Turner. In fact I believe there should be two little dots over the u, as in a German umlaut. But since we all found it rather difficult to pronounce—'

'Ah, yes.' Dobie recalled having experienced some difficulty himself and practised cautiously for a while. 'Üüüüüüüü. Üüüüüüüü. Üüüüüüüü.'

Traynor glanced nervously over his shoulder. Several other of their colleagues were sitting around in the staff room; not all of them were as accustomed as he was to Dobie's modes

33

of expression and there had been a considerable fuss made in the media of late about mad-cow disease and its possible transmissibility to the human species. 'In any case,' he said, 'the name is Seymour now. Or *was* Seymour, I suppose I should say. Did you ever meet her husband?'

'I did, yes,' Dobie said, abandoning his linguistic experimentation with some reluctance. 'At least, he was her fiancé at the time. But yes, I did. He was attending our School of Dramatic Studies, I seem to remember. Held to be brilliant, all the same. By some.'

'She had interests in that field herself, of course.'

'She did?'

'I'm surprised that it's slipped your memory.' Untrue. He would have been more surprised if it had acted otherwise. 'Quite a promising actress, or so I believe. Don't you remember we all went to that rather odd dramatic society production in which she played the, ah, leading lady? And Borrodaile got rather disgracefully sloshed and hiccuped loudly throughout the entire performance?'

'That wasn't Borrodaile. That was me.'

'You see? You *do* remember.'

'Of course I do. And I most certainly wasn't sloshed. Very far from it. What happened was that an inadvertently swallowed potato crisp—'

'Quite so. Very embarrassing.'

'I wasn't in the least embarrassed.'

'I didn't mean for *you*,' Traynor said.

Dobie was silent for a few moments, reflecting. The occasion upon which he was reflecting had now receded into the distant past, having taken place all of five or six years ago, but his recollection of it was moderately clear, at least by his own somewhat unexacting standards. 'Sort of a Greek thing, was it not? All the girls romping around in see-through nighties?'

'Could you really . . . ? Or rather . . . that's to say . . . I suppose, yes, it might be so described.' Traynor pulled himself together with a visible effort. 'Very short tunics, anyway. Or what you might call Freudian slips.'

34

This was a shaft of wit which Dobie, inevitably, missed, or rather ignored completely, his gaze remaining expressive only of untold suffering recollected in tranquillity. It was true that, faced with the altogether daunting horrors of an entire evening spent observing an amateur, indeed an undergraduate theatrical performance in the company of his departmental colleagues, he had fortified himself against the prospective abyss of excruciating boredom not wisely, as some fool or other had once put it, but too well; *disgracefully sloshed*, however, was in his view overstating the case. And the performance had, in the event, revealed certain redeeming qualities – in Derya Tüner's case, indeed, very nearly all of them. A promising actress, was she, then? Well, yes. Dobie vaguely remembered various announcements and proclamations as having emerged from her other end in a clear and resonant voice. Obviously a lot of highbrow tosh, probably literature or something like that. But the legs, of course . . . Phenomenal . . .

'What was she doing in Cyprus, then? It said in that letter they sent me—'

'She *was* Cypriot,' Traynor said patiently. 'Turkish Cypriot. Hence the peculiar configurations of the vowel-sound which you were earlier and vainly seeking to reproduce.'

'Eh?'

'That's why she had a funny name.'

'Seymour? What's funny about that?'

Traynor gave it up. 'Anyway, that's why she was working in Cyprus. Which is what you asked me.'

'Yes, at Sauerkraut University or whatever it's called. In effect, I'm supposed to be her replacement.'

'That's my understanding of the situation also.'

'But why isn't she there *now*, is what I'm getting at? What happened to her?'

'She's dead.'

'*Dead?*'

Traynor moved his head from side to side, not in negation of his previous statement but with a lugubrious motion expressive of sadness and regret. 'I'm afraid so.'

'But that's awful,' Dobie said.

'Yes.'

'She couldn't have been . . . She was so young. Couldn't have been much more than thirty.'

'Or thereabouts. Yes.'

'Well, that's terrible.'

Traynor was aware that the sudden death of attractive young women in their early thirties (as Jenny Dobie had been) had to be something of a delicate topic where his friend was concerned and sought at once unskilfully to change the subject. 'Of course, you'll be missed here. Sadly missed. But I intend to postpone your Physics III lectures to the Hilary term and Wain, I think, can manage to cover your other courses if Gwyn Merrick takes over the first year, which I'd planned to have him do anyway. So you needn't have any worries on that score. Indeed you ought to find a change of scenery altogether beneficial, and I've every confidence you'll return to us next term like a giant refreshed.'

'A giant what?'

'Refreshed. Full of get up and go.'

'Oh, I see.' Dobie stared for a while at the raindrops pinging happily against the staff room windows. 'What's the scenery going to be like there, I wonder?'

'Delightful, John. Delightful. There'll be . . . Roman ruins and so forth. Peaceful bucolic orange groves and sandy beaches and things. And an ideal climate. Or so they tell me.'

'Aren't the people there always shooting at each other?'

'Good heavens, no. Not any more.' Traynor laughed heartily. 'It's a former British possession, after all. No, you'll just have the odd bomb going off, as I suppose, maybe a very small hand grenade chucked in through the window every so often. Quite like London, in fact, except that everyone there speaks English so you won't have an language problem.'

Beyond the rain-misted window-panes a wild and stormy Welsh sky extended a gloomy overcast and a gust of seasonably violent wind rattled the window-frame.

36

Dobie sighed plaintively. 'Well,' he said, 'I'll think about it.'

Feeling the need for rather more exact information than that which Traynor had provided, Dobie went round to the university library and looked up *Salamis* in the encyclopedia. He returned to Kate's place an hour or so later and not, as Kate couldn't help but notice, in a particularly gruntled frame of mind.

'It was founded,' he said, 'by refugees from Troy. You know the Trojan Wars? That lot.'

'What, the university?'

'No, *no*. Salamis. Then they had an earthquake and it all fell down. Then they rebuilt it and the same thing happened again. They gave up eventually as who wouldn't? So now there's nothing left but a lot of ruins. And the university, apparently.'

'Some people,' Kate said, 'never learn.'

'Well, the incidence of earthquakes and tidal waves seems to have diminished of late. But you're right in principle. In fact, you've hit the nail on the head. Done much the same thing to Cardiff, haven't they? Without the need for any earthquakes at all.'

Dobie was obviously as grumpy as ever. He had had to consult no reference books to perceive from the outset a very weighty drawback to Bill Traynor's proposal. He had realised from the first that acceptance of it would of necessity involve him in all the stomach-churning horrors of a lengthy air flight, and the risks of being eventually dismembered in some major seismic disturbance affecting the eastern Cypriot coast might after all be virtually discounted if one rated one's chances of arriving there in the first place as minimal. As Dobie did.

Always did. The prospect of air travel invariably induced in him all the symptoms of what the psychiatrists casually refer to as 'panic syndrome' – the forehead moist with fever-dew, the wildly staring eyes and dishevelled locks, the tendency to leap suddenly high into the air upon the announcement

37

of the arrival of the early morning jumbo jet from Karachi. Certain of the circumstances attendant upon the recent death of Dobie's wife had accentuated his ingrained dislike of aircraft to the point where it now verged on the traumatic: he was still visited all too frequently by the recollection of Jenny as he had last seen her, a small figure half-turned towards him as she walked towards the waiting 727, carrying her weekend bag in one hand and waving the other in the air in cheerfully nonchalant farewell; and his occasional nightmares were these days invariably accompanied by the rising whining roar of jet engines passing overhead, to the sound of which, sweating and stiff-limbed, he would finally awake. Not feeling, be it said, particularly groovy.

'You've just got to look on it as something up to which you have to face,' Kate said. Formerly a bit of a vulgarian in grammatical matters, she had decided that she ought to pay more attention to formal syntax now that she was getting laid by a university professor, the fact that Dobie was a Professor of Mathematics being, in her opinion, beside the point and the fact that she wasn't getting laid all that often being, also in her opinion, even more so. 'Part of the treatment, you might say. Psychotherapeutic. Right?'

'Wrong.'

He was being more than usually obstreperous that morning. 'How so?'

'My objections to flying are eminently reasonable. I regard the whole thing as anti-natural. I mean, you've only got to look out of that porthole thing to see that sooner or later the damned thing's wings are going to fall off, and probably just when you least expect it. These hijacker chaps are doing a useful public service, the way I see it. Drawing attention to the . . . They must feel just the same way as I do about it. And besides,' Dobie said, 'the seats are too small and I never know where to put my feet.'

'You never know where to put your feet anyway. You tripped over the kitchen table only yesterday.'

'Yes, but that's *different*.'

The truth of the matter was that Kate to some extent shared Dobie's concern. Hijackers indeed represented very much less of a serious menace to any reputable airline than did Dobie himself, when in characteristic form. And this, of course, was something to be borne in mind.

She didn't, of course, think it probable that any aircraft in which he might be briefly incarcerated would take it into its head to hurl itself incontinently downwards (or upwards, or sideways) in the way that he so trepidantly anticipated; she considered it, on the other hand, highly probable that it might transport him to Reykjavik or Addis Ababa or to practically any destination other than the one for which he had booked his ticket. Dobie's propensity always to make for the check-in desk with the shortest queue rather than that presided over by the airline issuing his ticket made such monumental balls-ups something of a matter of course.

Convinced as she was that Dobie, like a clockwork mouse, would need to be pointed in the right direction and given a gentle nudge before proceeding on his way, Kate said, 'Of course I'll drive you to the airport. And see you off in the proper style. Noblesse oblige.'

'What *is* the proper style?'

'You'll see when we get there.'

'I was afraid you'd say that,' Dobie said.

Having thus made all possible preparations – or more exactly taken all possible precautions – Kate was none the less further relieved to learn later that day that Dobie, once aboard the lugger, would be accompanied throughout the flight by a seemingly reliable nursemaid. The nursemaid rang their number while Dobie was taking his evening constitutional but Kate was able, with her usual competence, to relay the message to him on his return. 'His name is Ozturk. It sounded like.'

Dobie was shaking puddles of water from his raincoat down on to the carpet. 'Whose name is?'

'Ozturk's is.'

'You can't have got it right.'

'Hang that damned thing up, Dobie, and listen to what I'm telling you.'

'I *am* listening,' Dobie said. Plaintively. He sat down in an armchair the better to do so.

'You're to call him Ozzie.'

'I am? How? When? Where?'

'When you meet him at the airport. He's to be a colleague of yours. Or you're to be a colleague of *his*, more exactly, since he's working in Cyprus already.'

'Yes, I think I follow that fine distinction. What's he working *at*? I mean, in what department?'

'He didn't say.'

'Speaks English, does he?'

'He has a rather attractive husky voice with a lilt of the Mediterranean about it. I visualise him as being tall and broad-shouldered, with nice crinkly black hair and brown eyes with an exciting luminous quality. He probably has impeccable taste and wears superbly tailored charcoal-grey suits—'

'Speaks Welsh, does he?'

'In actual fact,' Kate said, 'he's got a cockney accent you could cut with a knife but he seemed to be a pleasant enough character. And at worst he'll be able to make sure you get off the bloody aircraft at the right stopover because you know what happened when you went on that day trip to Weston-super-Mare and that was on a bus, for heaven's sake.'

'I still insist the confusion was due to a simple misunder-standing—'

'And *I* still say that Belgian customs officer had every right to cut up rough. Look, just suppose you were to end up on the Greek side of Cyprus by mistake . . . No. The mind boggles. You stick with Ozzie and you'll be all right. I hope.'

'The Greek side? What Greek side?'

'I expect,' Kate said, 'he'll explain all that to you when he's got you safely on the aircraft. *Someone* had better.'

* * *

40

'Ah, yes. Them Greeks,' Ozzie explained. 'Right efficacious bastards, they are.' Yes, he spoke English all right. After a fashion. 'You don't want to give a second thought to *that* side of things, china. Don't let it trouble you one way or the other. 'S a fact of life, like we all got to rub along with. Shouldn't ever even *mention* the buggers. Only hets people up an' to no good purpose. Got enough problems of our own these days, ain't we, with interest rates an' all, Gawd help us.'

'Funny you should say that. Only the other day—' Dobie, inadvertently glancing out of the observation window as he spoke, stopped short and closed his eyes up tightly. Unmentionably horrid things were going on down there, where a pleasantly green and perfectly respectable part of England had apparently and also to no good purpose been tilted over on its side at an angle of approximately ninety degrees. Dobie desired nothing more ardently at that moment than to be safely back there, storm clouds, interest rates and all.

'Anything the matter?'

'No, no. Not at all.'

'Not too keen on air travel, right?'

'Air travel? Who, me?' Dobie tossed back his locks with a light-hearted gesture and giggled girlishly. 'Oh, well. Done enough of it in my time, y'know.' This was neither more nor less than the truth.

'Mebbe,' Ozzie said. 'I got a forced impression from summink your young lady said, as led me to suppose—'

'Ah? Oh, Kate. A notorious rumour-monger.'

''S all right then. We'll be flyin' pretty high on this trip, anyway, so's to stay above the disturbance.'

'Eh? What? What, what disturbance? Who said anything about a disturbance? On the weather forecast was it? No one said anything to *me* about a disturbance. I mean, good God, hasn't anyone told the pilot?'

'Pilot?' Ozzie stared at him. 'What pilot?'

Surely he didn't . . . Ha ha! No. Of course not. A pilot-less . . . ? Ridiculous. A joke. It must be. Whoever heard of a . . . Though the idea of being closeted for something like seven hours in this metal coffin with a man possessed of such an appallingly perverted sense of humour was in its way almost equally disturbing. No, there'd be a pilot all right. Who presumably had been given firm instructions to turn back and head for home in the event of encountering adverse weather conditions. Lightning bolts and such. Ah, but had the instructions been firm *enough*? Or worse still, could he conceivably have *forgotten* them?

An alarming thought. Since Dobie himself almost certainly would have done.

A polite reminder, Dobie thought, would certainly do no harm. *Dear Sir*, or no, *Dear Captain* as he believed these people quaintly entitled themselves . . . He drew from his inside pocket a used envelope covered in abstruse mathematical squigglings and began to scrawl on it hastily. 'Scuse me,' he said indistinctly. 'I'm just composing a little message.'

'Message?'

'For the pilot.'

'Ah.'

'The air-hostess seems to be an intelligent girl. I'm sure she'll deliver it to him safely.'

'Oh, I shouldn't give no messages to the air-hostess,' Ozzie said. 'Some bloke got quite seriously injured the other day. Doin' just that.'

'Injured? How?'

'Beaten up by the security guys. Thought he was a hijacker, ha ha ha. Turned out he was only inquirin' as to his prospecks for a quickie on the stopover but there you go, shows you can't be too careful. Reassurin', though, innit, when you know that any geezer steppin' out of line is goin' to get his toes stamped on? An' his skull beaten in, like as not.'

Dobie unobtrusively tucked his feet even further underneath the aircraft seat. Good heavens, what a narrow escape. He had always known that overseas travel would inevitably be fraught with peril, but . . . He slid the envelope back into his pocket and sat back, breathing deeply, or as deeply as an over-tightened safely belt permitted.

'Not to worry, old chum,' Ozzie said. 'We don't let the Greeks get hold of you on this trip, ho ho ho ho.'

Dobie shrank yet further back into his cushioned recess. As far as he was concerned, carefree laughter had no takers today. He hadn't yet arrived at anything like a settled opinion with regard to his present companion, settled opinions being (in his case) invariably slowly arrived at. Ozturk might well be regarded in the circles he normally frequented as an inveterate prankster and great old josher or there again, he might not. Dobie had, as yet, no idea at all what circles Ozzie normally *did* inhabit. Kate had in fact hit the bell in hypothesising a charcoal-grey suit of irreproachable cut; Ozzie's outward appearance conformed in every way to that of your average umbrella-swinging City commuter, but then, Dobie thought, quite a high percentage of pillars of the Stock Exchange have to be of Levantine extraction. 'Forgive my asking but . . . you *are* a Cypriot?'

'Not really. No, I'm from Bethnal Green.'

'Oh, I see. It's just that—'

'Lived in the Smoke all my life. Look, I'm only workin' on the island now because duty calls, no other reason. Certainly not for the lolly. Bloody 'ell, they pay me twenty per cent of what I was makin' with Snow Electronics and that's in Mickey Mouse money. Turkish lira. But my parents are living in Cyprus now the old man's retired and what with one thing and another, that's how it is.'

Dobie nodded sagely. He was, of course, aware that Britishness was an outmoded ethnic concept and especially in London; this, in fact, was the chief reason why he never went near the place if he could help it, though probably this admission was not one to be appropriately made at the present juncture. 'So you've been visiting London? I mean, on holiday?'

'Just calling on my ex, really. And seeing the kids. Looking up a few old pals. That sort of thing.'

'I see. Yes. At least—'

'Wife didn't fancy life in Cyprus all that rotten. Well, it's

43

a bit strange to a London girl, you can understand that. So she went back home. No hard feelings, though. Nothing like that.'

'Well, but couldn't you have—'

'I know what you're thinking. Well, we had other problems besides but I won't go into that. Troof of the matter is,' Ozzie said, sighing deeply, 'I'm pretty well stuck with this job in Cyprus for a bit; it's like I said . . . duty calls. Or old Arkin does, anyway. Which puts me on the spot, so to speak.'

He seemed, Dobie thought, to be a garrulous sort of a chap. And while his English was perfectly comprehensible, not all of his utterances seemed to be so. Soon the air-hostess would be serving them with drinks and such. Dobie needed one. 'In what way, on the spot? I'm afraid I don't—'

'Called me up on the dog an' bone he did, a couple of years ago. Old Arkin did. In person. Asked me if I felt like doing something for the yoof of the country, was how he put it. So, well, I just felt I couldn't refuse. I mean, if someone like Arkin makes that sort of an appeal to you, talkin' man to man, it ain't easy to say no. So I didn't. I said OK, I'll give it a whirl an' he said ta very much and there you go, that's how it was. In a nutshell.'

'Arkin?'

'No one else but.'

'Who's he?'

Ozzie, who had been nodding portentously, paused in mid-nod, his eyes – which were slightly bulbous anyway – starting from their spheres with a stupefied incredulity. 'Who's *he*? You mean who's Arkin? Mean to say you've never heard of Tolga Arkin? Nobel Prize a few years back? '85, I think it was. Only Cypriot ever to win it. It was in all the papers. Like, he's *famous*.'

The name, thus earnestly repeated, did indeed seem to ring some sort of a bell in the hollow echoing fastnesses of Dobie's mind. 'Oh. I mean, ah! *That* Tolga Arkin.' Lights were now going on and off the length of the cabin and with a soft grunt of satisfaction Dobie grabbed for his cigarette packet. Maybe

44

after all Kate was right. His nerves weren't steady, not steady at all. Having lit up and exhaled, he risked another glance out of the porthole. Nothing to be seen out there but thick grey cloud. That was better . . .

'Well, you ought to know something about him, as he's your boss.'

'He is?'

'And mine, of course. Indirectly. He's the Minister of Education. President's appointment. And,' Ozzie said, warming to his theme, 'his son's the Vice-Rector of the university. Big tall bloke. Not a bad sort. You'll be meeting *him* soon enough.'

'I'll have to get all these names sorted out. They seem a bit . . . you know . . . strange, at first.'

'Cem Arkin. He's a good lad. Bit of a hot shot, too. Professor of Information Technology or something like that before he was thirty: Lancaster I think it was or mebbe Leicester. Anyway he went back to Cyprus for the same reason as I did though he's more of a real Cypriot than me; I mean he was born there and so forth. An' I'm not sayin' I'm in that class myself. I'm not what you'd call an intellectual. Just an 'ardnosed engineerin' consultant, really, but then we need engineers, too. An' plenty of them.'

'And mathematicians, I suppose.'

'Goes without saying. Basis of everything nowadays, isn't it? But they're not so easy to find, y'know – mathematics professors aren't. That's why Berry Berry's invited *you* along to the party an' you'll be made very welcome, don't have any worries on that score.'

Dobie's worries were in fact of a much more immediate nature but now and at last they were being slightly eased. The aircraft hadn't actually crashed, or not as yet, and the cabin crew, he saw, were indeed commencing to serve the passengers with strengthening beverages, an encouraging development. 'But what,' he asked, 'happened to that girl?'

'What girl? The air-hostess? Look, if I was you—'

'No, no, the *girl*, or young lady, perhaps I should

45

have . . . The one who had the job before me. She used to be one of my graduate students, you see, and that's why I . . . Derya, her name was. In fact she married another student called Seymour—'

'Ah, Derya. Yes.'

Dobie waited for further comment, but Ozzie's streak of garrulity seemed to have fizzled out. He was looking down now at the folded newspaper he held across his lap and might indeed have been glancing through the headlines, though he obviously wasn't. Dobie tried again. 'I understand she . . . well . . . died. And that's why I was sent for, in a manner of speaking. Not very pleasant circumstances, really, in which to take up a post. But of course it happens sometimes and life must go on, I quite see that.'

'You're right about the circumstances. Not very pleasant, no, not pleasant at all.'

'Oh dear. A painful illness, was it?'

'Did you ever meet her husband?'

'Yes. Before they were married. Why?'

''Cos it looks very much,' Ozzie said, 'as if he went an' croaked her.'

'*Croakter?*' Dobie was flabbergasted.

'Shouldn't really prejudge the bloke. The case hasn't come up yet. But there ain't very much doubt about it, far as I can see. I mean, they say he's confessed to it an' all. Bit of a bloomin' tragedy all the same.' Ozzie sucked in his lower lip and released it with a little plopping sound. 'Nice little bit of stuff like that, an' intelligent with it. Very popular girl, Derya was. Mebbe a bit *too* popular but that's by the way.'

Dobie's flabbergastification had now turned to something like petrifaction. 'My God, if I'd known *that*, I'd never have taken the job.'

'Oh, no need to look at it like that. Life has to go on, like you said, students have to be given leckchers an' so on. No one's goin' to resent it because you . . . I mean, we may be a bit thick in Cyprus but we ain't *that* stupid.'

'It isn't that,' Dobie said 'It's . . . Oh, well. Never mind.'

Ozzie wouldn't understand. Naturally not. Nobody would understand, except Kate. Dobie tried to check that line of thought, though, as soon as it occurred to him. Fifteen minutes into the flight, and he was missing Kate already. It was ridiculous.

2

Dear Kate, Dobie wrote. Subsequently pausing. Oddly enough, this was the first letter he had ever written to Kate . . . or perhaps not oddly at all, since they'd been living in the same house virtually from the time of their first meeting . . . and he wondered if perhaps this opening might not be better rephrased a little more effusively. Having considered various alternatives, however, he let the heading stand. Kate wasn't, after all, an effusive person. Neither was he.

How's the medical profession? The teaching profession seems to be doing all right. At least I haven't fallen over anything yet, not even off the aeroplane, though I had a perfectly terrible trip and my companion, the chap who spoke to you on the phone that time, wasn't at all reassuring. Never mind, I'm here now and quite low down on the ground I'm happy to say, indeed just about at sea level which is the way I like it. In fact the house they've given me is very close to the sea, though right behind me there's an uncommonly precipitous slope called in Turkish, and I hope without ironic intent, the Two-Finger Mountain. The university is some five miles distant. Also located in the same general area are about 150,000 prickly-looking bushes interspersed with bare patches and beyond this outbreak of luxuriant vegetation a rather barren plain extends into what most people would call infinity (though I wouldn't). On the left this flat expanse changes abruptly to acres and acres of rather nice blue sea, in fact to the Bay of Salamis, where

I can see various hotels and suchlike structures and, in the far distance, Famagusta. I'm afraid I'm not much good at describing places but I hope this is the sort of thing you wanted to know. So there it is. They've given me a car on loan and three free days to settle in with and there's a restaurant bar sort of place round the corner where I can get nosh so you don't have to worry about that; I'm being fed all right. Mutton chops, mostly. Of course the house has a kitchen and a fridge and all that so I'll be able to do some cooking when I feel like getting down to it. There's also a telephone on which I plan to give you a ring quite soon: 90-357-31962 for when you reciprocate. You can also call me at the U during office hours but as we don't kick off for another couple of weeks yet I'll only be checking in there in the mornings. Or so I should think. It's pretty damned hot here in the afternoons.

Dobie chewed the end of his felt-tip reflectively and after a while spat, also reflectively. He'd been chewing the wrong end. It tasted awful. His somewhat hazy concepts of the rules of prose composition suggested to him that the commencement of a new paragraph might well be desirable some way back. Oh, well. Better late than never. Sucking the other end of his pen, he stared out of the window in search of inspiration. Since it was now night, the views he had just endeavoured to describe were no longer visible. Nothing out there at all. Only a star-roofed night, a velvety blackness. Anyway it was time, he felt, to move on to some other topic. The human element, perhaps. Though he wasn't particularly at ease with that subject either.

I haven't met many of my colleagues yet, except for Ozturk on the plane (you know about) and Prof Berry who met us at the airport and brought me here, I mean to this house. His first name is Bernard so he's known here as Berry Berry, so Ozzie tells me. Sounds more like your field than mine. In fact he did look rather sleepy but as the bloody plane got in

49

at two o'clock in the morning (three hours late) I suppose that was to be expected.

There are six houses here in this sort of compound: Ozturk, Berry, me and obviously three other chaps I haven't met yet. The house is OK like I said, but apparently it belonged to my predecessor, that ex-student of mine I told you about, and her husband. Well, it's a bit embarrassing or rather awkward as there's lots of their stuff all over the place and I don't know what to do with it. I suppose I'll have to leave it where it is for the time being. He murdered her by the way. I mean I'm only going by what I've been told so far but I'm inclined to believe it because there are smears of fingerprint powder all over the place as well and as you must know I've had just about all I want of that sort of thing and if I'd known about it I certainly wouldn't have taken on the job which I'll be bound is why nobody saw fit to mention it . . .

Paragraphs, Dobie. Paragraphs. We're in danger of getting carried away on a wave of emotion, aren't we? Conduct that ill becomes a mathematician. All the same . . .

until I got here. But it's a bit bloody much. Don't you think?

There. And conveniently enough at the end of the page. Dobie tore the sheet off the pad and crouched, pen poised, ready to continue.

Well? What next?

Writer's block, wasn't that what they called it? Nowhere to go. Not to be compared with the dreaded mathematician's block, but an uncomfortable state of affairs all the same, especially when a chatty letter to your lady friend was all you were supposed to be writing. Ridiculous, really. Maybe in his present nervous state . . . Only he didn't have anything much to be nervous about now, did he?

Dobie stared for a while at the virgin sheet on the table in front of him and then reluctantly put his pen down. All you did was sit back and relax. Something would come.

He did. Only it didn't. Or wouldn't.

A remarkable thing. A simple letter to a close personal friend shouldn't be beyond the capacities of your average university professor, assuming your a.u.p. to have any personal friends, close or otherwise. Dobie knew of quite a few who didn't. He looked with his usual mildly beneficent air around the room, looking no longer for inspiration but for something else. What?

An explanation, maybe? For this sudden choking-up of his far from exuberant epistolary flow? Although it hadn't been going badly just then. The felt-tip had been fairly whizzing across that last page. Yet now, confronted with a clean and unmarked sheet . . .

He picked up his pen once more.

For all I know she could have been killed in here, I mean right where I'm sitting. Mind you, I've no reason to think so. The walls aren't exuding evil at me or anything like that. They're just holding the ceiling up as usual. All the same I can't help feeling . . .

No.

Kate wasn't into psychic phenomena and neither was he. Whatever it was that he was feeling at this moment, it was something that couldn't be very easily described and might in any case be attributed to the effects of residual jet lag. Dobie tore off the page and crumpled it up and threw it into the wastepaper-basket.

Yes. Jet lag, probably. Even now in the stillness of the Mediterranean night he was sometimes conscious of the sullen, whining roar of aircraft engines. Indeed, listening carefully he thought he could hear them now, though the sound had to exist only in his imagination since underneath that constant thrumming crepitation he could also hear a voice, a low yet confident voice with an underlying cockney whine. 'Bit of a

51

bloomin' tragedy all the same . . . Nice little bit of stuff like that . . . '

A *tragedy*, yes, you could call it that and even consider it appropriate – she'd been an actress, hadn't she? as well as a mathematician . . . and a nice little bit of stuff, if you thought in such terms. A talented girl, anyway. And popular. Maybe *too* popular – hadn't he said that? Yes. He had. Dobie wondered what he'd meant by it. Probably not very much.

He got to his feet and wandered aimlessly across the sitting-room towards the bookshelf.

There were quite a few mathematical textbooks there, including – as he'd already noticed – one of his own. *Dobie on Paradox*. Not exactly a textbook, of course, but something of a standard work and not yet completely outdated, like so much else in that particular field. Twenty years old, though. One of the sad things about being a mathematician is that if you haven't done your best work before you're thirty, the chances are you'll never come to anything. So Derya wouldn't have. Not that the statistical evidence had ever been properly worked out . . .

He took the book down from the shelf and looked at the flyleaf, observing his own scrawly signature there with some surprise. *All best wishes for the future. John Dobie*. A relic of her postgraduate course, no doubt. He hadn't been notably effusive in those days, either. He couldn't remember having ever signed the copy for her, but that in itself was hardly surprising. And around the room were other reminders of a colder, wetter and windier existence a few years back in the past, of a time that after all she must have enjoyed or she wouldn't have . . . Those framed photographs, for instance, pegged to the wall beside the bookshelf. Student groups. The acting casts of university productions, by the look of them, with herself invariably positioned at or near the centre. Or was that female vanity?

A harmless form of vanity, if so, and as such forgivable. Unlike the academic kind. Not in the least surprising, either; she'd been an inordinately attractive young woman, as the photographs made clear. *Nice little bit of stuff*, indeed; Ozzie had to have picked up the notorious British passion for understatement. The last thing you'd have guessed from those rather over-formalised studio shots was that . . . Dobie looked like a professor of mathematics. He knew it. Inasmuch as he looked like anything. Derya certainly didn't, or hadn't. She looked like . . .

Well . . .

Especially in that very low-cut and diaphanous tunic thing. It really didn't . . . But *yes*, Dobie thought, a recent memory interlocking with a considerably older one somewhere within the little grey cells, we *did* go to that performance. Some mythical rubbish or other. Parts of it highly indecent. A Restoration comedy, didn't they call it? A comedy, and now a tragedy. A terrible thing, of course, but . . .

But I don't want to know anything about it, Dobie told himself firmly. I don't want to be concerned in any way. That was how the other thing had started, with Sammy Cantwell killing himself, only he hadn't; Gwyn Merrick had used that very word, a *tragedy*, talking about it. Another ex-student . . .

'There ain't very much doubt about it . . . They say he's confessed to it an' all.'

There hadn't been much doubt about how Sammy had met his death, either. Not at first. But this, too, was ridiculous. There wasn't the slightest reason to suppose . . .

Almost with relief, Dobie heard the doorbell. He pushed the book back on the shelf and went to answer it.

'You shouldn't have been put here,' Cem Arkin said. 'Nothing personal, of course. Delightful to have you with us. You shouldn't have been put in *here* is all.'

Quite a sizable fellow, Cem Arkin. His hefty body completely filled one of the sitting-room armchairs and his legs seemed to stretch a preposterous distance across the carpet. Dobie, six foot two in his Argyle socks, was maybe slightly taller but didn't begin to match the other's impressive bulk.

53

He didn't have a heavy blond Zapata moustache on top of a jutting Kirk Douglas chin, either. But then he lacked charisma. Cem Arkin seemed to have it, in abundance.

'I understood,' Dobie said, with a diffidence that in the circumstances he felt was becoming, 'that there wasn't anything else immediately available. If it's inconvenient, I expect I can find a hotel—'

'It's the inconvenience to *you* I'm thinking of.'

'Oh.'

'The place hasn't been properly cleaned out, let alone tidied up.' Arkin cast piercing glances to left and right, as though assuming command of a Viking ship and finding the scuppers to be devoid of running blood and the state of the starboard gunwales equally unsatisfactory. 'It's a bit of a pigsty, in fact. Had the police in, you see. I suppose they'll have told you about that?'

'I gather there was a . . . tragedy, yes.'

'A crime, if we're to call a spade a spade.'

'Er, yes.'

Arkin, Dobie thought, was probably in reality more of a bloody shovel man, accustomed to saying what he thought and being, no doubt, in a position to be able to do so. Whatever it was he said, however, he said it in excellent English, insofar as anyone can be held to speak excellent English with a sharply clipped public school accent. 'Which is all the more reason for you to have been put somewhere else. Not a very pleasant place to be, if you're the imaginative type.'

Dobie wasn't. 'You don't have to worry on that account. I'm not.'

'Seymour was, to put it mildly.'

'A writer, wasn't he?'

'He claimed to be. Well, yes, he was. Highly thought of, I believe, in some circles. But . . . '

But not, it would appear, in this locality. Arkin probably had the usual scientist's opinion of arty-farty literary types. Dobie shared that opinion up to a point. He didn't recall Seymour all that clearly, but he wouldn't have used the word *imaginative* to describe him. *Obstreperous*, more like. Somewhat of a berk, to be frank. His attention, for some reason, had again been taken up by that photograph over by the bookshelf and Arkin had noted the direction of his gaze.

'Taken in England, that photograph?'

'Yes,' Dobie said. 'In fact I . . . Some kind of university production. I saw it myself.'

Arkin's formidable eyebrows rocketed upwards like Patriot missiles and then descended again. 'Was she any good?'

'I don't really know. I mean, I'm not much of a judge of acting and anyway I was somewhat pissed at the time. But her performance seemed to be well enough received.'

'If she was wearing *that* outfit,' Arkin said, 'I'm not surprised.'

'She was. Did she take part in any amateur theatricals while she was here?'

'Not in the way you mean.'

'I meant plays and things.'

'Plays and things, no sirree. Histrionics generally, yes. What you might call *scenes* – oh, yes, indeed. Plenty.'

It seemed evident that Arkin hadn't fancied Dobie's protégée all that rotten. Well, protégée – she'd hardly been that. But one of his few academic successes, yes. 'You mean domestic tiffs? Private quarrels? That sort of thing?'

'The sort of quarrels that should have been kept private but weren't. I mean, I'm in the house just across the way, as I told you. It must be all of twenty yards distant from here but I could often hear them slanging one another. Shocking language that girl used, too – you'd have been surprised. I know I was, to begin with. Sometimes I walked across and told them both to shut up. Complete waste of time, naturally. Of course they probably enjoyed it but it was damned annoying, all the same, when I had work to get on with. Not to say embarrassing. You can imagine.'

Dobie could, just about. It wasn't difficult. And after all, when a husband murders his wife one normally assumes a certain unfortunate lack of marital accord. Dobies's own short

55

married life had fully convinced him that the conjugal state had its ups and downs, but Jenny had never presented him with any problems of *that* kind. A gentle, quietly spoken girl, Jenny. He'd never quarrelled with her. Not once.

'I think she'd have upped and left him,' Arkin said, 'if he hadn't . . . Well. Done what he did. Left him *and* us. She didn't intend to stay with us for very much longer, in my opinion.'

'Where was she planning to go?'

'The UK, maybe, or the States. Somewhere with better prospects. We awarded her an Assistant Professorship so that gave her a foot in the door. And she was always an ambitious little bitch. Not that you can blame her for that, not altogether.'

Dobie thought of quoting some consolatory lines from a poem about a field mouse, of all things, which he had had to learn at school and with which he was therefore familiar. These were indeed almost the only lines of English verse with which he *was* familiar and therefore he refrained from citing them, not wishing to give an impression of intellectual omniscience that would be all too inevitably later subject to eventual and total deflation. Anyway they weren't even written in proper English, now he thought about it, having been composed by some bloody Scotsman or other on his way back from the local boozer. So, 'Yes, well,' he said in the end. This was neither a sparkling nor an original contribution to the conversation but had at least the considerable merit of not, as far as he could see, committing him to anything very definite.

'People come and go,' Arkin said. That was hardly an original observation, either. 'You expect that of any university. But of course we'd prefer them not to go feet first, if it can be avoided. The truth of the matter is that this business with Derya has given rise to an awful lot of talk and . . . I suppose I have to say scandal.' He stared glumly for a few moments at his toecaps, away over there in the middle distance. 'We really don't need that sort of thing. It's bad for the corporate image, as you'll appreciate.'

56

'What exactly has . . . '
'Yes?'
'What's happened to him? To Seymour?'
'He's in jug, of course.'
'I suppose I should have asked, what *will* happen to him? I mean, in Cyprus is there a . . . ?'
'Death penalty? Yes, there is. In theory.'
'I see.'
'But it hasn't been invoked in years and I don't suppose for a moment it will be in this case. No, he'll plead extreme provocation or temporary insanity or something and in point of fact it probably *was* just that; I mean both those things. What's more, I'll bet he was flying higher than a kite when he did it because he often was. Stoned out of his mind.'
'He drank a lot?'
'I meant drugs.'
'Oh. I see,' Dobie said again.
'The cops took away about a hundredweight of crack or crunch or whatever you call it and of course that complicates matters a bit. The Rector's trying to keep that part of it hushed up but I doubt if he'll manage it. Though he just might. No one wants to give those sods over on the Greek side that kind of a handle because God only knows what a meal they'd make of it, the Turkish mafia flooding Cyprus with boatloads of shit and all our students turned into junkies. They've got vivid imaginations, those boys. And *very* lively newspaper coverage, when they get the bit between their teeth.'
'But that's not what's really happening?'
'Good God, no.'
'I'm pleased to hear it.'
'Oh, now and again a courier gets picked up by the customs but it isn't any kind of a serious problem. It's a tiny little island after all; the big dealers just aren't interested and it *is* an island which makes things difficult for them in any case. No, they're not bothered and why should they be? It's just the small-time guys who try it. Now and again.'

57

'And the students? A lot of them come over from Turkey, or so Berry told me.'

'Yes, they do. About ninety per cent of them, in fact.'

'Could they be bringing any in? Of course, I don't know why one automatically thinks of students whenever drugs are mentioned. It's most unfair.'

'All the same it's a good point and don't think the police haven't thought of it. Seymour got the stuff from *somewhere* and nobody knows where, or if they do they're not saying. It could have been a student. Indeed it's quite likely that it was. But of course there weren't any students around at that time, not from Turkey anyway, because it was the middle of the summer vac and they'd all gone home. So that has to be a completely separate issue.'

Shaking his head unamusedly, Arkin rose to his feet and lumbered towards the door, a big shambly man in loose white shirt and linen trousers. 'Let me know if there's anything I can do, I mean I'm right next door if there's . . . And you're quite sure you don't mind staying here? I'll get you down in the flats tomorrow if this place makes you feel in any way uncomfortable. And either way it should have been tidied up. Of course it's a terrible thing to have happened but we shouldn't have let it throw everything out of kilter like this. It's disgraceful, really.'

'You said the flats?'

'What?'

'What flats?'

'Oh, the *flats*, the university flats, yes, you can move in down there any time you like, there have to be quite a few vacancies. Reason why old Berry didn't take you there first off is because they're supposed to be for lecturers and others of the lower orders; these villas are for senior staff and Berry Berry tends to be fussy about things like that. In fact he's a bit too fussy about almost everything. Reflects on the Department of Mathematics, in his opinion, if the Visiting Professor doesn't rate a villa – this one used to be Derya's so now it's yours. He's not an imaginative feller, either. But you can see his point.'

'Yes,' Dobie said. 'And I'm perfectly happy here, I can assure you. I don't want to cause any inconvenience. Tell me, who's my neighbour on the other side?'

'Ah. Eng Lit chap. Dr Hillyer. Yes, that may well have been another factor, they may have reckoned you'd like to have another Brit next door. I don't have all that many dealings with him but he's pleasant enough.'

Dobie pressed the doorbell and nothing happened. A couple of minutes passed. Then, just as he was about to turn away, the porch light came on and faint Mr Badger-like shufflings became audible within. Eventually the door opened and Hillyer peered out, his eyes blinking anxiously from behind his glasses as though in expectation of an immediate and violent assault. In contradistinction to Arkin's casual mode of attire, he wore an ancient but very well-tailored tweed suit, an MCC eggs-and-bacon tie and, Dobie observed, carpet slippers with holes through which his blue-besocked toes coyly pointed. 'Yes?'

'My name's Dobie. John Dobie. I've just arrived. I was wondering if—'

'Of course. Of course. Yes. Come in, why don't you?'

Muttering the usual polite acknowledgments, Dobie entered, to find himself in a drawing-room that was, except for the incidental accoutrements, an exact replica of the one he had just left. The same somewhat creaky pseudo-modern furniture, the same Formica-topped coffee table, the same plastic striped blinds hanging over the window. Hotel furniture, one would have said, and the twin rows of books in the bookcase, the sports magazines strewn over the sofa and the remnants of an obviously bachelor supper littering the table seemed to accentuate rather than to alleviate this overall lack of individuality. There was, however, a faint scent of something hanging in the air which Dobie's undiscriminating nose was unable at first to identify. On being waved by his host to an armchair and sitting cautiously down on it, a sudden increase in the effluence caused him to appreciate that someone, probably the aforesaid host, had either emptied or spilt the better part of

59

a bottle of peppermint cordial over the cushions. This didn't strike him as being in any way odd. He was always doing that sort of thing himself.

'Fancy my tie?'

Dobie wasn't disposed to be over-critical. 'MCC, isn't it? Very nice.'

'But perhaps you'd prefer John Collins'?'

Dobie was puzzled. 'I don't think I've met him.'

'Or a grasshopper? Or maybe a gin daiquiri? Extremely refreshing, y'know, in this steamy weather.'

Something at once well practised and very familiar in Hillyer's stance enabled Dobie to leap to the wild surmise that beverages rather than sartorial matters were germane to this present issue. 'Well, perhaps . . . one of those grasscutter things . . . '

'A wise choice. A very prudent choice. And how was your trip?'

'Appalling.'

Dobie watched his host slide open the door of the corner cabinet and commence to mix various liquids together with gay abandon, squeezing oodles of sticky fruit juice obscenely out of a tube. Truly appalling, yes, and he was still aware of the after-effects; but a small snifter of something might, he thought, help to settle his stomach. He looked vaguely about Hillyer's sitting-room, wondering what he was doing there. Obedience to the impulse of the moment wasn't usually a Dobeian characteristic but he couldn't convincingly attribute his presence here to anything else.

Hillyer turned and reapproached him, bearing a brimming glass before him like some bespectacled and soberly suited Ganymede. 'Do you?'

'Do I what?'

'No, will *this* do you?'

'Oh, yes. Rather. Thank you.'

Having delivered his cargo, Hillyer placed a second similarly brimful tumbler on the side table and placed himself in the other armchair alongside, flinging one bony knee high up into the air before folding it untidily over the other. 'A beaker,' he observed, 'full of the warm south. Welcome to Cyprus.'

'Thanks very much.'

'Though I don't suppose it was *any* old beaker that he had in mind. Some delicate Etruscan ware, most likely. Conceivably a della Robbia. Something like that.'

In addition to wondering what he was doing here, Dobie had now to wonder what the fuck his host was talking about. 'I'm afraid I . . . You see I've only just got here and it's all a bit new to me.'

'Of course. And you say they've put you next door? I'd no idea. Or I'd have made a point of dropping in. But there it is. No one tells me anything. You flew straight out from the UK?'

'Not exactly *straight*, no. There was a considerable wobble factor. The adverse climatic conditions—'

'Pissing down, was it? When you left?'

'It was humid, certainly.'

'Well, at least you've got away from all that for a while. You can relax in the sun and so forth. We won't be kicking off with the classes for another three weeks yet, so you'll have plenty of time to get settled in. I don't think you'll find it too difficult once you've . . . What's your field, by the way?'

'My field?'

'Yes, what's your—'

'Oh, my *field*. I'm a mathematician, I do sums and all that kind of thing.'

'Of course you would be. Silly of me. As you're little Derya's replacement.' Hillyer sampled his own wares and smacked his lips noisily, somehow contriving to make the resultant sound seem thoughtful and even pensive. 'I take it you've heard about . . . ?'

'Yes, I have. Very sad and . . . tragic.'

'And very *disturbing*, what's more, when it happens in the next house to yours. Those two didn't get on, we all knew that. In fact we could hardly help knowing it. The rows and so on. In a close-knit little community like this one. But if

61

we'd had any reason to think . . . Plenty of married couples have the most awful rows without ending up strangling one another and they were both very young, after all, very young indeed, so it was really a . . . I take it you're not a married man yourself?'

'I'm a widower,' Dobie said. 'A recent widower in fact. That's partly why I'm here.'

'Ah. Very sorry to hear it. I'm divorced myself. Second time round. I must say I find the single man's mode of existence a great deal more . . . But of course one has certain problems, yes, especially in Cyprus. I've been here twelve years now, so I should know. However, that's by the way. Can I offer you another little . . . ?'

Dobie saw with some mild surprise that his glass was indeed already empty. 'Why, yes. Please. Er . . . Delicious.'

'Splendid. Splendid.' Hillyer ambled back towards the corner cabinet with notable alacrity. His mode of progress was totally dissimilar, Dobie noted, to that of Cem Arkin, not resembling that of a grizzly bear so much as that of a secretary bird stalking a tasty viper with its knees bumping together at irregular intervals; he might well, Dobie thought, have sunk one or two before his guest's arrival. Or three or four, for that matter. 'Perhaps,' Hillyer said, looking back over his shoulder as he spoke and crashing inadvertently into a footstool, 'perhaps I shouldn't say this, but in a way . . . Of course one would wish the *circumstances* to have been otherwise . . . ' One would indeed, Dobie thought gloomily. Further obfuscations seemed to be imminent. Odd, though, as Hillyer's previous question he had found to be readily comprehensible and even delicately phrased. ' . . . But all the same I'm on the whole greatly relieved to have *you* as a neighbour this coming term. Married couples are always . . . And besides, you're British. One thing to be said for the British. You know where you are with them.'

'Seymour,' Dobie objected, 'was British.'

'So he was, so he was. And so was *she*, technically. Or by birth, anyway. A surprising number of Cypriots manage to get born in the UK, you know . . . the middle-class ones, anyway.' Dobie accepted his replenished glass and hastened to test its content. Delicious, as before. 'But he wasn't a very likable man, I'm afraid. Seymour wasn't. Brusque and offhand in his manner. Not very popular. And bad-tempered with it. I don't say we never chatted together, of course we did. But he wasn't the sort of fellow you'd ever want to get on first-name terms with. Nobody ever called him Adrian that I can remember, much less Ade or anything like that. He was always so argumentative, it was almost as though he . . . I remember his making some particularly vitriolic comments about David Gower to which I had to take violent exception and I remain convinced he made those comments with the intention of annoying me. *That*'s the sort of man he was.'

'I don't think I've . . . Is he in the Mathematics Department?'

'Who?'

'The chap you mentioned. David—'

'David Gower is a *cricketer* and one who in my opinion should be the present England captain.' Hillyer's normally mild countenance had turned, Dobie saw with some alarm, to a violent shade of puce, rivalling in intensity that of the content of his upraised glass. 'Seymour made the utterly preposterous claim that Gower couldn't bat for toffee. I'd have said that the Test averages alone provided a more than sufficient refutation, but to offer such an unwarranted opinion about the most elegant batsman in the England team seemed to me indicative of so profound an ignorance that I preferred simply to ignore the remark. I walked away, more or less. With dignity, I hope. No, there's no gainsaying the fact that the man was an idiot.'

'I must admit I'm not too well informed about cricket, either.'

'So I'd inferred. But that's another matter. I know absolutely nothing about mathematics and wouldn't be so ill advised as to offer any kind of an opinion on the subject. Seymour, on the other hand—'

'Derya didn't make any effort to enlighten you?'

'In what respect?'

'About mathematics, for instance.'

'Good heavens, no. And I sincerely trust you won't, either. No, Derya was always enlivening rather than enlightening. Though not in a way that I myself could readily appreciate.'

'I'm not sure that I . . . You mean her conversation wasn't . . . ?'

'No, I wouldn't have called her a great conversationalist, not at all, but I didn't mean *that*. It was more the way she . . . I mean, she'd do things like . . . well, sunbathing on the terrace with nothing on. Where I and just about anyone else could see her. I don't think of myself as a killjoy and I'm well aware that the tourists in the beach hotels here all do that sort of thing, but in her case it showed to my mind a certain . . . a certain . . . '

'Lack of consideration?'

'Exactly. Other people could just pass by, I suppose, and regard it as a mildly enjoyable experience, but living next door I had no choice but to . . . '

'Regard it.'

'Just so.'

'And no doubt it would somewhat exacerbate the rather personal problems you mentioned earlier.'

'Indeed,' Hillyer said, emitting a surprisingly high-pitched giggle. 'This is of course the island of Aphrodite, as Kaya never tires of telling us. He runs the Archaeology Department, by the way, my next-door neighbour on the other side; you'll meet him pretty soon. Where was I? Ah, yes. Aphrodite. Well, even allowing for the classical associations of the place . . . there *are* limits.'

'Well,' Dobie said, regretfully lowering his once again empty tumbler. 'I don't intend to explore them, I can assure you. I'm hoping to have a quiet time here and avoid all excitement. On my doctor's recommendation.' Since it was in fact his doctor, i.e. Kate, who had in recent weeks been providing most of the excitement of that nature to have come his way, Dobie was being more than a little disingenuous. But it hardly mattered.

'Oh, you'll find things are quiet enough here. Extremely quiet. Abysmally quiet. There's very little in the way of entertainment, even in Nicosia. No cinemas, you know, no theatres or concerts, nothing like that. So we've all rather got into the habit of providing our own entertainment. We're always dropping in on one another for a chat. It's quite the done thing. That's one of the reasons why Seymour—'

'Even so,' Dobie said, 'I think I should maybe be toddling back now. Having some, ah . . . unpacking to do. And letters to write.'

'Well, look. Most days a few of us get together for lunch in the little lokanta place by the main entrance. On the left as you come in – you've noticed it? Good. Do feel free to join us tomorrow if you wish.'

'Fine,' Dobie said. 'I'd like that. Thank you.'

Hillyer's hospitality had been rather more extensive than he'd at first realised. Powerful stuff, these lawnmowers or Mao Thai Tongs or whatchamaycallums. His head swam a little as he levered himself up from his chair.

He'd unload his suitcase, he decided, and then head for bed.

But it wasn't just the drink, of course. He knew perfectly well what the trouble really was. Over-excitement. A natural consequence of all that flurry of movement, of packing and unpacking and being intemperately whizzed from place to place. His was a sedentary mode of existence and he wasn't used to this sort of thing. It's one thing to head for bed and another to get to sleep – but at least as an academic mathematician he was no stranger to insomnia. It worried him not at all. He took it only to mean that his mind was active – which is the way a mathematician's mind ought to be – and needed the equivalent of another hour's solid workout on the parallel bars. A few vigorous press-ups against some problem or other. There were plenty to choose from. No shortage of foxes to hunt, in mathematics. Evasive little creatures who might lead you a rare old chase through the undergrowth of Dirac equations before disappearing down a hole, by which time however they would have served their purpose and have exhausted you completely. Dobie was an old hand at the game.

So old that sometimes his brain seemed to be taking up the hunt on its own, so to speak, to be coursing up and down with its nose to the ground but more like some electrical device than a foxhound . . . like a computerised tuner, maybe, searching for some distant station that it hadn't been programmed to identify and therefore wouldn't recognise even if it managed to catch up on it. On the face of it, a thoroughly pointless procedure. But Dobie wasn't really using a computerised tuner, he was using a human brain and human brains have their quirks and oddities and Dobie's, as any of his friends would have told you, was quirkier and rather odder than most. This was because it was his frequent practice to let it off the leash and see where it ended up. Doing so now, it instructed him to get his butt end off the bed and to provide needed stimulants, such as a cup of black coffee. Dobie sighed, and rolled off the bed, and headed for the kitchen.

While waiting for the electric kettle to boil he switched on the radio that stood on one of the shelves and nodded his head more or less in time to the music that obediently emerged. One of the BBC World Service's late-night jazz programmes, as was evident, with the incomparable Kid Ory snorting away and Johnny Dodds weaving clarinet magic in the background. Dobie would have preferred something rather more soothing, or even somnolent, but once the mind is off the leash you have to let it work with whatever comes along and what was coming along of course was Satchmo's trumpet in one of its growlier gutbucket moods and a misty visualisation of someone's undergraduate digs and one of the old blue-labelled Parlophone 78s spinning on a turntable. Oxford, 1960, and Dobie's own student days with the LP revolution well under way and Humphrey Lyttelton still playing at the Eights Week

66

balls and Dobie himself cutting a notably inelegant rug with, with . . . what was her name? Fiona something; they'd all been bloody Fionas in the Sixties and the face was there in his memory but ill-defined, the faces of so many other students having in the interim been interposed.

Photographs of Derya, yes. Four or five of them, neatly framed and placed on the walls. But none of the husband. Seymour. Not even in a wedding photograph or as a member of a group. Strange, that, though there was probably some simple explanation. In fact Dobie remembered his face quite distinctly. Sharp, triangular, with a heavy forelock of reddish hair falling across the forehead; not unlike a little fox, when you thought about it. But with blue eyes transparently lacking in guile; not innocent, exactly; unrevealing, rather. They observed without reflecting any reaction. But that, of course, had been four or five years ago and in another country. Seymour might have changed. People do.

Dobie very arguably had, and in the space of three or four months. The way you look at things can very quickly change when your wife gets murdered. It can change even more quickly and completely when you're suspected of having done it. In point of fact, Dobie hadn't done it, and it looked very much as if Seymour had. All the same, one of the things that changes when something like that happens is the way you look at little foxes. And how they run. The hounds will go after them anyway, whether they've eaten the farmer's chickens or not. Dobie hadn't, but the hounds had been after him ever since. That was the real reason why he'd come to Cyprus, after all. To get away from them.

Run, Dobie, run . . .

But that couldn't have been the reason why he'd been invited. He was wondering about that. Maybe he should have wondered a little earlier but there again, there wasn't any reason why he should have. It wasn't the first invitation to a Visiting Professorship he'd ever received and it wasn't the first one he'd ever accepted. He'd been to MIT. He'd been to the Max Planck Institute. He'd been to Vienna. But in all those places the circumstances had been different . . . and so had the climate, of course. He hadn't been anywhere where you could placate a bout of insomnia by taking your coffee out on to the terrace at half past midnight and sit there in your cotton pyjamas savouring the immensity of the southern night with Louis playing W.C. Handy fifteen feet away in the kitchen. The terrace faced downslope, away from the other houses. That trumpet wasn't disturbing anybody. Those rows of which Arkia had spoken must have been really loud-voiced affairs but then Derya's vocal cords would probably have been in splendid nick, being an actress as well as a lecturer and hence well accustomed to turning up the volume. Not an unpleasant voice, as Dobie remembered it, and clear as a bell. But Seymour must have found it so in the end.

Nothing anyone does can irritate you more than their voices can, even when they're doing no more than hum Cole Porter tunes slightly off-key (which had been one of Dobie's wife's failings). Dobie drank his coffee slowly, thoughtfully, gazing the while at the distant stars and at the pale moonglow reflected from the long flat mirror of the sea. There seemed to be clouds to the south but not very many and not very much of a wind to move them. When he had finished the coffee he went indoors and sat down at the desk to finish his letter. There didn't seem to be very much to add so he wrote a few more lines and then signed off.

Afterwards, he thought for a minute or two and then added a short postscript. A very short postscript. Two words only. *Miss you . . .*

And why not? he thought. It was true.

3

The car they had placed at his disposal was a clapped-out navy blue Cortina which, however, usually seemed to start at the first turn of the switch and which, having been started, seemed to keep going. Dobie had been assured that the road from the professorial compound led directly to the university but he drove with some caution none the less, the road in question being narrow and bumpy. Very shortly, however, the university complex came into view, a sprawling conglomeration of sparklingly modern buildings backed by the blue flatness of the bay and by a proliferation of pine trees running the length of the beach. As Dobie drove onwards he detected occasional bright slivers of light gleaming disconcertingly amongst the trees and was soon able to relate this phenomenon to the presence of what appeared to be a very large number of polished white marble columns uprearing from the sandy soil and pushing their convoluted capitals above the level of the pine boughs. This was Dobie's first view of Salamis. But he didn't realise this at once because it wasn't what he'd expected.

He continued unperturbed on his way, clutching the unfamiliar steering wheel tightly and blinking anxiously in the sharp sunlight. The air entering by the side window seemed to be very warm – it wasn't yet quite eight o'clock in the morning – and to be impregnated with a very fine white dust, a dust that was already coating the outer surface of the car with a filmy layer. Welcome to the Mediterranean, Dobie thought. Mucky old Cardiff had gone a long way away, in time as much as in space, though he'd only been on the island some thirty hours. He found it difficult to dispel from his mind the intangible sensation that he was going on holiday rather than driving to work. Not that he'd be starting work just yet. That had been made quite clear to him. The so-called Protestant work ethic hadn't yet penetrated to these backward parts. But then these people weren't Protestants, were they? No. They were Muslims. Of a sort. Or most of them, anyway.

All the same there were formalities he had to observe. Check in at his office. Call on the Rector. Shake a few hands here and there. Noblesse oblige, as Kate would have said. Meaning, politeness pays. Rarely more than .005 per cent, but every little counts, or does if you're a mathematician anyway. By the same token, Dobie was pleased to find the Mathematics Department located on the ground floor. An upstairs step saved is an upstairs step earned, the way he saw it, and especially in this fast-increasing heat. His office, once he'd found it, seemed to be pleasant and cool enough. The plaque on the door said:

Assistant Prof DERYA SEYMOUR

and the bookshelves inside were laden with tomes of a mathematical nature mostly, formerly the property of

Assistant Prof DERYA SEYMOUR

and the computer set-up on the side table bore a red stick-on label saying:

Assistant Prof DERYA SEYMOUR

so one way or another Dobie was able to form a clear and rationally based opinion as to whom the previous occupant of the office had been.

He assumed that at least for the time being no one would be likely to object if he made use of the books and the computer; other items in the desk drawer, such as a half-used lipstick and a bottle of blush-pink nail varnish, would doubtless be rather more subject to adverse comment were he to put them to employment and after a few moments' consideration he relegated them and a few other less readily identifiable but obviously feminine oddments to the wastepaper-basket. He then tucked up his Julio Iglesias-length trouser-cuffs, sat down in the revolving chair and spun it round once or twice, surveying through this means his new kingdom. On the whole he approved of it, though sooner or later the resident ghost would surely demand rather more drastic forms of exorcism. Dobie didn't feel that he was conspicuously lacking in respect for the dead, but he didn't propose to allow himself to be *haunted* by the bloody girl.

Or her husband, either.

And anyway he still had those formal calls to make. Starting off, as was customary, with his Head of Department.

'You won't have seen the Salamis tombs yet,' Berry Berry said. 'Only just got here. Quite. Well worth taking a look at, all the same. Hundreds of them, hundreds. Only a mile or so down the road. Amazing what they buried along with the corpses. Horses, even chariots, believe it or not. And all kinds of armour and pottery and personal belongings. Weird. For use in the after-life, as I understand it. I'd ask Kaya about it if I were you. Not too clear on the point myself. Well worth seeing, anyway. Gives you a real insight into something or other, I mean the way those people . . . And things aren't so different now, after all.'

'There's a song about it.'

'What?'

'A negro spiritual, don't they call 'em? *Swing* low,' Dobie carolled unmusically, '*sweeee-eeet* chariot, Coming for to carry me *hooooome* . . . '

Berry Berry listened, obviously deeply impressed, marking time on the surface of his desk with his fingertips. Not the *same* tempo, of course. That could hardly have been expected of two mathematicians. ' . . . I say! Yes! You're absolutely right! Interesting survival, that. But then these primitive forms of belief—'

'And then it goes, *Swing* low, *sweeee-eeet*—'

'Yes indeed. Quite right. Well, there it is. And it's a bit like that *here*, you see. For all our veneer of what d'you call it . . . civilisation. Of course we don't *bury* the things any more but nobody wants to touch them. Or do anything with them. That's why all that stuff of Derya's is still in her office, which is *your* office now. Do just what you want with them, arrange everything to your convenience. But don't ask any of the cleaning ladies to tidy up anything of Derya's, because they won't. I know it seems damned silly but that's how it is.'

Professor Berry was small and easily agitated, as heads of university departments often are. He had a short, white and extremely bristly moustache which also seemed to be easily agitated and which projected across the walnut brown of his face as though signposting the general direction of his ears. His office was the same size as Dobie's but had a better view. As he sat with his back to the window, however, he gained no particular advantage from this.

'What I'm saying is that I don't want you to feel too miffed because things haven't been properly prepared for you in there. Or in the house either. It's just that the circumstances are a bit unusual and we have to make allowances for local feeling in these matters. Or superstitions, if you like. Zeynep used to clean for the Seymours and I'm sure she'd be willing to do the same for you. A very nice woman. She's the wife of the chap who runs that little restaurant round the corner, Ali his name is, and she does the cleaning for Cem Arkin and Bob Hillyer as well. *And* for Ozzie, now that his wife's no longer here. She'll keep the house spotless for you *but* she won't touch anything that belonged to the Seymours. You'll have to tidy their stuff up yourself, I'm afraid. Just pack it away anywhere you like.'

'Is that a Moslem tradition or something?'

'Nothing to do with Islam whatsoever. It's like I'm telling you – Islam's only been here about four centuries. Skin deep. And mixed in with Greek Orthodoxy at that. The fact is that all the locals are pagans at heart, if you want to know the truth. That's why they take so easily to the secular way of life.

Religion here – it's just passed them by. But then . . . you're only going to be here for three months or so. No reason why you should take much interest.'

'Oh, I'm interested,' Dobie said. 'But as you say, I don't suppose I'll have much time to find out very much about these things.'

'Quite right. Quite right. Of course, if we can persuade you to stay a bit longer, everyone'll be delighted. The crying need here is for long-term staff; visiting professors are all very well but . . . That's where old Arkin's proved to be such a shot in the arm. But for him, the Faculty of Science'd be creeping about in the Stone Age, no question of it. You've met him, I suppose?'

'Well, no. Not yet.'

'You'll meet him this week in any case. He makes a point of it with new arrivals. An energetic sort of fellow altogether. He's really taken things by the scruff of the neck since he took over the Min of Ed, and between you and me, this crowd needed a good shaking up. Wonderful people, the Cypriots, but a little lethargic. Lacking in initiative. Stuck in the mud of all those old ideas of theirs, as I was explaining.'

Half past nine, according to the clock on the wall of the office, and the heat was building up. Dobie found that his attention was drifting. It tended to do that at the best of times.

'You'll have to make allowances when you start teaching the students here. But don't confuse lethargy with laziness. They've been cut off, you see, for so long from the so-called international community . . . but then that's just what Tolga Arkin's doing. Bringing them back again. It can't be done at once, of course. After sixteen years of being a backwater and maybe something rather worse than that, academically speaking it's bound to be a bit of a struggle. But we're starting to get the kind of staff we need now, as your own arrival indicates. And the rest will follow.'

Dobie, who had always found academic work of any kind to be a struggle, couldn't think of anything to say so he nodded

73

sagely. Berry's remarks were probably very pertinent but also seemed to be a little too well rehearsed. And a quiet backwater was in any case exactly what Dobie felt he needed, somewhere sedately remote from the depredations of investigative journalists and television interviewers and . . . Yes. 'No. It's quite all right. Just something I thought I'd forgotten but in fact I hadn't.'

In fact he'd been within an ace of nodding off.

'Ah. Happens to us all, on occasion. Where was I now?'

'You were commenting on the lethargy of the locals.'

'Was I? Perhaps I was emphasising the point unduly. Because of course there's the after-effects of '74 to be borne in mind. They actually speak of a war, you know, that's how they think of it, but it's best not to talk about it at all if the subject can be avoided. To Arkin, for example. *Young* Arkin, that is. He lost his mother, you see, and his uncle, of course, and several other members of his family were . . . And quite a few others here would tell you the same story if they talked about it much. Which they don't.'

'His mother? Tolga Arkin's wife?'

Berry Berry nodded sombrely. 'Very sad business, that was. I don't think Tolga ever really got over it. He left the country almost at once, of course, and never got married again, which rather suggests . . . and his brother was killed as well.' He stopped nodding and shook his head instead, no less sombrely. 'Something of a national hero, his brother was, as I expect you've gathered.'

'A little odd he should have wanted to come back here, don't you think? Tolga, I mean. He can't have very many happy memories.'

'No, but he's very patriotic in his way. He isn't really into politics the way his brother was, but he's probably done a great deal more for his country than Uktu ever did. Hardly a fair comparison, as Uktu died very young, but you'll follow my meaning.'

Not really. Dobie was getting even more than ordinarily confused with all these Tolgas and Mai Tais and Uktus and

74

whatever but then, he told himself, it had to be remembered that these chaps were foreigners, after all, and shouldn't therefore be expected to make too much sense, at any rate to begin with. 'I'm not into politics, either,' he said. 'Though I did vote Labour in the last election.'

'Things are a little different here. You could almost say the word has a different meaning.'

'They lost, of course. By a convincing margin.'

'Well, you may have better luck next time.'

'I very much doubt it,' Dobie said.

In fact nobody really wanted to talk about politics. Everybody seemed to want to talk about the murder. Well, that was human nature for you, Dobie decided. Violent death seems to be a staple subject of conversation everywhere, a subject of perennial and sometimes morbid interest. But then he knew that already. He'd had every opportunity recently to discover that fact for himself.

At least this time it was the death of someone else's wife – and not his own – constituting the topic of general interest. The topic was still, for Dobie, a somewhat delicate one. And chiefly, he didn't want to become involved. There was no reason why he should be. He wasn't here to talk about murders or politics either. He was here to lecture on mathematics. He was a jolly good mathematician, that nobody could deny. Not a politician. Not a detective, amateur or otherwise. Ensconced once again in his armchair in his hot little sitting-room, Dobie stared for a while at the photograph on the wall. Cardiff, 1986, or thereabouts. Not so long ago. Yet now the girl in the photograph was dead and the photograph itself had become somehow dateless, had become imperceptibly a tiny part of the curious time-capsule effect that life in Cyprus appeared to have upon the unsuspecting arrival from the UK, who found himself pitched into an ambience where the events of 1985 and 1974 and 1960 and of 1985 BC seemed to be virtually coetaneous because equally relevant to the present moment. Or equally irrelevant, as the case might be.

75

Not a politician. Not a detective. And not, of course, any kind of an archaeologist or researcher into pagan and unpalatable mythologies. He wondered who Amphitryon was when he was at home. Or wasn't the point about him that he often wasn't? And when he was, was prone to receive unpleasant and improbable surprises? Dobie, who also in the not-so-distant past had made disagreeable discoveries of a (broadly) similar nature, sighed plaintively and wondered what to do next.

Normally he'd have expected to find plenty to do down at his office. Routine preparations. But Derya's wall planner and lecture notes had indicated a perfectly straightforward teaching programme that he could, he felt sure, conduct while standing on his head, though any such feat of gymnastics would hardly be necessary here in this Alice-in-Wonderlandish island where everything appeared in any case to be upside down. And he had, of course, already run Derya's mini-discs through the computer, rather in the spirit of a Test-class spin bowler (Derek Gower, maybe, or someone like that) idly entertaining himself at a schoolboy practice net. Nothing much there for him, either, except for run-throughs of familiar calculi and derivations from the Hundred Best-Loved Equations; oh, and a set of what looked like geometrical variants belonging or anyway relating to someone called HARRY O, this being the name entered on the starter access code. Having further leafed through a couple of textbooks and having thus exhausted the immediate resources of his office (and very possibly of the entire department), Dobie had found himself free to pursue his own devices, which had consisted of a series of small squiggly loops and circles drawn on a sheet of paper over a period of some twenty minutes. Outside, the sun had been shining in a virtually cloudless sky and the gentle waves of the Mediterranean had lapped insidiously on a white and sandy beach. To hell with it, Dobie had thought.

Back to square one. Why not?

Square one being much as he'd described it in his letter to Kate, now duly completed, stamped and posted. A pleasant

76

two-storey villa of inoffensive design, placed amongst other
seemingly identical villas in a gated compound beside another
white and sandy beach some eight miles from Famagusta
or Gazi Magusa. Every damned place in Cyprus, Dobie
had discovered, had two different names, one Turkish and
one Greek, together with a third name you used when you
wanted to refer to it in ordinary converse, this particular
villa complex (Tuzla Gardens) being thus generally known
as the Bughole – a succinct if unfair appellation suggestive,
as was so much in North Cyprus, of frowsty Junior Common
Rooms in minor English public schools and of pork pies being
toasted on cold winter evenings in the midst of a seasonable
fug. Dobie's own bughole, of course, bore no resemblance to
any schoolboy study he had ever inhabited: the ground floor
consisted of a sizable living-room (with terrace) from whence
a passageway led past a small bedroom (used by Seymour
as a study) to an equally small kitchen, this last redolent of
burnt cooking oil and rotten tomatoes. Dobie had managed last
night to locate the tomatoes in a plastic bag inside a cupboard
and had promptly re-located them in the dustbin outside the
back door, which had rather surprisingly seemed to be full of
paper ash. The melody, however, lingered on despite the open
kitchen windows and meantime Dobie was making a point of
eating out, in the small bar-cum-restaurant just outside the
compound gate, where indeed he intended in a few minutes'
time to respond to Hillyer's invitation of the previous evening
and join some of the others in the dismemberment of a sirloin
steak or some such delicacy. He was starting to feel a little
peckish.

   He was also, though for a different reason, making something of a point of avoiding the main bedroom upstairs,
which still bore numerous unmistakable signs of previous
occupancy. A wardrobe full of Derya's clothes, for a start,
with her husband's rather less ostentatious trousseau hanging
forlornly from a crossbar to one side of it. Dobie, suitcase
in hand, had opened the wardrobe, closed it again and at
once had plodded downstairs to set up shop in the other

bedroom; Seymour's things were all over the place here, too, but Seymour at least was still alive and . . . Well, Dobie felt more comfortable there, that was all.

There was a desk with a typewriter standing on it and a filing tray full of sheets of blank paper. There was a well-laden bookcase and there were a lot more books strewn over the floor beside the desk. There was also, of course, a single bed. Dobie, a tidy man at heart, had in fact picked up the books and had relegated them not to the dustbin outside but to the top shelf of the bookcase, which was where they had probably originally been stacked; he had made an exception, however, in the case of a paperback volume entitled *Hot Sex in the Sauna*, bearing on its cover the luridly coloured depiction of several unclothed ladies disporting themselves variously (and uninhibitedly) around a recumbent figure whose facial features, at least, bore a striking resemblance to those of the rector of Dobie's home university. The resemblance in other regions was very much less marked but Dobie set the book reverently aside on the table beside the bed, where he felt it might come in useful should he feel the need for a little enlightenment and/or improving uplift in the small hours of the night.

He was on the whole a tidy but not, as he'd already said, an imaginative man. Which wasn't to say that he felt completely at ease in this particular . . . bughole. He didn't. It was hard to say why. But it wasn't because the former châtelaine of the house had been from all accounts somewhat spectacularly bumped off in the upstairs bedroom. Rather was it because the other occupant of the house was still alive, if not exactly kicking, and Dobie was unable to rid himself of an uneasy feeling that he might at any moment walk in through the front door prepared to oust the present usurper through bodily violence, as after all he presumably had a certain right to do. Even if your actual grievous bodily harm was not involved, his entry, Dobie thought, would almost certainly be an *emphatic* one; Seymour, he remembered, had always been a decidedly emphatic young man, dogmatic in his opinions and often

78

over-aggressive in his presentation of them. And Benthall or whatever his name was had intimated clearly enough that his manner hadn't changed in that respect. He and all the other people Dobie had so far conversed with had expressed various degrees of courteous regret and even shock about the bumping-off, but nobody had seemed to be particularly *surprised*. In the undertones of Cem Arkin's comments Dobie had even detected the lurking suggestion that she might, to employ an inappropriate vulgarism, have had it coming. That wasn't, however, a topic upon which Dobie wished to speculate.

Or, if he did, not right now.

Glancing, as it were instinctively, towards the photograph again, he suddenly remembered who it was that Derya, in that particular posture, reminded him of. The physical resemblance could hardly have been slighter, but there was something about the carriage of the head and the marginally over-confident what-she-tells-all-the-boys expression that had caused Dobie to make the connection. Unconsciously, no doubt. Most of Dobie's mental processes took place on that level, as Kate assured him. Arguably they were doing so now. And since the person of whom he was being thus reminded was in fact his late wife Jenny, Dobie wished that they wouldn't.

Ah, but there was no real resemblance, not really. No real resemblance at all. One thing that having achieved notoriety as a Professor Bluebeard does for your unconscious mental processes is render you, perhaps, a little over-sensitive in such matters, and also more than ordinarily sympathetic to other unfortunate ex-husbands in similar cases. Dobie had already determined now that he was in Cyprus to make a point of visiting the Othello Tower in Famagusta; Othello he now felt to be a much-maligned and misunderstood character who had thrown up, clearly in a fit of pique, what was clearly an excellent chance of beating the rap.

And Seymour's chances, if it came to that, had to be rather more than non-existent. This was a Mediterranean country, after all, where murdering a wife or two might well be regarded in certain circumstances as being the only gentlemanly thing

79

to do. Dobie, it was true, was aware of a certain essential difference between himself and Seymour: he, when all was said and dun, hadn't dunnit. Seymour apparently had. Well, he'd confessed to it, at any rate.

So it wasn't, as in Dobie's case, a matter of sneaky and meretricious innuendoes appearing in the popular organs of the tabloid press. A statement made to the police would have been another matter entirely, and that, it had to be supposed, was what Seymour had offered up. Under duress? It didn't seem likely. While bemused by the intensity of his emotions? Possible, but also improbable. While under the influence of narcotic drugs? Well, if what that what's-his-name chap, yes, *Arkin* had said was true, and there seemed to be no reason to doubt it . . .

But of course there'd be a lawyer, someone who'd have looked into all that side of things and . . . And a British consular representative, there'd have been someone like that. The Cypriot police would be civilised and well-trained officers, not like that bunch in *Midnight Express* though the kid in that film (to which Dobie, by the way, had once been dragged under emphatic protest, since he wasn't in any way interested in train-spotting) had been fingered for drug offences, hadn't he? They might call it a Turkish Republic but Cyprus wasn't Turkey. And if it came to that, Seymour . . .

It isn't as though I *liked* the man, Dobie thought (almost in desperation). I hardly even knew him. And what I *did* know of him I didn't like at all. Of course they all said he was enormously talented but not in my field he wasn't and anyway that had nothing to do with it. What he did was to divert Derya's attention at a crucial point in her studies with all that acting and theatrical nonsense and *that* was how he got me pissed off. Of course it was serious in a way – they got married which might be held to prove it – but the final year of a doctoral assignment isn't a good moment for that sort of thing and even if her thesis had been duly approved it didn't seem that the marriage had been too much of a success if they'd . . .

80

Dobie sighed. Don't say it, Kate, he thought . . .

'Dobie, you're a prick.'

Yes. In some ways, it's true. But old habits of thought die very hard. And new ones—

He looked up, suddenly alert. The telephone was ringing. He hoped it was Kate.

But it wasn't.

4

He had been prepared for the car and even for the uniformed
driver but not for the twin flags to either side of the bonnet
that fluttered gaily in the wind and made flicking, snapping
noises like hungry terrapins as they drove at high speed down
the main road towards Pirhan. Together with the comfortably
appointed car interior they made Dobie feel like an American
politician on his way to an assassination date. He gazed out
of the window towards the mountains to his far right with
a definite sense of foreboding, wishing he could have found
it in him to be less accommodating to the nice lady with
the cultured (not to say sexy) voice who had called him up
on the telephone and who now, barely a half-hour later, sat
beside him on the back seat. 'It's really very good of you,' the
nice lady said, possibly sensing a certain recalcitrance in her
chosen victim and sounding even drawlier and Roedeanier than
before, 'to find the time for this visit. I have to say that not all
Mr Seymour's compatriots here have been so co-operative.'

Dobie shifted the angle of his gaze to take in, no less glumly,
the nearer of the red-crescented flags on the car bonnet. 'Well,
I understood you to say the Foreign Office—'

'Yes, that's quite right.'

'But I thought you meant *ours*, you see.'

'Maybe I should have said the Ministry of Foreign Affairs,
but that always sounds so cumbersome. And it isn't a
very exact translation anyway. I'm afraid that as a British
subject you don't have any formal diplomatic representation
in North Cyprus, other than through the High Commission,

and neither, of course, does Mr Seymour. That's rather the point.'

'So how do *you* come into it?'

The nice lady exhaled a sweetly perfumed breath with a sound that in a less refined context might have passed for a groan. 'I'm in charge of the English section of the Ministry and I'm able to liaise semi-officially with the British people over the other side. Between us we're able to sort out most of the problems that arise when all those fat-headed tourists get themselves into some kind of trouble Turk-side. Provided there's no criminal charges involved, smuggling or espionage or anything like that, it's not so very difficult. It just keeps me busy, that's all. But Mr Seymour . . . ' The nice lady sighed. 'That's a different kettle of fish.'

'Or can of worms.'

'Or can of worms, yes. I suppose you know something about the background to the whole business?'

'Something, yes.' The nice lady had very nice legs, which she had at that moment elected to cross, but they offered, Dobie sadly thought, inadequate compensation for his own prospective involvement in this *business*, as she called it. And with a local government department, furthermore. 'What I don't know is what you want me to do about it.'

'Just talk to him, that's all.' The voice now held a faint undertone of surprise. 'I thought I'd made that clear. We're hoping that if you do that, he'll talk to you. He did ask to see you, after all.'

'How did he get to know I was here?'

'He read about your appointment in the local paper. He reads a lot. He reads all the time. He just won't speak to anyone, that's the trouble.'

'I'm surprised he remembered my name,' Dobie said. 'He never knew me all that well.'

'They tell me you supervised his wife's thesis some years back.'

'So I did.'

'You see, he won't talk to *anyone*. Not to his lawyer, or

to me, or to anybody else. That's been the problem all along – or part of it, anyway. Right now they've got him in this military hospital and under guard, of course, but the people there don't really seem to know how to treat him. They're not too experienced in the use of modern psychiatric techniques, as you can imagine.'

'Oh, but I'm not, either. I'm not a psychologist if that's what you thought. No, no. I teach mathematics.'

'Well, but let me explain. They managed to get him off his drug dependence all right, they gave him cold chicken or whatever they call it, but he went through a really bad time one way or another and now they're talking about catatonic states and withdrawal syndromes and so forth and what they seem to mean by all that is that he won't talk to anyone any more. Like I said. He just sits around and listens to the radio and reads the papers but he won't *talk*, he won't tell us what happened or talk about anything concerned with it. And that's making it pretty damned difficult for the lawyer who's preparing his defence. And,' the nice lady said, 'it's indirectly embarrassing for the Ministry, too.'

'I suppose he *can* talk? I mean, when you say he asked to see me—'

'Oh, yes, he *speaks*, he can tell them what he'd like for breakfast, he can ask for a clean shirt, he'll even converse with the medical orderlies up to a point. In Turkish. But he won't tell us what we want to know. The doctor says he's incapable of facing up to what he's done, we're up against some kind of a mental block. I suppose that could be true. But he *did* ask to see you, that's the whole point, and maybe if he sees someone he used to know in England, someone who isn't connected with his life in Cyprus or with his marriage in any way at all—'

'But I *am* connected with Derya. Not very closely, of course. But more closely than with him, if you take my meaning.'

'Yes. It may not seem very logical,' the nice lady said, 'but then he isn't in a logical frame of mind. He's obviously very seriously mentally disturbed. And . . . it's just something that seems to be worth trying.'

After a while Dobie said, 'I was told he wrote some kind of a confession.'

'So he did. Or, at least, dictated and signed it, if we have to be exact. It's a confession all right, but the police seem to be happier with it than maybe they should be.'

Dobie wondered what she meant by that. 'You've seen it yourself?'

'A transcript, yes, of course. Bilsel – his lawyer – has a copy.'

'And how incriminating is it?'

'Bilsel thinks we can maintain that he dictated it while the balance of his mind was disturbed and if so, then he can get it thrown out of court. But of course, to maintain that convincingly—'

'He wants Seymour to tell you more about it.'

'Exactly.'

'Um,' Dobie said.

Ahead of the car he saw trees, crossroads, a petrol station sign cutting across the long flat line of the empty horizon. A khaki-clad, white-helmeted guard came to attention and saluted as the car turned sharply into what was clearly a military encampment. A curious place to put a foreign subject awaiting trial on a serious civil charge, but then not many things in Cyprus seemed to be done by the book. Dobie wasn't even sure that there *was* a book. Instead there was a row of huts, a lorry park, a grassless football pitch, everything seemingly stupefied in the noonday heat. Even the flags on the bonnet drooped limply downwards now.

'Well,' Dobie said grumpily, 'I suppose if he really wants to talk to me, I can't stop him.'

His thoughts were still dwelling lustfully on that sirloin steak but he didn't see any way he was going to get his gnashers into one right now.

* * *

85

Seymour sat stoop-shouldered at the table, his forearms resting on his knees and his hands dangling loosely between them. Bony-knuckled hands with long thin fingers. He seemed indeed to be greatly changed from Cardiff days, though that, Dobie thought, was to be expected. The beard, for a start. Rather a ragged affair, with reddish patches here and there. Probably they hadn't allowed him the use of a razor; you could see why they might have thought it wise to enforce such a prohibition. Something about the way his eyes moved constantly here and there without ever seeming to focus clearly on anything . . .

The only thing that struck Dobie as instantly familiar was the broad frontal bar that ran across his forehead, raising the auburn-coloured eyebrows and giving his expression, then as now, a certain lowering, almost a threatening quality. His present posture, however, wasn't at all threatening, and as he hadn't as yet looked towards Dobie it was hard to be sure whether he'd recognised his visitor or not. He hadn't said anything, either, to indicate that he had.

Then, just as Dobie himself was about to speak, 'Well,' Seymour said. 'So now you can see what's become of Waring.' He lifted his hands, palms turned upwards, about six inches, then dropped them to hang loose again.

'What?' Dobie said, taken by surprise. 'Sorry, I didn't—'

'Since I gave them all the slip.' Wearing a slip? What? Under the straggling edges of face fungus the corners of his mouth seemed to have lifted very slightly. 'The glory is departed, right enough. Ichabod, Ichabod.'

'Oh, right.' Dobie nodded emphatically. That was certainly one way of putting it.

'You don't follow me?'

'Not completely.'

'Browning.'

'Who? Me? Oh no, I don't think so. No more than a touch of suntan, surely.'

A faint expression of disbelief crossed Seymour's face, or as much of it as was visible under the beard. He changed position to sit with his elbows on the table surface and with his chin dropped on to the knuckles of his interlinked hands, a posture of comfortably relaxed intellectual alertness that somehow conveyed a totally opposite, or anyway a totally different, impression. Possibly he'd picked it up from someone. From Derya, conceivably. It wasn't a posture that seemed natural to him, somehow. 'D'you believe in telepathy?'

'Telepathy? Well . . . '

'*I* believe in telepathy. I believe in fairies and Father Christmas and unidentified flying objects and the Athanasian Creed and the doctrine of Papal Infallibility. I mean, I'm a real fruitcake, didn't they tell you? That's the logical explanation for it all and I believe in logical explanations. Yes. *That*'s what I believe in.'

'So do I,' Dobie said. 'I'm a mathematician.'

'And also a bit of a weirdo. Derya always said so.'

'She did?'

'Said you were brilliant. But barmy. Just like me.'

Dobie had heard this view expressed on previous occasions. He nodded again, though much less emphatically. 'Is that why you wanted to see me?'

'Look,' Seymour said. 'I told them what happened but words are no good and I don't want to talk about it any more. I don't need a mathematician. Don't think that.'

'What *do* you need?'

'Out.'

'Out?'

'Just *out* of here. A woman. A fix. You name it. Anything so it's out of this bloody dump. No, OK, it isn't on, I know that. They got to keep me here. It's OK.'

His ideas, of course, were disjointed to the point of incoherence but might well seem less so to Dobie than to most other people, conversational incoherence being one of Dobie's specialities. And it can't be easy when you're hooked on an addictive drug and they put you on cold turkey; it can't be easy to think rationally or to do anything else other than try to fight off the shakes. In a curious way, though, Dobie felt that he could see what

87

Seymour was getting at. Words were no good. He could understand that.

'I *was* thinking about you,' he said, 'when that woman rang. I doubt if it was telepathy, though. Just a curious coincidence.'

'What woman?'

'The one from the Foreign Office or whatever it's called. The one who's looking after . . . your interests.'

'Ah. *That* woman. And you were thinking about me, you say? In what sort of a connection?'

'Well, they've put me in your house, you see.' Dobie was apologetic. 'I mean, to live. For the time being. Another coincidence, in a way. Though not very considerate, either.'

Seymour blinked, perhaps being a little taken aback to encounter someone whose conversational gambits appeared to be almost as desultory as his own. More probably, however, this was a nervous habit of recent development. 'So why did she ring you?'

'Who?'

'That woman.'

'What woman?'

'The one who you said rang you.'

'Ah. She knew of the connection, you see.'

That made it Seymour's turn to play the lob to the back of the court. 'What connection?'

'Between . . . You do *remember* me, don't you?'

'Of course I do. You were Derya's supervisor, back in Cardiff.'

'Well. There you are. That's it.'

'That's what?'

'The connection.'

'Ah,' Seymour said, mis-hitting the ball weakly into the net. For a while they both sat there, surveying it glumly.

In the end Seymour said, or at any rate appeared to say, ' . . . Excavating for a mine.'

Dobie (for once) was familiar with the quotation and indeed even able to identify its source, but wasn't immediately able

88

to perceive its relevance. He therefore let that one whizz past him without even attempting a stroke. 'Sorry?' he said, belatedly.

'Hesketh Basinger was mine. My *supervisor*. I expect you knew him.'

'Oh, Hesketh, yes. He went on somewhere. Birmingham or some out-of-the-way place like that.'

'Wouldn't know. Didn't keep in touch. What with one thing and another.'

The Old-Collegians'-Reunion aspect of all this was of course deeply touching but the whole drift of the interview seemed to Dobie to be getting out of hand. He'd expected something more on the lines of the initial confrontation of Lord Peter Wimsey with Harriet Vane, though omitting, naturally, any overt or for that matter covert proposal of marriage. Seymour's attitude, on the contrary, suggested rather that of a dyspeptic don conducting a tutorial with a sullenly recalcitrant student; perhaps, Dobie thought, he'd been too much in the society of university lecturers of late. Immersion in such an ambience is often of itself enough to drive an inexperienced young fellow right up the wall. 'Such as going to Cyprus, I suppose.'

'Eh?'

'You said, what with one thing and another. Going to Cyprus, I mean, could be one of those things.'

'Oh, I don't know,' Seymour said.

Dobie wondered what he meant by that and then decided that it didn't much matter. 'I suppose it was Derya. Who brought you here.'

'Yes. Well, she got that job.'

'Quite.'

'And I didn't have one. And I thought it mightn't be a bad place to settle in and write a novel, bearing in mind what a hopeless mess the UK is in nowadays . . . '

His voice tailed away. Dobie waited for him to continue. But he didn't.

'And was it? A good place?'

'I don't know,' Seymour said again. 'It didn't seem to work. Nothing did. Or maybe it was me. I don't know. Or perhaps it was the pattern that was wrong.'

'The pattern?'

'Yes. You know. Everything here's that little bit out of date, out of kilter. It's like a regression, coming here. Like going back to . . . But I thought that didn't matter. Regression's more interesting than evolution in lots of ways. Look at Hemingway. What he got out of Spain and the Civil War.' Seymour was blinking again, while moving his chin jerkily to and fro across the backs of his hands. 'Bitter lemons there all right, wouldn't you say?'

Well, Dobie had heard of Hemingway. Just. Nobel Prize et cetera. Like old whatname. 'But—'

'You know what Cyril Connolly said?'

'Er . . . No.'

'Well, I think he got it exactly right. He said that while Hemingway was so good at getting surface textures, at writing about bulls and girls and wine and the heat and the *alegría* and so on, his *real* subject was always the shadow of those things, the dark shadows cast by the sunlight . . . a sort of inner sadness, if you like. A melancholy. You'll find that here, too. Because this is a Mediterranean culture, after all.'

The Turkish military policeman standing by the door had just changed position, his boots scraping noisily on the tiled floor. Now he was statue-still again. Dobie couldn't help wondering why Seymour was being kept under quite so close a guard; they couldn't imagine that he was *dangerous*, surely? Loony, yes, perhaps. But dangerous, no.

'They've had their political troubles here, too,' Dobie said. 'Or so I understand.'

'Oh, don't ever think you *understand*.'

'Perhaps I should have said—'

'At first you think that's the cause of it. Of the sadness. But it isn't. It goes far deeper than that. It's like when Aeneas arrives at Carthage, you know, and looks around him and decides that these people, whoever they are, must be a civilised lot

90

because they obviously understand the *lacrimae rerum* – the tears of things, the *sadness* of human life. And *they* were a Mediterranean race, you see. That's how I feel here in Cyprus. Like Aeneas.'

'Look,' Dobie said. 'What I really wanted to know—'

'Even the tourists feel it sometimes. They don't really come here to laze about on the beaches and pick up a suntan. Browning. That's a good one.' Seymour snickered briefly. 'No, it's the elixir of bloody youth they're after. A beaker full of the warm south. Maybe even a Grecian urn. With the tears of life winking away at the brim.'

'Is that what Derya had?'

'What?'

'The elixir?'

Seymour stopped blinking and stared instead fixedly at the far wall. 'I was right, then. You *do* understand. At least . . . something. No one else does. They can't. They're all too close to it, they can't see the hole for the trees. *Wood* for the trees, I mean. I tell them what happened and . . . no. They don't get it.'

Perhaps the room where he was usually kept didn't get much sunlight. Perhaps the sunshine coming in through the side window was a little too bright. At any rate, now that he'd stopped blinking his eyes seemed to be moist.

'And, ah . . . the novel?'

'Novel?'

'The one you were writing . . . '

'Yes. What about it?'

'You said it didn't work out.'

'It didn't. *Nothing* has. That's the point. I put it aside and did something else, instead. Sort of a . . . guidebook, what the hell . . . ' For the first time Seymour sat back in his chair, letting his hands slide down to lie flat palms downwards on the table. A more relaxed posture, but one that seemed as unnatural as the other. 'Look, forget about all this Greek-and-Turk nonsense. Christian, Moslem, whatever. What they are, they're *pagans*. Derya and all the rest of them.

91

That's why they have this feeling, this sense of sorrow. They know this life is all they've got, that's why. That's how they can see the shadow as well as the sunlight, how they can see things the way *we* can't unless of course you're someone like . . . But then he was a pagan, too. Hemingway was. He shot himself, didn't he? To prove it. But he didn't have to do that. He'd proved it already by writing the way he did.'

'And Derya?' Dobie grabbed rather clumsily for the only handle he could perceive in all this rigmarole. 'Was *she* a pagan?'

'Oh, yes. That's how I know about . . . Well, the little that I *do* know. Which isn't much. But—'

'Was that why you killed her? To prove something?'

The hands pressing hard down upon the table's surface didn't move. After a while Seymour said, 'What could it prove?'

'Maybe something to yourself?'

'No,' Seymour said. 'Nothing like that. No. No.' He shook his head and went on shaking it for some little time. 'It wasn't like that at all. I explained all *that* part of it. I wrote it all down.'

'It's the part you *didn't* explain . . . '

'Because I can't. I told you. Words are no good.'

'But you signed a confession. That's the trouble. If you'd had proper legal advice—'

'No, no, not *that*. I wrote it all down, before and after, it's in the drawer. Desk drawer, I think. Everything else I burnt, all that rubbish. It's in the desk drawer. And in the book. The publishers have the book, it should be . . . It's a mystery, you know. There's no doubt about that.'

His tone was showing for the first time signs of serious perturbation. And for the rest, it had to be rambling. Maybe the interview had gone on too long, but for some reason Dobie refrained from glancing down at his wrist-watch. He felt that if only for a minute or two he could get Seymour to keep to the point . . . 'They say you were stoned.'

'What?'

92

'When you did it. They say you were stoned out of your mind.'

'Yes. Flying. OK. Right. I was. I didn't know what I was doing. That's true. Like I was someone else but still me. Amphitryon. You know? Me and not me. Multiple personality, maybe. I've read about that. I've read of cases. Telepathy, no. That's shit. But *that* I can believe in. Because that's how it was. Me up there in the sunlight and underneath . . . the shadow. Another kind of being. It's like that with all of us, I'm convinced of it. Deep down we're all pagans, because that's what we all were, once. I mean, it wasn't just old Hemingway. Look at Lawrence. *He* knew. He knew about the underworld, Hades and that. He knew it existed. He'd been there.' Seymour surveyed his visitor cagily, his head cocked to one side like a bird's. 'So have I.'

'What's it like?'

'Oh, dark,' Seymour said. 'Amid the blaze of noon. Dark and deeper than any sea-dingle. It's horrible. I'll never go there again.'

'Would *you* say he was loopy?'

'A little unbalanced, certainly. But not noticeably more so than certain other of my colleagues back home.'

'That's where I'd very much like to see him sent,' the nice lady said. 'Because here, he's a serious embarrassment to everyone. He really is.'

Dobie was disposed to be wary. 'In what way?'

'Every which way. Legally. Politically. Medically. At least he *spoke* to you. That's something.'

'Yes, but he seems to have a very literary sort of mentality. He made a lot of allusions, or I think they were allusions, that I couldn't recognise. But then lots of people express themselves very abstrusely nowadays, don't you find?'

'*He* certainly does. But the psychiatrist regards that as a manifestation of the withdrawal syndrome.'

'Exactly,' Dobie said. 'That's what I mean.'

93

The nice lady elucidated the matter further. 'They've taken him off the hard stuff so he's flipping his lid.'

'Ah,' Dobie said. 'Gotcha.'

The car was trundling them both comfortably back to Salamis. The road was straight and almost empty of traffic. Away to the right and on the horizon he could see the low hills over Greek-side. Even with the air-conditioning ticking over, it was hot and sticky on the back seat.

He felt a little drowsy.

'But of course' – the nice lady wasn't paying any attention to the passing scenery, having no doubt seen it all before; many times – 'he isn't getting any intensive psychiatric attention. I told Bilsel he should fly in an expert in criminal psychiatry to help him prepare the defence, but he wouldn't agree. Of course that'd be expensive and Mr Seymour's financial resources are very limited. But even so.'

'Bilsel?'

'Mr Seymour's lawyer. He says that the tribunals aren't too impressed by that kind of evidence and I expect he's right. He knows his own system, after all, and he's supposed to be good.'

'Psychiatrists,' Dobie said, '*are* inclined to be . . . '

'Abstruse.'

'Yes. But then, so are lawyers.'

'When it suits them to be so, no doubt. Which is most of the time. But Bilsel reckons that if he claims his client went and knocked off his wife in the heat of the moment, after a flaming quarrel, that's the sort of thing the local people can understand – and maybe even sympathise with, up to a point. Especially if the defence can show that Mrs Seymour was consistently unfaithful and Bilsel seems to think that won't be difficult. Whereas if he puts forward a whole load of psychological jargon . . . '

'I can see his point.'

Dobie could also see that whatever the financial state of Bilsel's client, the nice lady didn't look as though she'd ever be pushed for want of a few bob. Nothing ostentatious, of course. All in the best of irreproachable Home Counties taste, twin-set and pearls without the pearls but wearing instead a rather attractive coral bracelet round her left wrist. Unlike Seymour, she kept her hands remarkably still, neatly folded on her beige-linen-skirted lap. 'And besides,' she said, 'he wants to keep the drug-addiction thing right out of it because that's bad publicity for this side of the island, politically speaking. Maybe he's even talked up a deal with the prosecution on that one. I wouldn't know.'

'So that's why he's an embarrassment.'

'That's *one* of the reasons why he's an embarrassment. Yes.'

Dobie considered the matter for a while. It certainly made better sense than Seymour himself did. 'But *was* there a flaming quarrel?'

'Oh, yes. On his own admission. It's all in the . . . But of course you haven't seen the transcript yet. I'll let you have a copy.'

'Of his confession?'

'If that's what you call it.'

'Isn't that what it is?'

The nice lady sighed. 'It amounts to that, yes. But it wouldn't stand up in a British court of law because it wasn't dictated under conditions that a British judge could possibly accept.'

'But this isn't the UK.'

'Indeed it isn't. And that embarrasses them, too. They're perfectly well aware that the legality of *all* their court decisions can be called into question outside the island. And sometimes is. Certainly they're going to be awfully reluctant to pass a death sentence on a British subject at the present moment in time. Bilsel's playing that card as well.'

'So that's in Seymour's favour.'

'Yes.'

'But you're not satisfied?'

'Would *you* be? If you were he?'

Dobie considered the matter. He found it easier to do so

if he lowered his eyelids slightly. Really it was never very easy to give matters serious thought here in Cyprus; there was something about the climate or the temperature or the atmosphere; no, he didn't know what to make of Cyprus at all, of the Turkish Republic as they called it, an imaginary garden, hadn't someone said? – with a real toad in it and while the legal system here also seemed to be in some respects also imaginary he didn't really know enough about it to . . .

'Well?'

'Eh? Oh, yes. Well.' He opened his eyes again with some reluctance. 'I suppose it would depend on the weight of the evidence against me. Him. And as he hasn't—'

'There isn't any. Apart from what he states in his so-called confession, it doesn't amount to anything and the police haven't done very much to uncover any. I mean – we've got a confession so why bother? That's their attitude.'

'It's um-derstandable.'

'Yes, but if there'd been even a suggestion of a not-guilty plea, they'd have gone into the whole thing a bit more thoroughly. As it is, the verdict'll be practically prearranged. Bilsel and the prosecuting counsel will fix up a deal that suits all parties. No scandal, no turning-over of stones with nasty crawly things underneath them, and in return . . . no death sentence. Just a minimal fifteen years that'll be six or eight in practice. It's all very convenient and even humane but . . . ' She paused. 'No, I'm not satisfied. I'm not satisfied that things have been done properly. You know what I mean?'

Yes. Dobie did. But where were they ever? 'If your main purpose is to act in Seymour's interests—'

'As he's a British subject, yes, it is. But you've got to remember that an awful lot of Cypriots are British subjects. Seymour's wife was, if it comes to that. The trouble is . . . ' She clicked her tongue. 'The law is the same but the application is different. Because the *pressures* that are put upon it are different. Perhaps you haven't been here long enough yet to understand.'

'I've only just got here.'

'That's an advantage in a way.'

'An advantage?'

'You may not understand the situation but at least you know the people. The university people. You're working with them, you're living among them. In fact you're actually living in Seymour's house.'

'Yes, but—'

'All I'm asking is that while you're here you look around a bit. Talk to people. Find out if what Seymour says . . . In other words, do what the police haven't done.'

'You mean . . . look for evidence sort of thing?'

'Look for something,' the nice lady said, 'that might persuade the lawyers to change their minds and run a proper trial instead of going through the motions. Not get him off. We can't do that. But at least give Bilsel something to work with so he can stop them from simply making a deal. He's a clever chap and he won't need much. But he does need something.'

Dobie sighed. He was tempted to say what he should have said much earlier, that all this had nothing to do with him and that he much preferred not to be in any way involved, because . . . But of course he didn't. 'I don't quite know what sort of evidence you had in mind. Those crawly things you were talking about . . . You weren't very specific, were you? But if they think there are a few stones lying around it would be best to leave unturned, you ought to consider the possibility that they might be right. There've been stones like that in every university I've ever worked in, I can assure you. There's nothing even remotely *unusual* about it, is all I'm saying.'

The nice lady was silent for a moment, staring thoughtfully out of the window as the car approached the Salamis turnoff without any slackening of speed.

'Or putting it another way,' Dobie added, 'why pick on *me*?'

'Because you're a stranger here, Dobie. That's the point. You see, Cyprus . . . There are stones that have been lying around here for hundreds of years and nobody even *notices*

97

them any more. People take them for granted. They pick up chunks of Roman temples and wall off their fields with them. They never ask any questions. They never stop and say to themselves, What's this? But *you* will. You're bound to. Like I said, you have an advantage.'

'I'm afraid,' Dobie said, 'I'm not very *good* at noticing things.' And he, too, was silent for a moment. The car took the turn and, committed to a new and bumpier route, raced off towards the not-far-distant mountains and the Karpaz hills, outlined now against a cloudless sky. 'But all right,' Dobie said. 'I'll try.'

5

THE MASK OF ZEUS

by Adrian Seymour

The moonlit nights were best, when without turning on the electric lights he could move quietly from room to room, everywhere in the house, upstairs, downstairs . . . Well, not quite everywhere, but everywhere he chose, which was what mattered, the important thing, that at night choice should become action in this way, become movement of feet and hands and eyes instead of lines of words on white paper. Of course, being what he was he had no need to move feet or hands or eyes . . .

In the desk drawer, exactly where Seymour had said it would be. In certain respects, then, it looked as though his word might be trusted, or as though at least he knew what he was talking about. It was all there in the desk drawer, pages and pages of it. Dobie read through it carefully, sitting at the desk where presumably Seymour had written it, one leg tucked angularly under the chair like a roosting stork's. When he had finished reading it, he read through it again.

Seymour, he then decided, might know what he was talking about but what he was writing about was something else again. It was all very . . . Well, it wasn't at all clear *what* it was. Not to Dobie, anyway. Was it supposed to be a story of some weird kind? Or . . . something pretty literary, anyway. Not the sort

99

of thing that Dobie was used to dealing with. Hillyer, on the other hand, might be.

Yes, Hillyer would be the man to see about it. Hillyer would know about Amphitheatre and Jupiter and people like that. Moreover, a sightseeing tour had been arranged with Hillyer for tomorrow morning, some kind of quick trip round the local fleshpots. There would be ample opportunities, surely, for raising the matter. But on the other hand . . .

Beauty, though, is sometimes a matter of unobvious things, like little undisciplined wisps of hair, the half-furtive rub of a shoe against the edge of a carpet. Often when you look for it somewhere, it's somewhere else . . .

Not only beauty, Dobie thought. But other things as well. Strange, though, that he too should remember Derya. Like that . . .

'This is where it happened.'

'What happened?'

'Where he killed her.'

'Ah.'

Hillyer, Dobie thought, was after all a Britisher like himself. A *British* Britisher, so to speak. And therefore, if the nice lady was right, someone who'd be good at observing rocks and ruins. They seemed to have observed an awful lot of them that morning.

'Though one wonders,' Hillyer said, 'why he didn't simply push her out the window. Quite a nasty drop, as you can see.'

Quite a nasty drop, and quite an impressive view. Brown roofs, palm trees, lion-coloured battlements: Famagusta, sweltering in the rays of a September sun. Dobie dabbed sweat from his forehead with a handkerchief. Quite unnecessary, he decided, to shove anyone out of the window; a tumble down the stairs they'd just surmounted would certainly have settled any young lady's hash. He found that for a very personal reason an unpleasant image and lowered his gaze, staring down at his own dust-smothered shoes. 'In fact he strangled her, as I believe.' What window? There wasn't any window. Just a flat stone space where they both stood, a stone floor hammered to dust by centuries under the sun. A ruin, in short, like everything else.

'She was suffocated, in point of fact. With a pillow. Though Shakespeare was never very accurate on points of fact. He was certainly never here, as goes without saying. It's generally held,' Hillyer said, 'that Othello wasn't a Moor at all. He was a Venetian general called Cristoforo Moro. Hence the misapprehension. Upon which, of course, the whole point of the play depends. Sometimes one wonders how many of the great works of literature owe their existence to total misapprehensions on the part of their authors. It's interesting, anyway, to speculate.'

Dobie shook his head sadly. He didn't really think so. It was kind of Hillyer to show him the sights of Famagusta, but it struck him as being a bit of a dump, really, and his guide and mentor certainly tended to drone on rather. Not to say drivel. He turned round. Directly behind them was the port; the eye of Cyprus, directed unblinkingly towards the exotic and mysterious Levant. Dobie saw rows of dilapidated warehouses, three or four equally dilapidated and rusting merchant ships; nothing moving. It was bloody hot. Not, surely, the scene that Shakespeare had envisaged; but then he couldn't envisage Shakespeare's version, either, or even remember much about the plot. Something about a handkerchief, wasn't it? Lost in the laundry? He looked at the sodden specimen still clutched in his right hand and returned it to his pocket.

'That's what Seymour did, of course,' Hillyer said, rather shortly. 'Smothered the girl. With a pillow. I must admit to having speculated on that subject, as well. As to whether he got the idea from . . . However.'

'Or maybe *he* was under some kind of misapprehension.'

'Yes. That's possible. The mind is prey to curious vagaries in times of stress, or so I understand.'

101

Dobie, whose mind was subject to curious vagaries at any time at all, didn't comment. The stairs were steep and dangerous enough to discourage further conversation as they descended them and Hillyer didn't speak again until they had passed through the gate of the citadel and were once again approaching the car, conveniently parked in a patch of shade. When he did, however, it was to put forward a practical rather than a purely speculative proposition. 'How about a beer?'

'A good idea,' Dobie said.

'Let's go to Petek's.'

'OK.'

Dobie cast a last glance backwards at Othello's Tower before clambering into the little Renault, at the dark shadowy gateway with the lion of St Mark prancing kittenishly over the low lintel. It was too damned hot for sightseeing, really, but interesting, no doubt, if history and all that turned you on. It was something, at any rate, that he could tell Kate about next time he wrote. And there were times, indeed, when he regretted the limited nature of his own interests. Not many times. But some. 'He was jealous of her, wasn't that it?'

'Seymour?'

'No, no, the other chap. Othello.'

Hillyer, manoeuvring the Renault out on to the empty road, glanced at him briefly and almost, Dobie thought, commiseratingly. 'He was. Though again, in consequence of a misunderstanding.'

'Because he had no reason to be?'

'Exactly. Though he thought he had. Are you genuinely unfamiliar with the play or are you having me on?'

'It's just that I don't remember things very well,' Dobie explained. 'Unless they're important, I mean equations and theorems and things like that, and even those I . . . So I may have been getting him mixed up with the other one.'

'The other one?'

'The one who *wasn't* married to what's-her-name.'

'You mean Iago.'

'No, no. The other one. Macdougal.'

102

'Macdougal?'

'The one who was married to *Lady* Macdougal. The lady in the nightie.'

'Ah.' Hillyer, whose mind had turned wildly in the direction of children's animated films, visibly relaxed, though only slightly. 'Yes. I'm with you now. Or I think I am. You allude to Macbeth, the eponymous hero of an altogether different dramatic work.'

'I do?'

'Yes, you do.'

Dobie sighed windily. He was tiring of this thrust and parry of intellectual rapier-work. Really, one might as well be sitting in the House of Commons. 'I expect I do, if you say so. But it's all very confusing. Not to say bemusing.'

'Lady Macbeth,' Hillyer said, braking the car rather sharply and tucking it neatly away into an altogether different patch of shade beside another battlement, 'was beset by vaulting ambition and egged her unfortunate husband on to a station in life beyond his true deserts. To be King of Scotland, in fact. She was,' he added, after a pause chiefly dedicated to applying the handbrake, 'rather like young Derya in that respect, though not in many others.'

'She was ambitious?'

'I've just said so.'

'I meant Derya.'

'So did I.'

'But Derya married an Englishman. Not a Scotsman.'

'Yes. You know, you're right? It's *most* confusing. And yet I'm sure I had it all clear in my mind before we started.'

Beer beckoned. In Petek's they served Pilsner lager ice-cold in long frosted glasses, a nasty Continental habit to which Dobie nevertheless felt he could quickly become accustomed. They could, while sinking these noggins, look down from the first-floor balcony on to the street and cracked pavements beneath, while (relatively) at ease in the comforting shade and cooled (comparatively) by the slow sea breezes that breathed, rather than blew, over the baking foreshore. Now and again a car drove unhurriedly by, but the pavements remained empty of life except for the occasional appearance and staggering passage of small groups of lightly clad sun-drugged tourists, arms and legs a rich tomato colour, returning to the air-conditioned safety of the hotel bus waiting round the corner.

'This used,' Hillyer said, 'to be called Shakespeare Road. Now it's Kalesi Kambulat. Kambulat Street. A Turkish general, he was. Regarded as a bit of a hero.'

Dobie drank more beer. 'Why?'

'Fell in battle. Facing fearful odds.'

He should then be regarded as a bit of a dickhead, in Dobie's opinion. But then Dobie was of resolutely unheroic a nature. 'Don't they have any local heroes? Cypriot ones?'

'Not really. I suppose they went through that phase three thousand years ago and just grew out of it. They think pretty highly of Asil Nadir, though.'

'The financier? The one who went bust?'

'They don't hold that against him. They maintain all those big Greek money-men in London got in the boot. The way they see it, if you don't come some kind of a cropper you're hardly a hero – their view of life is quite Shakespearean in that respect. Fail or fall in battle, it's all the same. They don't admire success here. Quite the opposite.'

'So they don't much admire Tolga Arkin?'

'Funny you should say that.' Hillyer removed a fleck of foam from his chin with a paper napkin. 'They don't, you know. Not nearly as much as Uktu. Though all *he* did was get himself shot by the Greeks in '74. Uktu's a local hero, if you like. And there it is. Brain has to give way to brawn every time, if it's heroes you're looking for.'

Dobie wasn't. The nice lady, he thought, had really been way off the mark with that theory of hers about strangers picking up stones. Why in heaven's name hadn't she asked Hillyer? Hillyer was clearly a knowledgeable person. And Seymour's next-door neighbour, for goodness' sake. Surely Hillyer would have been far more suitable. 'Uktu?'

'Cem Arkin'll tell you all about him if you really want

104

to know. Anything Cem says, you can believe. The rest is mostly fantasy and rumour. A stick to beat the Greeks with, in fact.'

'Did Cem know him?'

'Of course Cem knew him. He was Cem's uncle. Tolga Arkin's brother. That's why we have the Uktu Hall in the university. Hasn't anyone taken you round there yet?'

'I don't think so.' Dobie was thinking that Seymour, after all, had also been a stranger to the island. Had he picked up a stone, or stones, that everybody else had missed? Was *that* the sort of thing his lawyer whatever-his-name-was had in mind? If so, it was all much too . . . 'I haven't completely got my bearings yet, to tell you the truth.'

'Well, you'll be seeing it this evening, anyway.'

'Will I? Why?'

'We're all going there for the meeting.'

'What meeting?'

'The senior staff bunfight. Didn't you see the notice in your pigeonhole?'

'What pigeonhole?'

Hillyer quite suddenly decided he needed another beer. He called the waiter over. 'Someone should have told you but obviously no one did. The administration people always get their knickers in a twist when the Rector's away in Turkey. And it's just an informal get-together, anyway.'

'Ah.' Dobie nodded. 'Casual. I see.'

'Well, not all *that* casual because Tolga Arkin will be looking in so we'll all be in our best bibs and tuckers. Full academic dress in fact. And you'll be the person he'll be chiefly wanting to meet because he always likes to have a word with the new arrivals. There'll be drinks, of course, and a spot of nosh and— Ah, yes. Two more lagers, please.'

Dobie now needed another beer, too. He had a deeply ingrained dislike of these social occasions, probably stemming from the time when as a newly appointed Assistant Lecturer he had inadvertently poured the best part of a sticky gin and tonic into the small gap at that moment inconveniently appearing at the waistband of the then Vice-Chancellor's fashionably tight-fitting trousers. He had been, he remembered, thinking about something else at the time.

Which was something that he still found it very easy to do, given the peculiarly fascinating nature of the problems with which he had made it his profession to be concerned. You might, by way of example, readily concede A to be a matrix with characteristic polynomial $P(gk) = (-1)^n (gk - gk_1) (gk - gk_2) \ldots (gk - gk_n)$, allowing J to be a Jordan matrix similar to A. Then if the formula $P(J) = Z$ be derived through those successive steps with which every schoolboy is familiar, the Hamiton-Cayley theorem can obviously be applied to obtain an alternative method of calculating the inverse of a non-singular matrix A. That, of course, would be clear as daylight to the meanest intelligence. Surely, then, the students might not unreasonably be requested to prove that the trace of A is self-evidently the sum of the kth powers of the characteristic values of A and, further, to prove various properties of the trace – always bearing in mind, naturally, that trace A is demonstrably the sum of the diagonal elements of A. However . . .

'Perhaps,' he said thoughtfully, 'I shouldn't assume the students to be familiar from the outset with the canonical forms for similarity. So I'll limit myself to the consideration of square matrices only when discussing linear transformations and so remain strictly within the requirements of the syllabus.'

'Yes, yes,' Berry Berry said, somewhat absently. 'Admirable, admirable.' One would have said that he had other matters on his mind. That was odd.

'And,' Dobie said, 'I'll assume the scalar field to consist of either the real or complex numbers. It shouldn't be difficult for them to discern which theorems can in fact be extended beyond these restrictions and I can direct investigation in such a way as to make heavy use of similarity.'

'Ah. Yes. Similarity . . . Similarity . . .' Berry Berry settled the glass of orange juice he was clutching in a nearby

niche, craning his neck the while to peer over Dobie's right
shoulder. 'I think that's . . . Yes, I think I'm being summoned
to the presence. Excuse me for a few moments, if you'll be
so good.'

He sidled away with a curious crab-like motion, leaving
Dobie soundlessly mouthing abstractions into the void. Aware
of the pointlessness of this procedure, Dobie turned to take
cognisance of his present surroundings, of which for the past
ten minutes he had been largely oblivious. Ah, yes (as Berry
Berry had said). The Uktu Hall. Quite so. During those ten
minutes, as he now saw, quite a large number of people had
entered the room and seemed to be cluttering up the place as
ineffectually as he was himself. Some faces he recognised,
but most of them he didn't. This was to be expected and
perfectly normal. He himself wasn't drinking orange juice
but was on his third (or was it his fourth?) Cuba Libre and
would soon have reached that satisfying stage wherein all
academics look exactly alike. It is, as he well knew, vitally
important to distinguish between the relations of equivalence
and similarity, but this is easier to do in mathematics than
in real life. For Dobie, anyway. 'Ah, yes,' he muttered to
himself. 'Equivalence. Similarity. Quite so.'

He could at least still distinguish his colleagues from the
two or three plain-clothes policemen at the far end of the room
who had taken up defensive positions rather like his own,
their backs to the wall. The security men weren't wearing
gowns and hoods, for a start, and were notably more nattily
dressed than most of the academics present, though Dobie
himself saw no cause for self-recrimination in that respect,
having earlier irreproachably attired himself in his lightweight
summer suiting, a subtly iridescent goose-turd green in colour,
with trendily heliotrope silk shirt and pale pink knitted wool
tie, his gown being safely if a little over-obviously secured at
the front with three large safety pins borrowed from the lady
who came in to do the cleaning. He had, of course, something
of a reputation as a snappy dresser. Apart from the security
policemen, the only person in the room who wasn't wearing

hood and gown was the large broad-shouldered gentleman with the Captain Haddock beard who was now approaching him at a rate of knots, towing Professor Berry in his wake like an attendant remora.

Tolga Arkin's eyes, Dobie thought (having found himself eventually able to focus upon them), were singular. Well, no, he had two, of course, one on each side of his nose, but they were . . . remarkable. Unusual. Of a peculiar dull opacity, almost as though their pupils were made of metal, and yet intense, as if looking out at you from the windows of a burnt-out spaceship. The eyes of one who travelled through strange seas of thought alone, or maybe of an Ancient Mariner or a Flying Dutchman, something like that. Dobie briefly had the sensation of being gripped by them as by a pair of powerful hands poised to squeeze the juice from him as from a lemon; strangely enough, it wasn't an altogether unpleasant feeling.

' . . . Professor Dobie, I believe. Delighted to welcome you to the island, Professor. You have to be one of our most valuable intellectual acquisitions to date.'

Dobie had not often been regarded in so flattering a light but a becoming modesty, he felt, might best be affected. 'It's a great pleasure to be here, Minister.'

'Your first visit?'

'Yes, it is.'

'I hope,' Tolga Arkin said, gripping Dobie lightly just above the elbow and drawing him a little to one side, 'you'll be able to do a great deal while you're here to widen our horizons.' It was a gesture that betokened confidentiality rather than secured it but was also, in its way, more than mildly flattering. 'What the Rector chiefly needs here are academics of international repute, figures of recognised standing. Such as yourself. They can deny this university political recognition for as long as they wish – and no doubt they will – but they can hardly deny us intellectual and cultural recognition with scholars of your calibre on our staff. And in the long run I regard that as more important. I hope you agree with me.'

His eyes continued to massage Dobie gently but firmly,

108

forcing Dobie to reject the possibility that these remarks were being addressed to someone else standing directly behind him. 'Er, well, mathematics . . . Yes. I mean yes. I do.'

'That's splendid. That's great. You know, your paper on matrix theory in the *American Mathematical Monthly* some years back . . . Really most enlightening. I think we must have several mutual friends at MIT. Professor Bridewell, for instance? Ray Bridewell?'

'Yes, I still hear from Ray Bridewell once in a while.'

'We must join forces,' Tolga Arkin said. 'We'll try to persuade Professor Bridewell to join us here. Might he be attracted, do you think? It's my experience that really first-rate academics are often more easily lured by clear-cut objectives than by inflated salaries. Worthwhile objectives, that is. Maybe your arrival here does something to prove my contention.' His eyes released Dobie for a few seconds, flickering across the room before flickering back again; the effect was that of a torch being swiftly directed otherwise, then as swiftly returning. 'That's what I find lacking in so many British and American universities these days. Any sense of an objective, a true *cultural* objective. I don't even see how you can develop such a sense in societies allegedly dedicated to the multicultural educational philosophy. You know, here in Cyprus we're very proud of our British heritage, our old-style British heritage. Since I came back here I've been constantly reminded of Wordsworth's great sonnet: "We must be free or die, who speak the tongue that Shakespeare spake . . . "'

'Um, ah,' Dobie said, mentally adopting the hedgehog-like posture with which he normally greeted citations of literary classics. He'd really had enough of that sort of thing from Hillyer that morning. 'Yes indeed.'

But Tolga Arkin hadn't finished yet. ' "The faith and morals hold which Milton held . . . " Well, Shakespeare's English gets pretty short shrift in London and Los Angeles these days, wouldn't you say? And as for faith and morals, bearing in mind that Milton was a Puritan . . . It's surprising, perhaps, that Wordsworth made no mention of Newton, another Cambridge man after all, though of course he did so elsewhere . . . '

Dobie brightened a little. He had certainly heard the name of Newton mentioned on several occasions; some kind of a bloody physicist or other with pretensions in the field of elementary mathematics, pre-Einsteinian of course and so virtually neolithic. But what had this *Milton* got to do with anything? Some vague connection with antiseptic medicine flickered for a moment at the back of his mind, only to be summarily dismissed. 'I see,' he said, untruthfully, 'what you're getting at. I think.'

'What I'm getting at,' Tolga Arkin said, allowing those deep-set eyes to twinkle jovially, 'is that whatever antics they may be getting up to in other places, British culture is alive and well and living right here in Cyprus, just as it is in India and Pakistan and quite a few parts of the world where the feminists and anti-élitists and deconstructionists haven't screwed things up yet. We're taking up the torch, so to speak, that you and the Americans have dropped. Not the *power*, of course, that you still possess – power in the political sense. We don't want that. No use to us. But the culture. The sense of tradition. The old-fashioned patriotism, if you like. The belief, the faith, the morals, all those things. Whatever it is those nignogs on the other side imagine they can get from Greece. But of course they're chasing mirages – pan-Hellenism, Byzantinism, all those figments of the past. And now they're beginning to realise it themselves. The torch they've been reaching for, it's been out for centuries. Nowadays you read the language of Aeschylus and Demosthenes on the cornflake packets. Without Makarios, they're like the Iranians without Khomeini. Headless chickens. No, it's *Western* culture that we want to model ourselves on. A scientific culture where humanistic values are still respected. Both here and in Turkey. But we've got the advantage of having had the British here for eighty years and we've learned a great deal already. A lot, but not enough. We've some catching up to do. That's where you come in, Professor, and my good friend Berry here, and Ray

110

Bridewell, too . . . If you want him, we'll get him. I promise you. I have an objective, too, you see. We all have.'

The lighthouse beam moved at last away from Dobie, focusing itself with an equally blank intensity upon Berry Berry.

'I don't say we never stumble. We do. We have our setbacks. But we recover from them. Right, Berry?'

'We certainly do our best, Minister.'

'I'm thinking, of course, of that unfortunate business with Derya Tüner. Even though we've secured so very adequate a replacement . . . Well, when all's said and done, it takes many years to develop a fine human intelligence and only a matter of seconds to dispose of one. That's the real tragedy of existence, isn't it? But even though we must be moved by it when it happens, we have to recognise it as inevitable. Part and parcel of the human lot. And I think we do, don't we? Everybody *here*, I mean?'

'Some more than others, of course.'

'That's to be expected,' Tolga Arkin said. Dobie had the impression none the less that this was not quite the answer he had expected; Berry's tone had certainly seemed a little morose.

A moment later Dobie found his hand being gripped again by Arkin's in a warm, dry, somehow conspiratorial clasp; the great man then moved away to rejoin various other attendant lords, grouped a little stiffly in their black gowns over by the far wall. The visitation, it appeared, was over. 'Phew,' Berry Berry said, confirming this supposition.

Some comment, Dobie felt, was required, but he didn't quite know what to say. 'Does he, er . . . *always* go on like that?'

'He rather got the bit between his teeth today.'

'He certainly makes an impression.'

'Yes, he does.' Berry had retrieved his orange juice and was golloping it greedily. 'Though somehow one always feels a little more comfortable when he's moved on somewhere else. I expect that's how people felt about Napoleon.'

'For very different reasons, surely.'

111

'I don't think reason comes into it very much. No, it's instinct, if anything.'

Dobie peered contemplatively past the rim of his own half-empty glass. Rather surprisingly, Tolga Arkin had left him with an after-impression of a profound and disturbing inner melancholy, a quality that his words and bearing had surely done nothing to reveal. Maybe that was what Seymour had meant by . . . 'He doesn't seem,' Dobie said, 'to be really at ease with himself. Perhaps that's it.'

Berry glanced sideways at him, almost in surprise. Dobie was quite familiar with that kind of a glance; Kate sometimes flashed her eyes towards him in just that way when she thought he'd said something percipient. Of course, that didn't happen very often. 'That's probably true. Tolga never relaxes. He pushes himself hard. He always has.'

'That's how you get to win a Nobel Prize.'

'I'm sure. But in fact I've never met any other. Have you?'

'Well, yes. There were seven Nobels at Harvard when I was a postgraduate. In fact I was at MIT but I used to sit in on Marcus Dowling's lectures.'

'Brilliant, no doubt.'

'I found them almost entirely unintelligible so they must have been. But he had this remarkably . . . *challenging* personality.'

'Like Arkin's?'

'No. Not really.'

Berry was now staring rather lugubriously at the oil portrait that hung on the wall almost directly behind them. Dobie had noticed it earlier; it was placed in so dominating a position that he could hardly have avoided doing so. But now that he had met the original, he felt himself to be in a better position to offer comment. 'He'd have been a good deal younger when *that* was painted, I suppose.' And of course the neat black beard made a difference. 'I can see that it's a pretty good likeness but it doesn't get that oddly perturbing quality . . . whatever it is.'

112

'But that isn't Tolga, you see.'

'Not . . . ?'

'No. That's his brother. Uktu. This is the Uktu Memorial Hall. Uktu was killed fighting the Greeks, back in '74.'

'Oh, of course.' Hence the peculiar paramilitary uniform, the beret tilted at an angle across the broad forehead, shading the deep-set eyes. 'Hillyer was telling me about it this morning but somehow I . . . Stupid of me.'

'Well, they were twin brothers. It was a natural mistake.'

There was, as Dobie had now seen, a small brass plaque underneath the portrait. Saying simply, UKTU 1943–1974.

'He led the resistance movement,' Berry said, 'when the Greeks tried to take over. It wasn't his real name, of course – he had a *nom de guerre* like Grivas and all those thugs with EOKA. *Uktu* means victory in Turkish. Actually it *is* a man's name in Turkish, a proper name, I mean. But not *his* name. His real name was Necdet. Not that it matters.'

'It doesn't matter but it's a little confusing.' Not more so, though, than everything else.

'Well, you know what happens to wartime heroes. They get forgotten. So we've got this Memorial Hall here, though really I suppose it's more to please Tolga than . . . And you're right, it's not a very good painting. It was done from a photograph, of course. Much later. After he was dead.'

Dobie turned away. His concern wasn't after all with dead heroes or murdered girls or with eccentric British junkies or even with Nobel prizewinners-cum-politicians; his concern wasn't either with the dead or with the living. He didn't know much about Milton and Wordsworth and he didn't remember much about the troubles of '74. He knew something about mathematics, though. Eternal verities, chalked on a black- board. OK, he was a specialist. A man of limited interests.

But he liked it that way.

6

Next morning while Dobie was breakfasting Zeynep brought him in a letter. Zeynep was a valuable acquisition – or Dobie thought so, anyway. Built somewhat on the lines of a roly-poly pudding with small sparkly blackcurrant eyes, she and her husband, a one-armed Cypriot bandit called Ali, ran the little lokanta bar just round the corner where, as Dobie had discovered, he and the other inhabitants of the compound might lunch on extremely tasty lamb chops with mezes. Ali also doubled as the compound porter, his chief task being to ensure that the main gate was (more or less) punctually closed and locked at midnight, while in the mornings Zeynep, as she would have put it, did for Dobie, Hillyer and Cem Arkin, sweeping out the tile floors energetically and providing on occasion certain useful articles, such as safety pins.

'Bloke on a bark jus' brought this in.'

'A bark?'

'A motor bark.'

'Oh, right,' Dobie said, propping the communication up against the coffee-pot to await his attention, this being for the moment exclusively directed towards his breakfast egg. Zeynep had spent, it seemed, some ten years of her joyous youth in Australia and curious things had happened to her native Turkish vowel sounds down there in Melbun. She always referred to him, for instance, as Derby. Dobie didn't mind this but found that he had to exercise caution, since her manner of speech was horribly infectious.

'Wotcha think of Sourpuss then, Derby?'

114

'Sorry?'

'I said 'ow yer lark living 'ere in Sourpuss? Not much lark England I don't suppose.'

'Well, no. No, it isn't. Not much like Strylia either I wooden have thought.'

On an earlier occasion he had questioned her about the house's previous occupants. ''Ow, I mean how did you use to get on with Mr Seymour? Was he narce?'

'Not to 'er 'e wozzen. Led 'er a dog's laugh.'

'Really?'

'Always farting together, they were. Gawd, we use to 'ear them farting right round the corner.'

'Good heavens.'

'Aunty social it woz.'

'I can well believe it.'

'An' then at times 'ed get varlant.'

'Beg pudden?'

'They'd 'ave reely varlant arguments. No, it wozzen narce.'

Zeynep's command of the English language, though vivid at times, was certainly totally different to Tolga Arkin's, whose fluency and phraseology had (if you discounted the lurking trace of a Californian nasality) struck Dobie as being almost perfect. Of course Arkin's concept of Sourpuss as an eventual repository of a fast-vanishing British culture and code of behaviour seemed far-fetched to the point of being preposterous, but wasn't it, Dobie thought (dismantling his second egg), in a way a logical extension of one of Seymour's less violent arguments? If throughout its history Cyprus had been able to do precisely that, accepting and adopting in succession the Greek, the Roman, the Venetian, the Ottoman and goodness knows what other cultures, then why not – eventually – the British? Dobie certainly couldn't see why not. They drove on the left here, didn't they?

But then cultural history was another of the things that Dobie didn't know very much about. He regarded it indeed as a new-fangled and altogether airy-fairy field of study, even worse than literature in some respects and lacking in all the essential qualities of a true academic discipline, such as mathematics. Yet even Berry Berry, who in his youth had produced some interesting work on the solution of equations in integers and who beyond all question was a competent, if not absolutely first-rate, mathematician – even Berry Berry, unprovoked, had burbled on interminably the other day about burial customs and pagan survivals and so forth. Perhaps that only meant that he was a Cypriot first and a mathematician second. That, if so, was reprehensible but understandable. Seymour, though, was surely different in every way.

Dobie poured himself out coffee and reached for the letter. It was, he thought, some missive from the university. He was wrong. It wasn't.

He unfolded the sheets of typescript and read them and then read through them again while his coffee got cold.

POLIS MÜDÜRLÜĞÜNE GAZI MAGUSA KUZEY KIBRIS
RECORDED STATEMENT OF—Mr A.L. Seymour
INVESTIGATING OFFICER—Insp. Ibrahim Kenan

I am Adrian Leigh Seymour, twenty-eight years old and currently resident at A6 Tuzla Gardens (University of Salamis compound), region of Famagusta.

Prior to her decease I was the legal husband of Derya Tüner (aged thirty-two) also resident at the above address and being employed as Assistant Professor of Mathematics at the University of Salamis.

I am a writer and occasional journalist and have otherwise no fixed employment in the Republic of North Cyprus.

I wish to make of my own volition the following statement.

WHEREAS

On the evening of Friday 20th July I was at home working in my study until my wife returned at some time shortly after midnight. She said that she had been visiting a friend. She prepared a meal which she ate but I did not as I was not at that time feeling hungry. My refusal to eat, however,

116

*provoked a quarrel between us. After the meal she retired
to her bedroom and I went back to my study. The time was
then approximately 1.15 a.m.*

*Being somewhat disturbed by the quarrel and finding
myself unable to settle down to work I took intravenously
a small quantity, approximately one gram, of a cocaine
derivative. This is my frequent practice on such occasions.
I then worked at my MS for as I estimate three or four hours
but I have the impression that I also slept intermittently. I
do not have a clear recollection of this period.*

*At the end of it I left the study intending to go to bed.
On reaching the top of the stairs I observed that the door of
my wife's bedroom was open. I looked in and saw that she
was asleep. I then entered the room and placed a pillow over
my wife's face and held it there until she died of asphyxia.
She made very little attempt to struggle.*

*I did not switch on the bedroom light on entering the
room because at that time I had no intention of disturbing
her sleep but as the curtains were drawn and there was
bright moonlight within the room I was able to observe
her and my own movements clearly. I may have moved
around the room for some little time before picking up the
pillow. I cannot say if when doing so I had the intention of
killing her. I assume that I must have. However throughout
this time I think that the work upon which I was engaged
was uppermost in my mind.*

*Afterwards I returned to my study and continued to work
for some little time before falling asleep in my armchair. I
did not return to the bedroom at any time to check on my
wife's condition or go upstairs again for any other reason.
I was satisfied that she was dead. But I felt no satisfaction
in the other sense of the word nor did I feel any regret or
remorse. I did not feel in any way personally involved. As I
recall it, my thoughts, as I have said, were uniquely centred
on the work I had in hand. I concede that this is very strange
and I cannot now offer any explanation for it.*

I awoke at around 7.30 a.m. the following morning in the

117

knowledge of what had been done and, having made myself
coffee in the kitchen and drunk it, I telephoned the Police
HQ in Famagusta and informed the duty sergeant that a
crime had been committed and of what nature. Inspector
Kenan and a police sergeant arrived half an hour later and
confirmed the truth of my statement.

In reply to Inspector Kenan's questions I stated further
that I was fully aware of my wife's infidelities to me on
various occasions, she herself having admitted them to me,
but that I attached no great importance to these and certainly
did not kill her for any such reason. I am a bad-tempered but
not a jealous person. Questioned further as to my motives
I could only say that I had felt a state of affairs to exist
that could not be allowed to continue. I acted therefore in
self-defence. I cannot explain the matter more precisely.

There followed Seymour's signature, a neurotic squiggle if
Dobie had ever seen one – not so very unlike his own, in
fact – and the name and signature of the officer who had
prepared the document, the latter illegible and the former
unpronounceable. Dobie sighed heavily and treated himself
to a mouthful of lukewarm coffee. It tasted horrible. He'd
have to make some more.

He wasn't familiar, to put it mildly, with every detail of
the Judges' Rules, which probably didn't apply here anyway,
but now that he had read the transcript (twice) he thought
he could see clearly enough what the nice lady had been
driving at. It was a most inadequate document. It wasn't even
properly dated. And apart from the issue of legality, the actual
wording was . . . Well, it was a great deal more intelligible
than all that Mask of Zeus rubbish, but that was about all you
could say for it. *Very strange* it was, in Seymour's opinion.
In Dobie's, too.

Of course you could account for the weirdness of his story
by claiming he'd been honked out of his skull when he'd
done it. *A small quantity of a cocaine derivative*, indeed.
But then you might equally claim that the confession had

118

been elicited from him under the same conditions, or at least before the effects of his drug intake had fully worn off. Reading it, that seemed quite likely. And even supposing him to have been really flying that night . . . that might explain the weirdness and most, if not all, of the discrepancies but it didn't explain . . . It was hard to explain what it didn't explain, even to yourself. It was just that you weren't – to use Seymour's own expression – satisfied. The nice lady obviously wasn't. And Dobie wasn't, either.

What *was* he, then?

Intrigued? Perplexed? Or . . . ?

He put the two pages of the typescript down on the table and stared for a while across the room. He wasn't good at finding the right words to express the more subtle of his thoughts and emotions. But Seymour was, or was supposed to be. That was the point.

THE MASK OF ZEUS

by Adrian Seymour

Of such moments was his own calendar composed; written not on perforated pages but across the heavens and in starry signs, moments foreordained, predeterminable, and yet . . . he chose them. He chose them as at this particular moment he chose to be made a man, to be made a man, in the likeness of Adrian Seymour, that pretentious fart Adrian Seymour . . . Pretentious? What nonsense. He didn't choose to pretend to be. He was . . .

Strangely enough these references to calendars and stars and to various obscure tamperings with the laws of temporality were the only elements in Seymour's narrative that Dobie found perfectly comprehensible, recent developments in general relativity theory being after all one of his things and a field to which he'd made some respectfully regarded contributions himself. And in fact it could, he thought, only be through some kind of time-warp or star-drive mechanism that the world of an undergraduate dramatic society and the world, say, of Tolga Arkin could be made to coincide . . . and he sensed, furthermore, that only through establishing some such coincidence, or maybe point of similarity, might the Tuzla Gardens mystery eventually be resolved. The difficulty was, of course, that there wasn't a mystery. The whole thing had been resolved from the start. But the nice lady had been absolutely right on one point: in mathematics, it isn't *what* you do, it's *how* you do it. The proper calculations hadn't been written in to one side of the examination paper; there'd been shoddy work somewhere. That ought to be put right.

There again, Dobie didn't possess a literary mind or a literary imagination, as Hillyer and Seymour – whatever their other points of difference – presumably did. Normally, he found this lack to be in no way regrettable. But he was now aware that he was being brought somehow into uncomfortably intimate contact with a different kind of mind to his own and this was, he realised, both alarming and stimulating, like meeting a Martian. Again, two foreign worlds were being brought into proximity, but how? And how did you bridge the gap? It was all very puzzling.

But it was clear that he was being – if you liked the word – challenged. Well, the life of a mathematician is a constant response to intellectual challenge, to the problems posed by an ultimately inscrutable universe. His reaction was therefore almost automatic. Or you could even say, predictable.

He wondered if the nice lady had realised that.

It's funny, Dobie thought (but also sad), how many people imagine that mathematics consists of interminably applying fixed formulae to clearly defined problems and so 'working them out'. Because it's not like that at all. Half the time you don't even know what you're looking for until you've found it. A great deal more than half the time you spend looking at a blank sheet of paper and chewing the end of a pencil – the blunt end, hopefully – while you're trying to see what the bloody problem *is*. You know it's there all right but no, you can't grasp it, you just can't quite perceive how to formulate it . . .

Mathematician's block . . .

Dobie didn't have a literary imagination but it wasn't difficult for him to envisage the frame of mind that Seymour's story, if that was what it was, had at least on the face of it seemed to portray. He was very familiar with that state of mind himself. Frustration. The block. The inability to get anything down on that sodding sheet of paper. The incapacity to formulate the problem. Seymour had written a story – if Dobie was right – about being unable to write a story. A paradox. That was all right, paradoxes were meat and drink to Dobie.

His special field.

Anticipation. Excitement. Of such things as these, he knew nothing, precisely because he knew everything . . .

I am great Jupiter. And my words are thunder . . .

'Oh, the idea's anything but original,' Hillyer said. 'It's been done many times before. But of course you have to relate the block to some other comparable situation in order to express it and . . . overcome it. Hemingway, Lawrence, Eliot. They've all done it. Indeed *The Waste Land*—'

'He mentioned Hemingway. Seymour did. *And* Lawrence. Are they . . . Are they writers he admires particularly?'

'Hemingway, yes. Certainly. Of course the tide of critical opinion has turned against Hemingway, and in my view, rightly so. But to be fair to Seymour, he didn't pay much attention to critical fads and fashions. Or to anyone else's opinion whatsoever. Self-centredness is a very valuable quality to a writer. So much so that not a few of them set out to cultivate it.'

'It's not a valuable quality in a husband, though.'

'No. Or in a wife. And Derya was very much that way, too. A formula for matrimonial disaster, really.'

But . . . of course, you have to relate the block to some other

121

comparable situation . . . such as physical impotence, maybe? Or blindness? An inability to see what's before your nose?

I myself, Dobie thought, may be suffering from that right now . . .

QWERTYUIOPASDFGHJKLZXCVBNM straight across the board.

All the letters you need, Dobie. You can formulate any problem and solve it with that little lot. Though 1234567890 may also come in useful. But:

it all came to the same in the end. Stuck.
Impotent . . .

Of course sex figured in the equation somewhere. That was obvious. You didn't need either the story or the confession to see that; all you had to do was study that photograph. Derya as Alcmena. What about Zeus? Well, you'd need some pretty obvious symbol of physical potency, wouldn't you? to carry you through the barrier. Dobie's recollections of classical mythology were hazy in the extreme but he was naturally aware, like everyone else, that Zeus had achieved considerable and deserved esteem amongst the ancients through his prowess in jumping just about every female in sight. The trouble was that this particular incident . . . Alcmena, now . . . She wasn't the one with the swan? No. That was Leda. Castor and Bollocks. It was coming back to him now. Alcmena was . . .

'She was the mother of Hercules,' Hillyer said, a little severely. Dobie, his manner suggested, was not going to be allowed to confuse him on *this* point. 'She was married to Amphitryon and Zeus took on the physical appearance of her husband in order to seduce her. With results to which I've already made allusion. Well, in fact she had twins, but Hercules did rather well for himself and not very much was later heard of the other fellow. Surely you're familiar with at least the outlines of the legend? It has,' he added hurriedly, 'nothing to do with Lady Macdougal. Nothing at all.'

'Except that there *is* this play,' Dobie said, 'that I'm sure you know something about. It seems that Derya—'

'Ah, Derya's famous *play*, yes, the Dryden version. Well, that's a travesty, of course. Dryden sent the whole thing up, as we'd say nowadays, for the benefit of a sophisticated but extremely lubriciously minded audience. I gather Seymour had a considerable success with it as a university production. Which doesn't surprise me.'

'There are other versions?'

'Oh, heavens, yes. Molière's is the most famous, and probably Dryden's model. But then there's Kleist, Giraudoux, oh, any number of others. It's a theme that seems to have a perennial fascination for dramatists, especially.'

'Why is that?'

'Because it raises the basic problem of what constitutes a human identity. Actors, you see, in playing a part, in a sense they become someone else. Which is what Zeus does. To the point of becoming totally indistinguishable from Amphitryon, the husband he's deceiving. You can even say that he *is* Amphitryon. In which case, then, where's the deception?'

Dobie found this hard to follow. 'You mean like Sean Connery *is* James Bond?'

Hillyer clicked his tongue, in sadness, however, rather than in irritation. 'No, not really. Because everyone knows that he isn't. Though perhaps you might say that the publicity people who used that slogan were trying to make the same point subliminally.'

Dobie gave it up.

No, he didn't. Being of the bulldog breed.

An actor becomes someone else when he's on the stage. Yes, he could see that. At least his audience are able to believe that he's someone else, however briefly. But surely a writer didn't believe he was someone else when he was creating a character, did he?

OK. These guys are weirdos. Perhaps they did. But the characters in Seymour's thing weren't characters at all, really, or didn't seem to be. They were real people. Seymour himself. And Derya herself. But there again, they weren't. Or Seymour wasn't. Half the time he was anything but real. He was Zeus or was imagining that he was. When he should have been Amphitryon, surely? Since he was the husband . . . But then according to Hillyer, Zeus *was* Amphitryon. The two were the same. Except one was effectively impotent and the other very much the opposite. One was a stoned-out writer with a mental block preventing him from writing and so the other was . . . What? The opposite. Shakespeare, maybe. Hemingway. Lawrence. Anyone you liked. Or admired. *Overcoming* was the word that Hillyer had used. That had to be how you overcame a writer's block. You became William Shakespeare for a bit. However briefly.

Dobie looked down at the photostatted sheets on the table and shook his head, as though in an effort to clear it. Ridiculous. It wouldn't work. Obviously not. It *hadn't* worked. No mathematician had ever solved a problem by imagining himself to be Henri Poincaré or Dirac. Life just wasn't like that. You couldn't go about things that way.

Yes, but suppose you had a different kind of block. You wanted to murder your wife but you couldn't. You didn't have the guts. Or whatever. That would be impotence of a kind, wouldn't it? And then suppose you stuffed yourself full of crack and persuaded yourself you were someone else, someone of infinite strength and will-power, someone godlike and completely ruthless . . . and supposing you wore the mask of Zeus . . .

Whatever that meant . . .

' . . . Oh, my God,' Hillyer said, his rubicund features screwing themselves up into what looked like a parody of alarm and acute distress. 'You don't want to talk about that lot. Just don't ever even mention them round here. And above all not to Cem Arkin. It's an unsavoury topic, if you know what I mean.'

Dobie didn't, and so stared at him. 'I don't.'

'These things haven't been forgotten, you know. Not in these parts. Surely you can understand that.'

'I'm afraid I . . . It's the *title* I'm talking about. *The Mask of Zeus*. It's what Seymour called this story.'

'What story?'

'The last one he wrote. The one he wrote the night when . . . it happened.'

'It's the first I've heard of it.'

'Well, I found it in his desk drawer, you see. And I've read it a couple of times and I just don't know what to make of it. It seems to be a sort of account—'

'He called it *The Mask of Zeus*?'

'Yes.'

'How extraordinary. What's the story about?'

'It's hard to say.' It was, but Dobie also thought it best to be cautious. 'It's very . . . imaginative. But Zeus comes into it, certainly, and that's why I asked you if—'

'You said, the *mask* of Zeus.'

'Yes. I don't understand that bit at all. But I thought it was maybe symbolical or something like that.'

'It's also,' Hillyer said, 'the name of a Greek terrorist group who operated round here in '74. It's what they called themselves, anyway. And there was nothing symbolical about *them*, I can assure you. A gang of murderers, basically. That's what they were.'

'Like EOKA?'

'Oh, there were quite a few of them on the rampage at the time. Arkritas, the EYP . . . Some worked with EOKA and some didn't. They worked in different areas is all I know. And the Mask of Zeus, they were the local scourge. They killed an awful lot of people in Famagusta – I'm not sure of the figures and I doubt if anyone is. Cem could tell you all about it but I certainly wouldn't ask him if I were you because his mother was one of them. Was murdered by them, I mean. At least, that's what's always been assumed.'

'But did Seymour know about this?'

'Of course. He must have done. Nobody likes to talk about it much but it's still common knowledge.'

'Well, the story's got nothing to do with all that. I mean, it isn't even mentioned. All those things . . . Well, 1974 . . . That all happened years before Seymour ever got

125

to Cyprus. No, there can't be any connection. How could there be?'

'Since I haven't read it, I can't say. And,' Hillyer said, 'I must say I'm mightily surprised to learn that at long last he managed to get something down on paper. The last few months he was getting quite desperate, nothing seemed to be working out for him. And I know that for a fact because he told me so himself. And because Derya . . . A *long* story, is it?'

'No, not very long. But very . . . what's the word? . . . disjointed. I think it's what authors call a draft but I'd be interested to have an expert opinion on that. I understand that nowadays a lot of writers jump about like that on purpose instead of . . . you know . . . saying what they have to say properly.'

'I'd like to read it, certainly,' Hillyer said. 'He did have a certain talent. No question of that. Those two novels he wrote before he came here—'

'So what went *wrong*?'

'How do you mean?'

'You said he couldn't—'

'Oh, what went *wrong*? Yes, well, he was having problems.'

'He told you he couldn't get anything down on paper but did he say *why*?'

'He said he thought it was wrong to make fictional capital out of political situations because all such situations are ephemeral and he wanted to give expression to some kind of permanent ethical truth.'

'Eh?'

'I thought myself he was trying to rationalise his way out of the dilemma. I still do.'

'But I don't quite understand—'

'Like the Cold War, for example. Now it's over, all the spy writers who used that situation are dead ducks, don't you think? Except for a few like le Carré and Deighton who dug a bit deeper and made points about human duplicity and nastiness that will always be true, irrespective of the situation

126

that provoked them. Or let's say that the truth about them will always be worth examining. So that kind of story doesn't *depend* on the situation, you see, it illuminates it, and that's what poor Seymour wanted to do but he couldn't see *how*. Maybe he was just too young. Didn't have enough experience.'

'But did he have to write about a political situation?'

'Cyprus *is* a political situation. My personal belief is that, as a writer, he shouldn't have come here. He couldn't come to terms with it, somehow. He felt he was being strangled here. Asphyxiated mentally.'

'Really?'

'Yes. Oh! Well . . . You don't want to make any connections of *that* kind. I was speaking metaphorically, of course.'

Dobie didn't feel as though he were being asphyxiated. Pouring himself out another cup of re-heated coffee, he felt rather as though he were sinking up to his oxters in an ooze of metaphysical mud. And that, when you thought about it, was a very odd thing. A detail, certainly, but that was the trouble with all those literary people. Sweeping their grandiloquent theories around their head, they never paid any attention to points of detail. Their souls were above things like, well . . .

Mud.

Bearing in mind that it had been the middle of the summer. Of course all that fiddle-faddle went way back to pre-Christian times, pagan rites and fertility rituals and goodness knows what, the sun and the shadow . . . Dobie frowned, sipping at his coffee. This terrible memory of his was a real curse; already he had almost forgotten what Seymour had said. Something about political troubles, yes, and something about the cause of them going much deeper, going right back to primitive beliefs and mythology and so forth. A lot of codswallop it had seemed at the time, but thinking again about what Hillyer had said, well, maybe in the end Seymour had seen a way to break the deadlock, to relate a political situation to a permanent truth,

127

though what the truth was that he'd tried to elaborate wasn't at all clear. All that was clear, or that seemed to be clear, was that at least for a few hours he'd managed to break through the block, and spilled words down on page after page, the proof of this lying still in the desk drawer where Dobie had left it. *The Mask of Zeus*. Maybe, yes, maybe Hillyer should read it. It'd be interesting to know what an expert thought of it. Because, Dobie thought, *I* can't make very much of it. Or of its author, either.

In one way, though, it had to be arguably a valuable document. Because unless Dobie had misunderstood it completely – which was very possible – towards the end of its composition its author had broken off in order to commit a murder and then had returned in order to complete it . . . if it *was* complete. That was what Seymour's so-called confession also seemed to imply. And if so, that surely made it something pretty well unique in literature. But where was the *political situation* that Hillyer had gone on and on about? There wasn't anything about politics at all, unless indeed the title . . . But perhaps Seymour, like Dobie himself, hadn't known about that terrorist group – it certainly seemed a weird name for a gang of Enosists to have hit upon – and had headed his story thus through sheer coincidence.

Hillyer shook his head vigorously, as though once again mildly annoyed at Dobie's obtuseness. 'But of course he knew about them. He's pretty well informed about Cyprus politics – a great deal better than I am, anyway. He married a Cypriot girl, for heaven's sake. He even wrote a book about Cyprus last year. He let me read a few chapters of it. He didn't think much of it himself but it was well researched, I can vouch for that.'

'I think I remember something about a guidebook.'

'That's it. He sent it off to his publisher . . . oh, some time last winter. It should be due out before very long.'

'Then he can't have had this block for as long as I thought.'

'Oh, it was purely creative, it was *fiction* he felt he

couldn't write. The Cyprus thing – he thought of that as being journalism. Hackwork. To earn some money.'

'A lot of money?'

'Oh, no. I wouldn't have thought so.'

'But surely it's all *writing*, isn't it?'

Hillyer shook his head again, this time more kindly. 'Perhaps you'd do best to stick to mathematics, Dobie. You have your way of thinking and I have mine and we have to suppose that these creative chaps have theirs. I think you're going to find it pretty difficult to get on to Seymour's wavelength, if that's what you're trying to do.'

'Derya,' Dobie said, 'was a mathematician. And a promising one at that.'

'Yes, she was, and that was probably part of the problem. Though in their case it was rather the other way round.'

'What way round?'

'I always felt he was doing his best to get on to *her* wavelength and failing to do it. Mainly because he didn't believe she was capable of getting on to *his* wavelength. And she knew that, of course. And resented it. As well she might.'

Dobie thought with a sudden sense of shock, That's pretty much what I feel about Kate. And pretty much what I suspect she thinks about me. He paused with the coffee-cup halfway to his mouth.

And further reflected: Of course we don't really quarrel. Not really *quarrel*. But unquestionably we're . . . let's say we're both aware of the seeds of future dispute being planted in our minds. And maybe getting over-anxious about it. Twiddling each other's tuning knobs too quickly and getting irritated by the constant crackle of static. It was hard to see, though, what you could do about it. How to get through the block, if that's what it was. He sipped at the coffee.

It had got cold again.

All this ratiocination. It was bad for you. He should, he thought, be doing something *practical*.

He got to his feet.

* * *

129

The Seymours' car, an unassuming Renault 12 similar to Hillyer's, was still in the garage, collecting dust. The police or someone had removed the ignition key but the car doors had been left unlocked, permitting Dobie to carry out his own inspection. The light bulb in the garage was weak and inadequate but he found a surprisingly powerful torch in the glove compartment of the car and with it was able to find what he had half expected to find on the surfaces of the brake and clutch pedals. Or to detect traces of it, anyway. Unfortunately, having successfully detected it, he couldn't see that it signified anything in particular. Detect? Who's kidding who, Dobie? Or *whom*, as Kate would say?

Kate was a detective, of a kind. A police pathologist, anyway. I'm not a detective, Dobie thought. So why am I making like one? A maths master in exile, that's what I am. Just plain inadequate, like that overhead light bulb.

Seymour, it seemed, had felt the same way. Words were no good either. Something happened to the vowel sounds and what you wrote down didn't make sense. Signified and signifier got all mixed up. It was a dog's laugh.

Unconsoled, Dobie went to his bedroom to change his yellow and mauve silk pyjamas for a slightly less resplendent sports shirt and black cotton trousers, a little crumpled from their sojourn in his suitcase. It ws hot outside, but not too hot for a pleasant Saturday morning stroll.

Tuzla Gardens. The senior staff compound. The houses had gardens all right, Dobie's included, but after four rainless months of high summer there wasn't much left in them and the earth in the flower-beds was dry and parched. A few tall eucalyptus trees, however, gave convenient shade as Dobie passed Cem Arkin's house and Ozzie Ozturk's, emerging then into the glare of the sun as he walked past Berry Berry's residence, the last in the line. He could hear music coming from a radio somewhere but nobody seemed to be about.

He looked briefly up towards the sky and, perceiving no lowering rainclouds in the vicinity, made his way down the path to the beach.

130

It was a narce beach, of course. Soft white gently yielding sand, waves lapping peaceably against the shoreline. Grey-green rocks rose above the surface of the sea some twenty yards out, forming a natural lagoon, a fine and private place for bathing and allied activities. Derya might well have come here, Dobie thought, to indulge her penchant for naturism. Then again, she might not. According to Zeynep, the army base down the road had offered alternative attractions. Five or six miles down the road and further up the coast. You could see the army buildings from the beach, a gaggle of low flat-roofed huts similar to the one where Seymour was now incarcerated and behind them a huddle of derelict buildings. The village . . . What was it called? Nobody lived there now, anyway. The Turkish army had taken the place over. Nobody lived there because of some wartime disaster or other. It was hard to imagine wartime disasters affecting a place like this. It was hard to conceive of bombs bursting here, shells exploding, machine-guns firing. You couldn't easily imagine anyone being murdered here, either.

'Well, I always said that one day she'd come home late once too orphen and that's just wot happened. A terrible crarm of course but in a way she arst for it.'

'She orphan, I mean often stayed out late, then?'

'Ooooooblimey yes. Well after midnart lark as not. My old man'd be forever staying up for her to get back before closing the gates; yeh, she'd always be the last to get in Friardays, we all knew that.'

'Was it a Friday when . . . ?'

'Course we all knew where she woz as well. Down the army base with the officer boys. Sure it was a Friarday. Nobody else went out at all and so nobody else came back. 'Cept for 'imself and that was free hours earlier.'

'Seymour?'

'Mr Seymour. Yus. Nobody else was 'ere that nart who wozzen suppose to be 'ere and Ali could tell the cops that for a certain fack.'

'They were asking him questions about it, were they?'

''Im and me. They 'ad to, see? It's their job.'

Dobie strolled on down to the water's edge and stood for a while gazing at its blue and barely ruffled surface. The tide, such as it was, was receding, leaving the sand where he now stood smooth and dark with moisture. After a minute or two he turned and went back above the highwater mark; stopped to raise his feet cautiously and (naturally) each in turn, peering downwards at the soles of his shoes. Traces of dampness; a few grains of sticky sand; that was all. That was all that anyone would have expected.

He climbed the narrow path back to the compound. To each side of the path and around the six houses the maquis grew, fenced back by strands of wire, thick and seemingly impene-trable. Thorn bushes, scrub, acacia, mimosa and a few taller holm oaks pushing their tops above the tangle. Just possibly some young and active person could force a passage through that mass of undergrowth and gain entrance to the gardens that way: an army officer, for example. But he'd have to be pretty thick-headed as well as rhinoceros-skinned. Whyever should he? And in the dark, too? Moonlight, yes, apparently; but moonlight could never have penetrated those thickets, those dark dingles. Dobie shook his head and plodded on.

As he reached his front door he heard the telephone ringing. And this time it *was*.

'Kate? . . . Gosh, I'm glad to hear your voice.'

'Why? What's happened?'

'Nothing. I'm just glad, that's all.'

'Come on, Dobie. What's up?'

'Well, when I said nothing, I didn't mean nothing, not exactly.'

'I thought as much. All right. So just what kind of a mess have you got yourself into now?'

'I'll tell you,' Dobie said.

132

7

When Dobie had concluded his somewhat convoluted account of recent events on the isle of Aphrodite and shortly afterwards had rung off, Kate gazed for a while out of the window, seeing there the smooth pearly sands of a tropical beach, a stretch of invitingly sparkling sea, and in the foreground a white table-top upon which a frosty daiquiri had been no less invitingly placed. Elsewhere, there were palm trees laden with coconuts, gaily coloured beach umbrellas and the like. This vision eventually cleared to reveal beyond the raindrop-misted window-pane the customary appurtenances of a wild Welsh September day: the grey blank frontages of neighbouring houses battened down against the approach of winter, leaf-stripped branches swaying anxiously in a howling gale, the occasional slate whizzing past as the wind lifted it off her roof. Sometimes when you hear about all these goings-on in foreign parts, Kate thought, you feel it's good to be British. Sometimes. But not very often.

Repressing other thoughts of an uncharitable nature about her friend Professor Dobie, she picked up the receiver again and dialled another number. When the duty desk replied, she asked for the CID Room extension number and got it. The next voice she heard was that of another old friend, Detective-Inspector Michael Jackson, also known – though rarely addressed – as Wacko Jacko. 'Yes?' the voice said. 'Jackson here.'

'It's Kate Coyle, Jacko.'

'Oh, hullo, Kate, I mean Dr Coyle.' The voice became at

133

once a little guarded. 'No corpses for you today, I'm afraid. I think we're undergoing a procession.'

'You mean a recession.'

'Yes, one of those. Things are pretty quiet at the shop, anyway.'

'I'm glad of that,' Kate said, 'because I want to draw on your profound knowledge and experience of the criminal mentality. Or more exactly, Dobie does.'

'Ah.' The voice became more guarded than ever. 'Thought we'd got Mr Dobie out of the country for a while. And not a moment too soon, in my opinion.'

'Out of the country doesn't mean out of trouble.'

'Be a bit too much to ask for, that would. Amazing how he stirs it up, one way or another. Saddam Hussein, the boys in the Records Office call him. Still, give him my regards when next you write.'

'I will. But I also want to give him some information.'

'What's he want to know?'

'He wants to know something about fake confessions.'

'Eh?'

'People who come along to you and confess to committing crimes which in fact they didn't do. Is it very common, that sort of thing?'

'You have,' Jackson said lugubriously, 'to be joking. Hardly a day goes by, you might say. What sort of crime are we talking about?'

'Murder.'

'Oh, no,' Jackson said. 'Not *again*.'

'I'm afraid so. But at least it's a long way away this time. Not your manor.'

'Nothing like far enough,' Jackson said, echoing the sentiments of the rector of Dobie's university. 'But wherever you go it has to be pretty much the same. Nutcases everywhere. Hang on a mo.'

A pause. Then at the other end of the line a resounding crash and a tinkle. Another pause. Then Jacko came back on.

'Great big bugger of a fly crawling over my teacup. Soon settled *his* hash. Where was I?'

'Nutcases.'

'Right. Anything that gets into the papers, along they come. By the dozen, sometimes. You wouldn't credit it. Most of them are harmless enough, though. Some of them we think of as regulars. Keep on coming back.'

'So you don't take them seriously?'

'Not those ones we don't. But some of them we have to. You never know.'

'Because they're convincing?'

'Oh, they can be *very* convincing. Often as not they've convinced themselves, you see. Sometimes you can only trip 'em up on some little error of fact they've gone and got wrong. I mean, it's all in their imaginations, see? So now and again they let their imaginations run away with them. So to speak. The loony blighters.'

A long deep-breathing silence. Kate knew what had happened.

'Jacko?'

'What?'

'Leave that fly alone.'

Jackson with his rolled-up newspaper, poised to strike. 'Look, they're nasty things, flies. They spread diseases. Money jitus and things like that. You ought to know. You're a doctor.' Another splintering crash in the earphone indicated the abrupt demise of another teacup. 'I hate their guts, to tell you the truth.'

'What, flies? Or teacups?'

'No, no. Those loonies we're talking about. What with the time they waste, checking out their stories.'

'Do they come and confess to other kinds of crime?'

'Lord, yes. Anything they've read about in the paper, like I said. Or seen on the telly. Murder's what really turns 'em on, though. So Mr Dobie's right about that.'

'Any special kind of murder, Jacko? I mean, one kind more than another?'

Jackson hesitated for a moment before replying. Kate took this to be a pause for cogitation rather than a preliminary to further unprovoked assault. ' . . . Yeah. Sex killings. Anything that's . . . you know . . . a bit off. Kinky like. Appeals to the psycho in them, I suppose. I can't account for it, mind. But it's a fact.'

'So they're mostly men?'

'Nine out of ten of 'em, I'd say. But I couldn't quote you the actual sadistics.'

'And you can't hazard a guess as to why they do it?'

'Not my place to, is it? They're barmy, is why.'

'Yes, but—'

'Foxy Boxy, he's always going on about guilt complexes and suchlike but he goes to the pictures a bit too often, in my opinion. Sees all them Hitchprick films or whatever they're called. No – they just want to draw attention to themselves is what I think. Having missed out on a mother's tender care when they was young. And a happy family atmosphere such as I enjoyed. Why, I betcha,' Jackson said, 'I got the marks of my old man's slipper on my backside yet. Discipline, see? That's what this country needs.'

'And more unbreakable teacups.'

'Ha ha ha,' Jackson said.

Kate rang off on that convivial note and looked at the notes she'd scribbled on the telephone pad. They didn't seem to add up to very much but then that silly chump Dobie hadn't told her very precisely what questions to ask. And her next commission was, if anything, even vaguer.

A London number, this time. She had to look it up in the directory before dialling it because naturally Dobie hadn't known it. It was *always* like this with bloody Dobie. He hadn't even been gone a week yet and . . .

Oh, dear.

The telephone clicked in her ear.

'Perriam and Webb,' said a bright female voice. 'Editorial office. How can I help you?'

* * *

136

'Of course people talk about it,' Cem Arkin said. 'They're bound to. Just about everything in Cyprus is based on gossip. We're a Middle Eastern country in that respect, no doubt about it.'

Ozzie apparently didn't disagree. 'A pre-litterit sossity really, innit?'

'Becoming less so, though, surely?'

Cem shrugged. 'Perhaps. We're doing our best. But old habits dies awfully hard. You've got to visualise two camel-drivers meeting in the middle of the desert and sitting down on the sand to exchange rumours for three or four hours; and then transpose that scene to a village community; and then to what to all outward appearance is a modern city centre: and then you've got an overall picture of Cyprus. It accounts for a lot of the things that happen here, because that's the thing about rumour. It's almost invariably alarmist.'

Dobie didn't feel the least bit alarmed. Nor was he disposed to visualise anything in particular, unless it be a second glass of cherry brandy. Zeynep's lamb chops had been excellent, as usual, and the bottle of Cankaya even better, and even in the heat of the day it was pleasant to sit in the cooling shade of the pergola outside Ali's bar chatting about this and that with some of his new colleagues, establishing friendly relations *und so weiter*. Berry Berry wasn't present, his lunchtime (and other) requirements being presumably catered for by his wife, and Hillyer, one gathered, had earlier gone into town, but the other bachelors and bachelors-in-effect of the compound were all now seated around the wooden table, Cem Arkin and Ozzie and a little guy of vaguely Japanese appearance whose name Dobie hadn't yet caught. He wasn't really Japanese, of course; it was probably just the effect of those rather narrow slit eyes behind the thick pebble lenses.

'But isn't the press alarmist? And the media in general? In the UK and just about everywhere else?'

'Of course. They carry on the great tradition, or they do if they want to sell a large number of copies. All the same, there's a difference between reading something in a newspaper and

137

hearing about it from your next-door neighbour. Both versions will be equally inaccurate but your neighbour's version is personal. He'll tell you what *he* thinks about it, as something between him and you. And you'll react in the same way. That's the point.'

'And that,' Ozzie said, 'is what you geezers don't understand about the PLO.'

'And terrorist groups generally. It's not publicity they want, in the modern sense. Newspaper reports don't terrify anyone – if they did, we'd all live in a constant state of fear. And most of us don't. No, it's the word-of-mouth stuff that does the trick. The rumours. They know that because they're primitive people themselves. They know white man's medicine won't cure black man's toothache. Pull the damned thing out and wave it in the air. *That'll* show them.'

Dobie, as a newcomer to this particular terrorist group, was finding that most of these interesting remarks were being addressed directly to him but, again as a newcomer, wasn't finding it easy to reply. Luckily, it didn't seem that he was required to do so. The second glass of cherry brandy had duly arrived and he could content himself by sipping at it somnolently.

'And,' Cem Arkin said, 'the spoken word hasn't very much relevance to time. You know that? Or to any known timescale. That's another thing that throws people when they first come here – people who're used to getting their information in a written form, that is. You listen to people chatting in any of the Famagusta cafés, just the way we're chatting now, and you'll realise they talk about things that happened last week and things that happened twenty years ago in the same breath. Even *I* found that odd when I came back here. The fact that they're talking about them *now* seems to make everything a part of the present, far as they're concerned. Mind you, the Turkish language encourages that attitude in a way, wouldn't you say?'

The little chap in the pebble lenses coughed modestly. 'I'd rather not start up that hare, if you don't mind. After all, the

138

past *is* part of the present and I don't see anything wrong in recognising that. Unless we want to discuss philosophical niceties—'

'Doesn't it depend on the nature of the past? And on the character of the people who're doing the talking? If you're obsessed with the bloody past like Makarios was—'

'No one can say that the Turks are obsessed with the past. Hell, it's all secularisation and modernisation and Europeanisation and has been for these past sixty years. That's what I complain about.' Removing his glasses and rubbing them vigorously with a napkin. 'This almost total disregard for our heritage – both there and here. Everything being allowed to fall into disrepair and ruin and even to collapse. It isn't lack of money, like they say. It's lack of a sensible and coherent conservation programme. *That*'s what it is.'

Dobie was once again allowing his eyelids to close in a reflective sort of way. This afternoon and for the first time he was beginning to feel at home here; this ambience of post-prandial donnish conversation, of an agreeable all-male grouping was so familiar to him. Here, too, he couldn't really figure out what everyone else was talking about and here, too, it didn't much matter. They certainly seemed to be great talkers, though. Especially Cem Arkin, who appeared to have inherited something of Tolga's liking, and talent, for oratory. Amazing, really, Dobie thought, how well everyone round here spoke English. Except Zeynep, of course. Here she came now, bearing what? More cherry brandies? Splendid.

'So what do we do? You said it yourself. We sit around talking. Exactly. When we should be doing something about it. Talk is the national vice, as far as I'm concerned. Talk is nothing but a disguise for, for . . . *lethargy*.'

He had put his glasses on again and they now wobbled up and down on the end of his over-excitable nose. *He* didn't seem to be at all lethargic. He rather gave the impression of a high-tension battery prepared to shoot off sparks at the

139

slightest touch upon a terminal. Dobie, however, didn't see much wrong with being lethargic. Now, for instance.

'They're an 'ell of a lot more progressive,' Ozzie said, 'over on the Greek side. You have to give 'em that.'

And Arkin, 'Yes, it's all back to front with the Greeks. A progressive attitude to life and a retrogressive philosophy. While we've got a progressive philosophy and a retrogressive attitude. No wonder so many people think the situation here is hopeless.'

Dobie said, 'How are they retrogressive?'

'Just like I said. Obsessed with the past. And an imaginary past at that. Obsessed with their own idea of the past that they think they can somehow drag into the present. That's what Enosis was all about. Back to Byzantium. Look, you may not believe this, Dobie, but never mind Cyprus, a lot of these bloody mainland Greeks still think they've got some claim on Istanbul. They want it *back*, as they put it. I know it's incredible but there is it. Time doesn't exist for them. Nothing ever changes. You can't deal with people like that and, of course, the trouble is . . . we're just the same.'

'Was Seymour . . . like that? Obsessed with the past?'

This question provoked a sudden and immediate silence, a silence in which the previously animated discussion group looked blankly round the table at each other. Cem Arkin. Ozzie. And the fellow with the wobbly nose. 'Well,' Cem said in the end. 'Who's going to answer *that* question?'

'Kaya,' Ozzie said. 'He's the flippin' expert.'

Kaya. That was it. Sitting back and adjusting his glasses before replying.

'He took a great deal of interest, certainly. But I wouldn't say obsessed. He was writing this book last year about the local antiquities and I remember he consulted me on quite a number of points where . . . where I hope I was able to help him. And then there was a little research project that Derya and I were working on together. He took an interest in that, too. Though that may have been because Derya was doing it rather than because of the subject's intrinsic fascination.

140

I wouldn't have thought it all that fascinating to a layman. Not really.'

'What sort of research?' Dobie was puzzled. 'I mean, Derya was a mathematician.'

'Yes, that's exactly why I wouldn't have thought . . . I wanted some computational analyses carried out, you see, and she very kindly agreed to help. It was all fairly straightforward stuff and not too time-consuming, but naturally I shall make the proper acknowledgments when my paper is published.'

'Nothing to do with mythology? Anything like that?'

'Mythology?' Kaya blinked, as though uncertain he had heard aright. 'No, no, what gave you that . . . ? Nothing of the sort. I mean, there's no secret about it. I had to have some proportions and ratios estimated, that was all. I've been trying to work out the actual dimensions of the principal buildings of Salamis and their extent – the original city, that is – and things like that. Things that might be of importance in future archaeological surveys of the site. Mythology,' he said, bristling a little, 'doesn't come into it, other than very indirectly, any more than theology would come into working out the dimensions of a ruined medieval cathedral. Archaeology is a science nowadays, Professor Dobie, whatever you may have been told to the contrary. With a mathematical basis. Like all the others.'

Dobie took off his glasses and rubbed the lenses with the corner of his handkerchief. They tended to mist up in this steamy weather. From the radio at the far corner of the bar a Turkish pop singer was grinding a mouthful of consonants to powder with her teeth before whining them out plaintively through her nose; Kaya sounded as though he would have done the same to any of the figures of classical myth so unwise as to present themselves before him. They'd be Greek mythical figures, of course. 'Oh, I see. Well,' Dobie said peaceably, 'if *I* can be of any assistance in the matter . . . '

Kaya's expression softened immediately. Dobie, he had perhaps remembered, was a new boy around the campus and allowances, in his case, would need to be made. 'That's very kind of you,' he said, bobbing his head up and down like an out-of-work samurai searching for casual employment as the village executioner. 'But in fact Derya managed to complete all the computations before she . . . That's to say, she completed them. I hope to finish the paper itself before the end of the year. Though I doubt,' Kaya said, his disputatious mood returning, 'if it'll excite any very great attention, least of all here, given the present administration's attitude of total indifference.'

'Quite a lot of us,' Cem Arkin said, 'would like to get away from all that isle-of-Venus crap. We can safely leave that stuff to the Ministry of Tourism. In my opinion.'

'Oh, I agree entirely,' Kaya said. He might just possibly have suddenly remembered the position occupied by Cem's father within the administration he had calumniated. 'Indeed, that's the very point I was making. All this emphasis on the mythological element—'

'And after all Seymour was a tourist. Or a visitor, anyway. His being married to a Cypriot made no difference. He saw everything from a visitor's viewpoint, as was only to be expected. Not,' Cem said, reaching across the table for his brandy glass, 'that it's necessarily a bad thing for us to see ourselves sometimes as others see us. Perhaps at the university we imagine ourselves to be very much more anglicised than we really are. Though not enough so, maybe, to satisfy Derya.'

'Oh, I dunno,' Ozzie said. 'I always thought she fitted in all right. It was only—'

'I'm not criticising the way in which she performed her professional duties. All I'm saying is that I felt her balance to be a little suspect. Her equilibrium, if you like. I know she spent all those years in England but so did you and I, Ozzie, and it wasn't any kind of culture shock that she went through or anything as straightforward as that. It was almost the opposite. As though she found she belonged here in a way that she didn't expect, found that she was being assimilated, so to speak . . . and didn't like it. That's why she always set out to shock people in that really rather childish way. And then of course Seymour, Seymour . . . '

142

A short silence, in which the pop singer produced more strange gargling sounds and Dobie put his glasses back on.

'I can see what you're gettin' at,' Ozzie said, and snorted. 'But I don't agree. Look, like you say, I been in that position meself, I had a few up-an'-downers with *my* wife when she was here so I know what it's like and what you just said, it's a load of cobblers. Derya might've *acted* like she thought she was Aphrodite but she didn't think that really. No danger. Had her head screwed on real tight if you ask me.'

'No, no, *no*. That's not what I meant at all. I wasn't commenting on her *behaviour*; it wouldn't be right for me to comment on her behaviour.' This was the first time Dobie had seen Cem Arkin even remotely discomfited and he hitched up his eyelids about an eighth of an inch in mild surprise. 'Of course she had that rather . . . oncoming manner that a lot of people here would tend to misconstrue. And I heard things, of course. We all did. Nasty remarks. But nothing to my knowledge was ever definitely . . . But there we are. Back where we started from. Rumours. That's all they were.'

'Mebbe. But all the same he croaked her.'

This remark provoked another disconcerted silence, this time less surprisingly. It was Dobie who broke it, though unobtrusively. 'Did anybody see them? Earlier that evening?'

The others looked at him. Taken aback.

'I mean, I gather you were all *around*. I wondered if any of you had seen them. Or either of them. That's all.'

'Yes, I did,' Cem said. 'I saw them leaving together. In the car. But that was much earlier. Maybe four o'clock.'

'They didn't say where they were going?'

'No. We didn't speak. She waved to me, that's all. She was driving. And that was the last I ever saw of her, come to think of it. I didn't see him again, either.'

'Not when he got back?'

'Well, I went out myself shortly after that. I saw the lights were on in their house that night but I never . . . Why do you ask?'

'People say different things,' Dobie said naïvely. 'I was

143

curious. I mean, you say that they went out together but then he must have come back a long time before *she* did and—'

'Nothin' unusual about that.'

Kaya's glasses were jumping up and down again. 'I must say this sort of thing annoys me. Nobody knows where Derya went and nobody cares . . . and it's her business and nobody else's, except maybe her husband's and we've no right to poke our noses into that side of things. Well, have we? All the rest is rumour, as Cem says, and I've got no time for it. It's just gossip. Gossip.'

'With no mathematical basis,' Ozzie said.

No one laughed.

After the others had departed Dobie hung around for a while, slumped in the chair with his hat tilted forwards over his eyes. He felt that he was running short of ideas, if he'd ever had any; but then he would have expected to feel that way after a half-bottle of wine and was it three or four brandies? It was quiet there under the pergola, anyway, very quiet indeed; hardly any cars seemed to pass by along the road just behind him, but then the road didn't really go anywhere, other than to that deserted village and the army camp. Of course there wasn't any mystery about the car; Derya had driven it back that night, as he had proved earlier that morning, at least to his own satisfaction. But she'd driven it out with Seymour, according to Cem. It wasn't strange that Cem was apparently the only witness of this event; Cem occupied the house directly opposite and facing the compound entrance, the other houses – including Hillyer's – being placed much further back. The question was, though, how had Seymour got back? It was a question that could be resolved fairly easily, but to do so Dobie would have to put himself to the considerable effort of straightening his knees and standing up. Frankly, it hardly seemed worth the trouble.

Some fifteen minutes later, however, he accomplished this feat and wandered through into the lokanta kitchen, where Ali was sitting in the corner reading that morning's *Bügun*, flipping the pages over expertly one-handed, and where Zeynep was standing by the sink drying the dishes, a perfectly normal and equitable division of labour. 'Oh 'ullo, Derby. Enjoy your murl?'

'My what? Oh, yes. My murl was excellent, thanks.'

She turned away from the sink towards him, vigorously wiping her dampened hands. 'Can I get you anyfink else?'

'Oh, no. Nothing else. It was just that I wanted to ask you something. You told me that you saw Mr Seymour come back that night, you know, the night of the . . . The night when he . . .'

'So I did then. Quite distinkly. It wasn't all that dark.'

'Well, *how* did he get back?'

'In a turksey.'

Yes. Well, he would have. How else?

'One of the university turkseys it woz. Old Raif's turksey lark I told 'em.'

'So he'd have come back here from the university?'

'Bound to've done.'

Ali-in-the-corner continued to read his newspaper throughout this exchange, ignoring it completely. He wasn't sulking. He didn't speak English.

Dobie lowered his tone respectfully all the same when he asked, 'How did your husband come to lose his arm, Zeynep? In the war?'

'The war? Him? Not bloody larkly. No, he use to work in the docks, see, when this fragging great packing case come slarding down on top of him. Lucky escape, the doctor said.'

That was one way of looking at it. 'All the same, it must have given him a bit of a frart.'

'Yes, scared him shitless, the pore old bugger. Put him off work for the rest of his laugh, he says.'

'Well, we all feel that way sometimes,' Dobie said.

It was, he thought, evidence of a kind. Zeynep seemed after all to be a truthful person and one incapable of doing serious

145

harm to anyone or anything, except the English language. Otherwise, all that he had to work with was rumour. Gossip. What people said. The nice lady should have known better than to ask him to look for evidence in a place like this. Everything you built here had to be built on sand. On the sound of voices, talking in the shade, circling round to return to the point they'd started from.

A pleasant way, though, to spend a hot afternoon. Eating a good murl and knocking back the wine and brandy. Listening to what people had to say. His future colleagues. He hadn't found any of them unlikeable. Just the little agile-nosed chap, the Professor of Archaeology, Kaya, had once or twice seemed inclined to get somewhat stroppy. Perhaps because the conversation at that point had impinged on his special field in a way that he'd disapproved of. And perhaps not. 'You don't want to take too much notice of Kaya,' Cem Arkin had told Dobie later, sotto voce. 'He's from Ankara.' Which didn't seem to explain very much. Unless he'd meant to imply that Kaya, too, was a visitor. Like Dobie. Like Seymour. Perhaps in a way like Derya . . .

Dobie was now in his late forties and, like most others in his age-group, was disposed to accept male dominance in academic life as a simple fact of everyday existence – especially on the professorial level. You didn't think of this as being either good or bad; you took it for granted, maybe as a part of that British tradition that Tolga Arkin went on about. Academic wives – Berry Berry's, for instance – had their place in it. But Derya had been an academic in her own right. That was different. And what I have to imagine, Dobie thought, is the effect she'd have had here in this virtually all-male enclave, upon all these affable but serious, maybe even rather portentous gentlemen . . . a cockatoo, let's say, in a cage of jackdaws. Showing off its stunning legs in bright-coloured miniskirts and on occasion, if Hillyer were to be believed, showing off a great deal more. Never mind the Turkish officers that Zeynep talked about. What kind of inner turmoils and commotions mightn't she have instigated right here?

Where she hadn't any business to have been, really. Professors everywhere, in Dobie's experience, get pretty uptight about things like status and incidental perks. The Tuzla Gardens houses were professorial accommodation. Derya was only an Assistant Professor; the scum of the earth. So she had to have wangled it, somehow. And perhaps it wouldn't be very prudent to enquire too closely into her methods. Even those who didn't enquire, though, might well still feel free to resent them. And Seymour, of course, as an academic husband . . .

Not what you'd call a privileged position to be in. And not really happy for Derya, either. No balance, Cem Arkin had said. Probably not. She'd jumped on to an obviously unstable stepping-stone. Maybe with a little more time, things would have settled down. Though more likely not.

Dobie wasn't finding it altogether easy. He still found it hard to get rid of the feeling that he was living in someone else's house, but that wasn't it. He'd settled down almost at once in Klaus Schindler's flat in Vienna on the European Cultural Centre's exchange arrangement, though it was true he'd been a trifle disconcerted to discover that Klaus's girlfriend had decided to include herself in on the deal. Vienna, after all, was notoriously a civilised city. Not like Cyprus. But that wasn't it, either. It was . . .

Yes. He was feeling lonely. *That* was it.

Of course this was a nice house, he couldn't deny it. Reasonably well appointed. Well worth wangling, maybe even worth the guessed-at spot of discreet sexual blackmail. But somehow it didn't add up to the cosy little kitchen in Ludlow Road and the clatter of the breakfast things as Kate laid the table. Dobie, the exile, pined for the known and familiar. He, personally, would take Kate in preference to those long Cypriot legs any day of the week. Kate was good value. That was why. Maybe she could even come up with something in London. He hoped so . . .

And meanwhile there was one other little thing that he could try, in pursuance of a stray thought that had that moment entered his mind. There was nothing unusual about *that*;

147

Dobie's mind was normally a crowded thoroughfare jostling with reflections about almost anything other than the subject he imagined himself to be at that moment thinking about, and this particular waif was no different. Except in that it might be possibly acted upon. Dobie rose from his chair and went upstairs, his hat still tilted forwards over his eyes. He had forgotten to take it off.

Upstairs, and into my lady's chamber. Where *it* had happened. My lady's wardrobe stood where, presumably, it had always stood, to one side of the room beside the bed, and Dobie stood for a few moments where Seymour, according to his narrative, had stood quietly at the threshold, before clumping heavily across the room to pull open the wardrobe door. My lady's shoes were arranged, not very tidily but at least in pairs, on a metal rack at the bottom. Dobie took them out, one pair at a time, to examine them.

They all seemed to be lightweight summer shoes, as might have been expected, flimsy little creations with high narrow heels, though one pair had much lower heels and seemed to be considerably stouter than the others. Kate, Dobie thought, would probably have designated them as walking shoes, though they were in fact more or less the kind of shoe she wore all the time. Except in bed, of course. Kate's shoes, though, were invariably spotless. These weren't. Clods of grey mud had been caught and held in the space between heel and sole on both shoes and there were dark mud splashes across the insteps. The mud had long since been converted by the dry heat within the wardrobe into lumps of solid dust which powdered and flaked at the touch of Dobie's fingers, but the shoes were muddy all right, although a clear patch on the right sole showed where fragments had been scraped or rubbed away on the pedals of the Renault. Black shoes with neat grey plastic buckles. The shoes she'd been wearing the night she'd been killed, then, if Seymour's story could be believed. And it was beginning to look as though on certain points of detail it could be.

Of course she hadn't been wearing them at the moment

148

she was killed. She wouldn't have worn shoes in bed, any more than Kate did. Or anyone else. Dobie turned to look at the stripped-down bed. Probably the police had tidied up in here; it wouldn't have been Zeynep. Berry Berry had been right about that: Zeynep was a vigorous and conscientious cleaner but she wouldn't touch anything of Derya's. Or even of Seymour's. Perhaps one of the investigating policemen had put the shoes away, had folded and hung up Derya's discarded clothes; perhaps she'd done those things herself, before going to bed; it didn't matter, did it? Not unless . . .

He looked down again at the shoes he was holding, one in each hand. There was something else unusual about them, or at any rate something that made them different to all the others. It looked as though she'd put in fitted cushion soles, either because she'd found them a little too big or else to make them more comfortable for . . . walking, of course. What else? Dobie's fidgety fingers, moving instinctively rather than in pursuit of anything concrete, (which in fact they weren't), picked contemplatively at one of the loose soles, freeing it, pulling it out, finally encountering beneath it . . . What?

A slip of paper. Folded.

Great Scot, Dobie thought. It has to be a *clue*. Just like in the . . . But how incredible. It had never occurred to him that these mildly ridiculous Sherlock Holmes caperings might actually uncover anything substantial. No, of course they hadn't. A scrap of folded paper, that was all, she must have put in there to give a little extra support to her instep . . . or something. All the same, his fingers moved slowly and carefully as he unfolded the paper; it was dry as the mud had been and set in its creases and might very easily disintegrate if he . . . Ah. It had been folded up like that for a long, long time, that was obvious. Which was strange if Derya . . . Ah, again. Yes. Yes. There . . .

Bloody hell. All in Turkish.

As might after all have been expected.

Some kind of an official document, though. Or at least it appeared to be. With a black and white photograph stapled to

149

the top of it, though the staple had long since rusted and fallen away and the photograph itself was badly faded. It showed the face of a woman and that was about all you could say for sure. Maybe in a better light, or with a magnifying glass . . . The document, whatever it was, was typewritten and a name, most probably the name of the woman in the photograph, had been entered in ink on the top line, opposite the heading *Isim*. Black printed capital letters. It was legible all right but it wasn't a name Dobie had ever heard of. SABIHA METTI.

Dobie switched on the bedside lamp and moved the photograph into the circle of light. A name he was sure he'd never heard of, and a photograph of a woman he was quite sure he'd never seen. All very disappointing. Clues were supposed to *mean* something, dammit. This one didn't, although the bright light from the bulb was showing up the face on the photograph much more clearly, picking out the over-all contours rather than any detail. The line of mouth, chin and neck had gone for ever, but enough remained to show that the original had been a very good-looking woman. Say in her middle thirties, at a wild guess. With fine dark eyes, Dobie thought, under attractively curved eyebrows, though something in their expression was . . . well, was hard to define. A passport-size photograph, head and shoulders only. Some kind of a fringed shawl had been drawn across the shoulders that otherwise might have been bare, and under the folds of the shawl she seemed to be wearing a necklace, maybe a silver necklace as it had caught the light of the photographer's flash; wide silver or maybe metal links supporting a curious pendant emblem that hung at the base of the woman's throat and that looked like a capital letter V but more probably . . . No. I'll need a magnifying lens for this, Dobie thought, and I doubt if it'll help much even if I can find one somewhere. The photograph was old and the tones had faded and only those dark searching eyes were still bold and clear. There was something about their level gaze that—

The open wardrobe door emitted a groaning creak, causing Dobie to look round in sudden alarm. It had given him a frart.

And it also made him aware that he was now inexplicably, well, no, not worried, not exactly *worried*, but filled for no reason with what if you wanted to be melodramatic you might have called a sense of foreboding, as though he had unthinkingly stepped – as Derya apparently had – into muddy waters, a dark and ominous pool that might reach up in a matter of moments to close chokingly over his head, leaving nothing but his hat floating on its clotted surface. His *hat*? What was he . . . Dobie clicked his tongue and took his hat off and then, having nowhere to put it, slipped it back on again.

Dark, he thought. That's the operative word. Dark eyes, dark eyebrows, dark hair. Shadows in the sun. That was what the photograph showed. A darkness. But not a quiet or a peaceful darkness: a darkness full of furtive movements, quick tapping footsteps, the sound of voices whispering in the night. Oh, God, Dobie thought, I'm a *visitor* here. A visitor by definition. A Visiting Professor. I've got no business to be poking my nose into other people's affairs, into other people's secrets, Seymour, Derya, Sabiha Metti whoever she is . . .

Or whoever she *was*.

Because looking down at the paper again he saw that it was dated. Down there in the bottom corner: 22.7.74. How long had Derya been keeping it, then? Because she'd only come to Cyprus herself three years ago and she certainly hadn't been keeping this paper under the sole of her shoe for anything like that length of time. It would surely have been worn to fragments there in three months, let alone three years. No, the shoe had to have been a temporary hiding-place; most probably she'd have slipped the paper in there under the sole as soon as she'd returned from . . . wherever it was she'd been that night. And got her shoes muddy.

Got something else, too. *Got myself laid*, she'd told Seymour. That part of it might well be true, too. She hadn't said who by. Probably it didn't matter. *I am a hot-tempered but not a jealous person.* And *I* did it, anyway. So there's no need to go into all that. No need to stir up any . . . mud.

But *mud*. In mid-July. In Cyprus. It just wasn't possible.

151

She might as easily have got her shoes covered in snowflakes while walking across the Empty Quarter. Dobie sat heavily down on the bed where she'd died and stared once again at Sabiha Metti's photograph. Outside the circle of light where it lay, he seemed to sense a darkness inexorably closing in on it. On it and on him . . .

I'm lonely, Dobie thought. Lonely and very confused. I wish I were back home.

8

Kate liked London for much the same reasons that Dobie would have given to account for his dislike of the place but didn't in fact go there very often, and when she did found it more and more difficult to make her way around it. London Bridge – of comparatively ready access via the tube station – didn't actually seem to be falling down but the rest of the joint was and a vast number of interested parties, clearly sharing Dobie's opinion rather than hers, were intent upon accelerating the progress of its deterioration, improving substantially on the efforts made by Hermann Goering and the Luftwaffe some fifty years ago.

As a former medical student at Guy's Kate was well habituated to the rabbit-like dodgings and jinkings through which as of necessity you proceeded from one ward to another and which might later be trusted, though not implicitly, to carry you past the various houses of ill repute (though this, too, was a matter of opinion) lying to either side of the narrow streets you circumnavigated while returning to your lodgings. All that, and various other attempted gropings, she had been prepared to accept in those days as good clean fun, it being easy to regard these things in such a light when you're young and healthy and sufficiently agile. But now it was all concrete blocks and metal girders and roped-off passageways and small dilapidated newspaper kiosks seemingly dedicated to quite different forms of Human Bondage; it was reassuring, however, to find that if you wanted to get anywhere you still had to walk, all other forms of transport being either intolerable or inoperative. The offices of Perriam and Webb,

153

publishers, weren't all that distant from the bridge, being located appropriately enough in Clink Street just beyond the Stoney Street junction, but were surrounded by ditches and wired fortifications of so impenetrable a nature that Kate finally arrived there ten minutes late for her appointment and, having in the last stages of her journey surmounted four flights of stairs, somewhat breathless.

'I know, I know,' Ms Walters said. 'The lift's been out of order for three weeks now. Sorry about that. I always feel the exercise helps to keep me in shape but you look as though you don't have to worry too much about that.' She allowed Kate a few moments to savour the implications of this decidedly double-edged compliment amd, while so doing, to sit herself down in a horrifically creaky armchair. 'It's Dr Coyle, isn't it? Are you a medical doctor or the other kind?'

'I'm a GP,' Kate said. 'In Cardiff.'

'Then you'd like some coffee I expect.'

The effect of this *non sequitur* as a follow-up to the previous *double entendre* left Kate a trifle nonplussed; she crossed her legs – having every reason to be confident as to the effect of these – and gazed rather blankly around the room.

It was a very small room so this didn't take long. The plaque on the desk said DEIRDRE WALTERS EDITORIAL ASST but otherwise the desk and the office itself reminded Kate quite vividly of Dobie's little rabbit-hutch in the Old Buildings of the university with its surreal chaos of papers, scripts, files, folders, dog-eared books, journals and miscellaneous paperasserie strewn with a fine careless rapture over shelves, chairs, side tables, filing cabinets and of course over the entire surface of the desk itself. Dobie, she thought, would have felt immediately at home here. She didn't. Or not altogether. But at least the coffee seemed to be drinkable. 'I was a little late anyway, I'm afraid.'

'That's all right,' Ms Walters said comfortably. Such of Ms Waters as was visible over the desk was plump and practical and bespectacled and very young – considerably younger than Kate, certainly. Kate decided that she didn't really approve of

154

those oversized Spanish earrings and thereafter felt a little better. 'I've no other appointments this morning. I'm not really sure I can be of much help because as I told you over the buzzer I've never actually met Mr Seymour but—'

'Perhaps there's someone else here who has?'

'Yes, Mr Webb, but you see Mr Webb has left us.'

'What about Mr Perriam?'

'Well, there's *two* Mr Perriams actually. I suppose it should really be called Perriam and Perriam now but it's hard to keep up with all these changes.'

'Which one do you work for?'

'Oh, I work for Perriam.'

'I hope he's nicer than Perriam.'

'Much, much nicer. Perriam's a bit of a turd actually.'

'Well, now we've got that little matter cleared up—'

'You see, actually,' Ms Walters said, deciding to come clean, 'I've only been with P and W these past four months. Actually. Before me, you see, there was someone else; Anthony Pollock his name was, well, it still is of course, and I think it was Anthony who arranged this Cyprus guidebook thing, though Patricia may have finalised the contract before she got here, or no, I mean after, don't I? So just possibly it's Anthony you should be talking to; he's with Connor and Cunningham now, or Patricia . . . But of course she's on holiday. So it's all a bit difficult.'

'This Anthony Pollock. Is *he* a bit of a turd?'

'Frankly, yes.'

'Then I don't think I'll bother.'

'No, being a doctor, I expect your time's pretty well taken up with . . . And I don't mean to say that nobody here is concerned about Mr Seymour's present position; of course we are, he's one of our authors after all and he does seem to be in a fearful jam. The trouble is we don't know much about it and we certainly haven't heard from him in quite a while, not since before my time here anyway, or been in contact with him or anything like that. And he's abroad, you see. So it's all very tricky.'

155

'Authors,' Kate said, 'must be almost as difficult as patients.'

'Authors *are* patients as far as I'm concerned. Publishing their books is only a temporary cure. Almost at once they'll go and do the same thing again.'

'You can't have many authors on your list who've murdered their wives. And confessed to it.'

'I have quite a few authors whose wives wouldn't at all mind murdering *them*. But that sort of thing has to be discouraged, I suppose. More's the pity. Would you like some more coffee?'

Ms Walters had a rather high squeaky voice that seemed none the less to have no very great penetrative quality, like a Chinese ballistic missile. Perhaps they all developed voices like that, working in these tiny little boltholes. Kate looked out of the window, where behind walls of tarnished brick some ten yards of one of the murkier reaches of the Thames was foggily visible. 'I suppose,' she said, clearing a pathway across the desk for the hospitable cup and saucer, 'it won't do his sales any harm? The publicity?'

'What publicity? There hasn't been any. Whoever gets to hear of what goes on in *Cyprus*? Maybe if he'd done a proper book . . . But anyway we're an old-fashioned firm in some respects. Perriam wouldn't like it. Nor would Perriam. Besides, if we started puffing authors who'd murdered their wives they'd *all* be doing it. No, we have a very decided negative error policy on that issue, I'm afraid.'

'If it were a novel . . . ?'

'That might be different. But a guidebook, and in my view not a very good one at that . . . '

'Hard to sell on a sex-and-violence ticket.'

'Hard to sell, period. And as far as I can make out he hasn't sent us any fiction for something like three or four years now. Of course he's still very young and Anthony reckoned that if we took the Cyprus thing we could tie down his future work on the contract and that's just what Patricia's done. But of course—'

'Problematical.'

'Yes. However,' Ms Walters said, brightening, 'quite a few people have done good work in quod. John Bunyan, for instance.'

'Oh? I haven't read much Australian literature.'

'How very enviable. But Mr Seymour isn't Australian. Is he?'

Kate had found herself getting involved in this kind of a conversation with increasing frequency since she'd started going around with bloody Dobie. It was of course *Bunyip* that she'd been thinking of, not Bunyan; who was this Bunyan anyway? She hadn't come here to talk about Bunyan. Or Bunyip, either. 'The point is,' she said, her small face expressive of a fixed determination at long last to get to it, 'I have this friend in Cyprus right now . . . Professor Dobie . . . '

'Oh, if Professor *Dobie* would write a book for us, that would be an altogether different matter. I don't know if you think he could be persuaded . . . '

Dobie was indeed and to Kate's certain knowledge the author of several books, mostly dealing with the applicability of inconceivably complex mathematical calculi to unutterably remote or even downright impossible physical contingencies. But this, she assumed, was not at all the sort of production that Ms Walters had in mind. Seymour she no doubt regarded as a common-or-garden criminal and – what was far worse – a failure; Dobie, on the other hand, was very widely regarded as having not only murdered his wife but having *got away with it*. Kate was naturally familiar enough with the contemporary yuppy's worship of success, but she still found it hard to get accustomed to being in so close a relationship to a national hero. 'Unfortunately, Dobie doesn't have any literary gifts.'

'*Quite* unnecessary,' Ms Walters said firmly. 'Hardly any of our authors do. In fact the whole problem is one of finding authors who can write badly enough to satisfy the general public and at the same time . . . ' She paused. An idea had obviously struck her. 'Or is he difficult?'

'Dobie? He's by far the most difficult man I've ever met.'

157

'Oh, dear. But then men *are*, aren't they? So you may as well have one who drives you up the wall all the time, so you don't have to . . . What exactly was it that he wanted to know?'

'He wants to know about something called the Mask of Zeus.'

'The mask of what?'

'Zeus.'

'You sure he didn't mean Zorro?'

'No. I mean yes. I mean no, not Zorro. Zeus.'

'Well, there you go. That's not something I get asked about every day; people don't come up to me and . . . I mean it's sort of *original*, if you see what I mean.'

'Oh, he's an original all right.'

'One might even say eccentric.'

'Indeed one might.'

'So OK. What is it?'

'What? What's what?'

'This mask thing you said.'

'The mask of Zeus.'

'Yes. That. What is it?'

'*I* don't know. I thought you might.'

'Might what?'

'Might know.'

'About the . . . ?'

'Yes.'

'Never heard of it.'

'No. Well, if it comes to that, neither have I.'

Ms Walters picked up a ballpoint pen as if wondering what it was doing there and, having studied the tip of it, put it down again. 'This is all getting a bit too much like Question Time in the House of Commons. I suppose you're going to tell me next that Professor Dobie doesn't know, either.'

'Of course he doesn't. But he thinks there may be something about it in the book, I mean in this guy Bunyip . . . in this guy Seymour's bloody *book*, for God's sake. If you follow.'

158

'Ah,' Ms Walters said. 'I'm with you now.'

'Oh, good.' Kate breathed deeply and through her nose.

'It just may be that I can help you on that one. The proofs came back from indexing only the other day. So let's,' Ms Walters said, searching for and discovering the telephone under a pile of discarded directories, 'see what we can do. Provided the copy editor's somewhere round, we could be in business.'

The copy editor was indeed around and came up with the goods and Kate was able to make her way back to Paddington with some ten or twelve photostated pages tucked away in her handbag. At least it would be something for her to read on the train.

CHAPTER 6

THE ZEUS MOSAIC

The famous decapitated statues of Salamis may indeed have been the victims of eighteenth-century head-hunters, impelled by the urge to 'collect' relics of classical antiquity for the Western European market. But no such simple answer suggests itself to the Mystery of the Missing Mosaic. You can't put a mosaic into a sack and walk off with it. And possibly for that reason a number of the Salamis mosaics survive in place, ravaged by the droughts and rains of a couple of millennia but with much of their cunning intricacy intact. Yet at some time in the past two hundred years one of the largest, and probably the most remarkable, has vanished. Under the ground, like Salamis itself? Into the sea, like the harbour fortifications? Who knows?

At least three earlier observers of the ruins have left written confirmation not only of its existence, but of its size, magnificence and subject-theme. But none of them – unfortunately and annoyingly – describes its exact location. Since prior to

159

the recent excavations and restorations this would have been like describing the position of a given burrow within a rabbit warren, this is understandable; nor would it have occurred to any of these witnesses that an object of such immense proportions might later be somehow unaccountably mislaid. Ten metres by five is probably a reasonable estimate.

Since by common consent the mosaic depicts the figure of Zeus engaged in the bedding of one of his numerous lady friends – or possibly Hera, his wife – it may be assumed that its probable location lies within the temple of Zeus and beside the Agora. All that remains of this temple, however, is the high podium and inchoate masses of buried and half-buried rubble. It's possible that some relatively recent collapse or subsidence has covered the Zeus mosaic under tons of loose and shifting earth and that future excavations will bring it once more to light, as was the case with the much smaller dove mosaics of Soli, to the west of the island. It's also possible that the god is at this moment conducting his amours somewhere else entirely.

What seems certain is that, wherever he may be, he is conducting them in an extremely uninhibited manner. The last person to have recorded his impressions of the Zeus mosaic appears to have been the British traveller William Bryce, who visited Famagusta in the summer of 1798. Being not only British but British to the core, he professed himself to be both deeply impressed and profoundly shocked, this in language that may recall to us Dickens's later diatribe on the Roman Colosseum. 'Surely,' he writes, 'we need seek no further cause for the sudden collapse of this once great city nor regard it as worthy of any other fate! Hardly can we suppose that any but a race of decadents could admire, adore, nay worship the depiction of the depraved and debased liaisons of a pagan deity! Yet may we still marvel at the paradox lying inherent in the Roman nature and seized upon by a greater and later bard than Virgil: – as Antony's infatuation for Cleopatra presages the fall of the greatest of the ancient Empires, so does the mindless and savage lust here delineated in all its

160

crudity presage no less colossal a fall, no less inevitable
a decline: – that of the Salamis of Constantine the Great,
shaken by earthquakes, riven by sea-raiders, and in the end
– alas, we must say deservedly! – destroyed.'

Doubtless the unmistakably injured tones of this eighteenth-
century Mary Whitehouse will suggest to us a reason for the
lack of later comment by less jaundiced travellers; Victorian
susceptibilities must be borne in mind, and Islamic attitudes
also. The stricter forms of fundamentalism have never been
practised in Cyprus, but it was, of course, an Islamic state and
part of the Ottoman empire; it's therefore not at all impossible
that, faced with the protests of the ineffable Bryce and his like,
the civic authorities took the appropriate steps and that, as a
result, the offending depiction was not merely sealed off from
public view – like the Pompeii frescos – but deliberately buried
or even dug up and, in Bryce's words, alas! destroyed . . .

It may well be that the activity displayed in the Zeus mosaic,
or more exactly the manner of its portrayal, would be offensive
even to some modern tastes. The Italian art historian Giacomo
Marinetti, who visited the site some eighty years earlier
in search of surviving relics of Venetian rule, spoke with
disapproval of 'open and naked copulation . . . a scene of
unbridled and indecent lust . . . ', but also confirmed 'the
combined power and subtlety of the overall composition,
dominated by the shades of blue and black . . . the sense of
tremendous physical energy conveyed . . . the faded yet still
glorious coloration of the flesh.' He was indeed moved, he tells
us, to make a detailed sketch of the composition; this also has
seemingly disappeared, but he further and interestingly claims
that his sketch was known to the famous (or infamous) Vasari,
who used it as a basis for one of his highly pornographic
pseudo-Classical reconstructions of the sexual encounters of
Greek gods and human mortals. Of these, the most likely
candidate is the well-known depiction of Neptune enjoying
the rather over-opulent favours of Gaia, though we must then
assume Vasari to have replaced the figure of Zeus with that
of the fishtailed sea-god to suit his own dubious purposes.

161

There can be no doubt at all that the original representation in the mosaic was that of Zeus (or Jupiter); the identity of his partner, on the other hand, has not been clearly established.

However, a curious and unique feature of this mosaic, commented upon both by Marinetti and Foscolo (another Italian observer), is that the male figure is clearly masked. Masked figures, both male and female, are of common occurrence in Greek representations of ritual orgies and symposia on urns and pottery fragments, but always in an unequivocally human context; masked divinities are unknown in such depictions, and such a concept might have had much the same effect upon Graeco-Roman susceptibilities as the visual representation of the act of sex had upon William Bryce – who clearly saw it as little short of blasphemous. According to Marinetti, moreover, the mask worn by Zeus here is neither the formal black face-covering of the orgiast, granting anonymity, nor the animal-mask sometimes worn by those engaged in the acting-out of some form or other of fertility rite; it is, Marinetti says, 'simply moulded to the form of a bearded human face of a certain severe or militaristic aspect . . . bearing the marks of an innate dignity disfigured by the intensity of a momentary passion.' Since it is normally the purpose of a mask to conceal rather than to reveal emotion, this struck him as being strange: 'Perhaps,' he adds, 'the mask may serve the obverse of its usual purpose and . . . serves to give a human semblance to that cold divine indifference the god's features might otherwise have untowardly revealed.' (An idea to be, curiously enough, taken up by Yeats in his 'Leda' sonnet and elsewhere in his work.)

Professor Kaya Caprioglio argues, as I think powerfully, from this evidence that Zeus's partner on this occasion can only be Amphitryon's wife Alcmena and that the scene represents the act of procreation of the greatest of Grecian heroes, Hercules. 'Zeus,' as Robert Graves puts it, 'honoured her so highly that, instead of roughly violating her, he disguised himself as Amphitryon and wooed her with affectionate words and caresses.' Zeus did not, as Professor Caprioglio points

162

*out, appear to any other of his many loves in human form,
and the mask in the Salamis representation is intended, in the
professor's view, to show that the form adopted by Zeus on
this occasion is not only human but specifically so, the face
revealed being that of Alcmena's cuckolded soldier-husband.
I myself find this argument fully convincing.*

*It is true that, as Kaya admits, no obvious connection exists
between Amphitryon, the King of Troezen, and Salamis, but
'no obvious connection' here means only 'no known connection'; the much-publicised Cypriot Aphrodite cult has tended
to obscure the complex network of religious inter-relationships
linking Cyprus to mainland Greece and to Asia Minor two
thousand years ago. Salamis was after all allegedly founded
by Teucer, a refugee from burning Troy; the names of Troy
and of Troezen might easily have been confused by later
generations and the liaison of Zeus with Alcmena celebrated
in Salamis – as many other such mythical events elsewhere
– in consequence of a simple linguistic error . . .*

Not really a guidebook at all, Kate had decided; more a
collection of historical curiosities and archaeological oddities.
A rather old-fashioned sort of book altogether and not one
she imagined she'd find of any great interest, should she ever
get around to reading the rest of it. The other photostatted
pages made reference to Zeus all right, as to numerous other
Classical dignitaries, but she couldn't find any other reference
to masks; so all this crap about a porn mosaic had to be what
Dobie wanted. She couldn't think why. But the train should
get her back to Cardiff in time to get to the nearest fax office,
though with not too many minutes to spare. She looked at her
wrist-watch.

The train was swaying dangerously to and fro now, thunder-
ing down the track like an outraged buffalo scenting the purple
sage of Bristol Parkway. Kate raised her head again to stare
out of the window at passing chimney-stacks and factory walls
smeared over with spraygunned graffiti. Surely, as William
Bryce would have said, this *couldn't* be what Dobie wanted?

Surely all that mythological guff could have no relevance to anything going on in the modern world? What could Dobie have gone and got himself into *now*?

Perhaps he'd already managed to cut himself off from the modern world, anyway; the world of Deirdre Walters, the world of brick walls and of aerosol cans and of the natural affinity existing between them. Perhaps in Cyprus you could get away from all that. It certainly seemed that Seymour had. Briefly, Kate tried to visualise a different world, a labyrinth of tall stone pillars and stone steps and of linked and writhing shapes, human and unhuman – a world very far removed from Dobie's comfortable certainties of x taken to the power of n and of πr^2. He'd better be careful, Kate thought; it mightn't be a good world in which to miss one's step, much less to lose one's way entirely. As to all appearances Seymour had done . . .

'Of course it's rubbish,' Kaya barked jovially. 'Written for a popular audience, as you'd expect. But accurate enough. The facts, as far as I know, are as he states them. After all he got them from me and Derya, all of them. Kind of him to give me a mention, though, I dare say.'

The professor seemed to be in a rather more amiable mood this morning, placated perhaps by Dobie's expression of interest in the gleaming architectural relics that towered to either side of them as they walked along. It hadn't been a very long walk from the university: not much more than fifteen minutes, in fact, at a leisurely pace along the beach and through the pine trees, and Dobie wasn't even sweating. His interest wasn't altogether feigned; at close range, Salamis was extremely impressive. Partly, Dobie decided, because of the remarkable way in which it had become assimilated by the terrain, the thirty-foot-high marble and granite columns thrusting upwards through the dark clumps of umbrella pine and ilex to juxtapose startlingly their antique and time-scoured artificiality upon the surging waves of natural growth, like the bones of a ship on the seabed encrusted with shells and wound about with waving seaweed.

164

'A lot of it *is* in the sea,' Kaya said. 'Or under it. You can still see the shape of the harbour walls in the bay if you look down through the water. And some of the port buildings. Of course they've been pillaged as well, by divers and such.'

'Perhaps it's lucky so much of it is underground, then,' Dobie said, 'where it's relatively safe.'

'Yes. But only relatively. People come and dig, you know; heaven knows what they find and what they take away. The whole site ought to be properly guarded, of course. But the area's so enormous. Something like twenty square miles if you include the burial areas, as of course you must. There's no immediate answer to the problem that I can see.'

Dobie looked around him. It was more like one of those weird Indian temples lost in the depths of the jungle than anything he'd seen in Europe, but in far more advanced a state of ruin and far, far bigger. There was a whole town here, under the clinging roots of the bushes and the sheltering trees. 'So if anyone wanted to look for this mosaic that's disappeared . . . ?'

'The Zeus mosaic?' Kaya vibrated his rather thick lips contemptuously; the Turkish equivalent of a snort, no doubt. 'Needle in a haystack, as the saying has it. Oh, there are quite a number of things we know about but have lost track of – the Athena statue, the Eurotas frieze – maybe they'll all turn up again but if they do it'll be through pure chance, as like as not. What you see here is the tip of the iceberg. Not even that.'

Dobie was still surveying it. In a clearing of the woods, a great bare square with the tall columns marching down all four sides; behind the square, a huge brown jumble of stone walls and of fallen rocks. 'Fantastic.'

'In the spring, the whole of this square is carpeted with flowers. It's a beautiful sight. Though originally it would have been paved over with mosaic patterns. You can still see vestiges of the stonework here and there.'

165

'And this is the gymnasium, I think you said.'

'That's right. And over there, the baths. Not much left of the buildings, they've mostly collapsed, but we've been able to work out the water supply lines and the heating system quite accurately. In their heyday they'd have been more than a match for the famous baths of Caracalla, believe me. Splendid engineering. Well, they made as much of a cult of bathing as we do nowadays and almost certainly a ritual as well. No bikinis, of course. He-he-he.'

They walked on to take a shufti at one of the bathing pools. It didn't seem to be very large. Or very deep. 'No bikinis, you said?'

'Nothing at all.'

'He-he-he,' Dobie said. His visualisation of a couple of dozen unclothed Deryas splashing about in the shallows was certainly intellectually stimulating. The water couldn't have reached much above their knees. There's more to this archaeology business, Dobie thought, than I'd suspected.

'Of course, they wouldn't have admitted tourists. Or the *hoi polloi*. All this area would have been reserved,' Kaya said, waving one hand around with a proprietorial gesture, 'for the local earwigs, no, *big*wigs, that's it. The town aristocracy, so to speak. I always tell my students to think of the gymnasium as another kind of temple, rather than to give the word its modern connotations. Because they worshipped physical perfection. That's what the gods exemplified to them – Zeus, Apollo, Aphrodite and the rest – although the idea sounds paradoxical to the modern mind. But what we now call spiritual values didn't really come into it. Or only indirectly.'

Dobie dredged up a vague memory from his schooldays. 'What about *mens sana in corpore sano*?'

'Ah, but *mens sana* to them was quite a materialistic concept. Rationality, we'd call it nowadays. Which of course implies a rejection of metaphysics and religious belief and all that sort of thing. Seymour was quite amused by that paradox, as I remember.'

166

'In what way?'

Kaya sat down on the chipped stone wall that surrounded the pool. Dobie followed suit. The dry stone felt pleasantly warm against his cotton-trousered buttocks – quite sybaritic, in fact. Yes, it was sensible to allow the old *corpore* a little room for expansion, once in a while.

'He said Molière and Dryden had got nearer to the truth of the matter than he'd supposed. To be honest, I'm not familiar with their works, but apparently they adopted a rather derisory approach to Classical myth and religion. Well, naturally the Greek gods and heroes must seem absurd if you attribute to them spiritual values that they didn't possess. They represented elemental and physical power. The women, beauty and fecundity. That was all. And that was considered to be enough.'

'Not by William Bryce.'

'Who? Oh, yes. Well, exactly. The representation of violent physical energy in the sexual act has never had much appeal to the Western mentality, has it? You prefer to have it symbolised in the form of the hydrogen bomb.'

'As a matter of fact,' Dobie said, 'the underlying math-ematical equations, as they were first formulated . . . ' But he hadn't come here to talk about *that*. 'I suppose the trouble is that nobody's perfect. Spiritually. Or physically either.'

'No. But in Salamis they *aimed* at perfection.'

'No harm in trying.'

'That, again, depends on how you look at it. There's some evidence they practised a rather radical system of practical eugenics. The children of the ruling classes who showed at birth any signs of imperfection . . . They got rid of them. Put them to death.'

'Sacrificed them?'

'Well, again, not in the modern sense. Though certainly there'd have been some form of ritual, in which I believe the Zeus mosaic would have played its part. I think the children were killed before it, or possibly on it. Seymour didn't mention that in his book but then he always found

167

the idea rather unpalatable. That's not to say that he found my conclusion unacceptable, however.'

'It *is* unpalatable,' Dobie said.

'To us, yes. Of course it is. Because we think quite differently upon these matters. *These* people related imperfection in new-born children not to hereditary defects, as we might do, but to some fault of execution in the moment of conception. Strabo is very clear and quite enlightening on that point. Well, the Zeus mosaic from all accounts shows Zeus in the act of conceiving Hercules, who became the peak of male physical perfection on the human level. In other words and putting it very crudely, he's showing how it's done. So the father of the child shouldn't make the same mistake again.'

'Are you saying it was the father of the child who . . . ?'

'Yes, of course. Since his was the responsibility.'

'Well,' Dobie said. 'All I can say is . . . '

But he decided not to. *Unpalatable* was no longer the word that he would have chosen. Old William Bryce's interpretation might be unduly moralistic but it seemed to him infinitely preferable to Kaya's.

'*Autres temps, autres moeurs.* One shouldn't judge too harshly. And as a scientist one shouldn't judge at all.'

'You discussed all this with Seymour, did you? At length?'

'With Seymour and Derya, yes, quite often. Seymour's views always interested me because he *wasn't* a scientist, and Derya, well, Derya was good enough to help me with some rather complex calculations. But I believe I mentioned that before.'

Kaya had risen to his feet. The tutorial appeared to have been concluded. Dobie also rose and fell more or less into step beside him as they strolled across the open space towards the amphitheatre. To their left the sea extended like a stretch of blue watered silk towards the horizon.

'It's an odd coincidence, but a few years ago Derya played a part in one of those works you mentioned earlier. A leading role, in fact. I don't know if her acting—'

'Oh, I know all about her acting,' Kaya said. 'She gave all

168

that nonsense up when she got here. Not much opportunity for it anyway. But Seymour was always telling me how good she was and in fact there's a photograph . . . But of course you must have seen it, you're living in that house so you must have done. Alcmena. Yes, an element of coincidence, I suppose, but Seymour really made too much of it, I always felt. After all, the Zeus mosaic is only one element in a really complex mythological mix-up. Cyprus has always been a hotchpotch of cultural confusions, then as now.'

'I was thinking rather that acting . . . It does demand a certain amount of, how did you put it? Raw physical energy. Wouldn't you agree?'

'Well, she had plenty of that. And she didn't employ it only on the stage either.'

'So there's been a certain amount of gossip.'

'Yes. And I think I made my opinion of all that quite clear the other day. Of course I'm not denying she was a . . . a highly sexed young lady. I don't think anyone here would dispute that.'

'But some might be better qualified to comment on the matter than others.'

Kaya emitted another high-pitched and definitely malicious little giggle. 'Some might, yes. He-he-he-he. But not, as I think, any of *us*. Any of our colleagues, that's to say, though I'm sure they'd find the suggestion extremely flattering. However, I've no reason at all to suppose that Derya's interest in antiquities was ever extended in our direction. She'd have found us a great deal too old for her, I fear. Youth calls to youth all the world over.'

'So who would have exercised a more insidious appeal?'

'Oh, well,' Kaya said. 'There's a Turkish army base in the village, you know; some of the younger officers . . . though I wouldn't have described their appeal as insidious, exactly. Or hers, either. No, Derya was always very direct in her methods. And her approach. Probably the result of her mathematical training and her appreciation of the geometrical qualities of the straight line. But you'd know more about that than I do.'

169

Kaya was pleased, Dobie thought, to be facetious, but for the first time that morning he was now perspiring lightly. The expression in his eyes was difficult to read behind those thick lenses; velly insclutable these oilyentals. 'How exactly was she helping you, Kaya?' Velly insclutable and not *that* old. Nor was Hillyer and nor was Ozzie and nor was Cem Arkin and nor, for that matter, was Dobie himself. An over-ingenuous disclaimer altogether.

'Now that you've seen the site I can explain a little more clearly. My students have been locating the positions of buried buildings through the use of Ponsonby meters, which work on the same principle as those little machines with which surveyors and estate agents now measure the walls of modern houses. All quite simple, but Salamis, like most ancient cities, is a kind of palimpsest – one town being built on top of another and so on through various layers. So the outline of the original *civitas* would normally be impossible to determine. However,' Kaya said, raising his broad bespectacled face towards the sky like Winnie the Pooh in search of a passing cloud, 'my contention has been that the foundations of the earliest city would have been laid out *per scamna et stryges*, in accordance with the geomantic principles accepted at the time. So I asked Derya to run our readings through the computer to see if any recurrent mathematical pattern might thereby be revealed. In which case, I would assume that the foundations and buildings corresponding to the pattern would appertain to the original city and all others to be later additions and accretions. A simple idea, really, but then many simple ideas turn out to be successful.'

'So she *did* discover such a pattern?'

'Oh, yes. And a most intriguing one. Since from it I shall be able to deduce the exact nature of those very early geomantic principles that have never been other than very vaguely understood.'

'To a layman,' Dobie said slowly, 'that sounds rather like a major discovery.'

'Since the same methods can be applied to all the major

170

urban archaeological sites throughout Turkey and the whole of the Middle East, yes – I rather think it is. And of course I shall make a full acknowledgment of Derya's contribution, as is only proper.'

'That might have been of no little help to her in her own career.'

'I suppose it might. Yes. It's all very sad.'

'Did she at any time try to show *you* . . . how it's done?'

'That is not a question,' Kaya said severely, 'that one gentleman asks of another.'

'I know. I'm asking it all the same.'

Kaya looked up towards the sky again. It was an aching blue and cloudless as ever. 'I have my pride,' he said. 'I have my pride.' Rather an odd answer, Dobie thought. If answer it was.

Away to the north and beyond the green clumps of umbrella pines the university buildings raised a distant bastion of glass and concrete. The university was here; Salamis, gone. Derya, too, was now disappeared; such physical perfection as had been hers was now vanished underground, like the Zeus mosaic itself, like William Bryce, Giacomo Marinetti and all those who at one time in the past had gazed upon it. What, Dobie asked himself, did it all matter? Why was he asking so many meaningless questions? It wasn't his habit to question the past. That might be Kaya's area of academic endeavour; it wasn't his. Time to him was a pure abstraction, expressed when necessary by the convenient symbol t; some, no doubt, might think of it as an ever-rolling stream, carrying all its sons away and all its daughters, too, but that wasn't how he was accustomed to look at it.

He needed, perhaps, to put in a few hours' work back in the department. That might restore to him a proper sense of values.

But work was just what he couldn't settle down to. Proper work. Everyone said that it would be different when the students arrived; well, he knew that. But there were still

171

two weeks to go before full term commenced; exactly two weeks if you thought of time in that way, and for some reason Dobie couldn't now do that, either. He felt disorientated. Usually before the beginning of term there was a certain amount of work, quite clearly specified, that had to be got through: classes to be prepared, lecture notes to be revised, programmes to be drawn up. Time could be measured in terms of a simple countdown to D-day, of leisurely but steady movement towards a concrete aim, a movement he'd executed many times before and could carry out with little expenditure of effort, almost unthinkingly. There was an aim and there was progress towards it, that was the point.

That didn't seem to be the situation here at all.

He had papers in his briefcase all right, plenty of them. Papers to be gone through. Their bulk seemed to be building up, if anything. He had several pages of an impenetrable type-script called, for some unfathomable reason, *The Mask of Zeus*. He had an official transcript recording the results of a police interrogation. And he had five pages of printed bumf that Kate had faxed to him from Cardiff, he didn't know why. Well, no, he knew why all right – because he had asked her to. That was why. What he didn't know was why he had asked her to. It was *all* like that. Papers, yes. Plenty.

Progress, zilch.

He had the faxed pages on the desk in front of him now, and again, he didn't know why. They didn't tell him anything. Together with the proofs Kate, with her customary thoroughness, had sent a copy of the biographical note on the back of the book's dust-jacket and of the accompanying photograph of the author, which naturally had come through rather badly smudged. All you could see was a vaguely oafish and heavily bearded face, almost as indeterminate in outline as that of the still unknown Sabiha Metti had been after her sojourn in the sole of Derya's shoe. To clarify matters the publishers had very considerately featured the author's name in bold capitals directly under the photograph, thus:

172

ADE SEYMOUR

. . . is a graduate of the University of Cardiff, which he left with a first-class honours degree in English and with a considerable reputation as an actor and producer of college plays. He has since written two highly praised novels and a stage play, awaiting West End production. For the past three years he has lived and worked in Cyprus and his profound knowledge and love of the island is displayed in this searching personal study of the place and its peoples – not a guidebook but, as he himself says, an 'investigation' of the island's many mysteries and hidden secrets. This book may, like Bitter Lemons, become itself a part of the troubled and turbulent history it graphically describes . . .

You see, Dobie? It doesn't tell you anything. Clarify matters? Not at all. Nobody had ever called Seymour 'Ade', that Dobie could remember, or even 'Adrian'. Well, maybe Derya had, but nobody else. No doubt Perriam and possibly even Perriam had favoured the shortened version as being more friendly and *Neighbours*-like, but that was just exactly what Seymour hadn't been. And still wasn't. Dobie pushed the top page aside and riffled through the pages of close-packed print underneath.

Hopeless.

No, the search for the mask of Zeus in London had been a waste of time, a pursuit of something that once had been but now wasn't, and his stroll round Salamis with Kaya no better; Seymour's story, if that was what it was, a boojum bird whizzing round in ever-decreasing circles before disappearing up its own back end. As for Derya's escapades and other peccadilloes, these were quite simply none of Dobie's business; what earthly point could there be in raking them up? Or digging down into all this archaeological rubbish? Sam Spade might have been the man for the job. He-he-he-he. But Dobie wasn't. That was for sure.

Unfortunately the nice lady still didn't seem to agree with this opinion. She rang through just as he was shovelling his papers back into the briefcase and she sounded a little het up. 'I've been trying to get hold of you all morning. Where have you been?'

'Oh, out,' Dobie said vaguely. 'Looking into this and that. You know, I've been thinking this matter over—'

'Well, listen. My clerk's identified that document you sent me and it's extremely interesting.'

'It is?'

'Yes, it is. Apparently it's a travel pass. A safe-conduct. They were used in '74, my clerk tells me, at the time of the Turkish invasion, when people were travelling from the Greek side over to the Turkish-controlled area. It was a clearance paper, really, to make sure that whoever had one wouldn't be stopped and sent back by the Turkish patrols.'

Dobie rubbed his eyes, which had begun to ache a little. 'So who *is* she?'

'Well, we don't know that yet, but my chap's working on it. No. Listen. We do know that whoever she was, she travelled from Nicosia to the Famagusta area and we know that she *did* go there because the pass has been stamped, and we know she went by car because the car registration number has been filled in, so if we can trace the owner's name which shouldn't be too difficult—'

'We know her name. Sabiha something. That's not what I meant. I meant, who *is* she? What's she got to do with Derya? Or with Seymour? Or with anything? 1974 . . . They were neither of them here. They'd both have been kids, for God's sake.'

'All the same it might be important. *Very* important. I'll get back to you as soon as I can.'

'Have you tried showing it to Seymour?'

But the telephone had already clicked in Dobie's ear. He put it down. Not a very sensible suggestion anyway. Seymour might or might not recognise the photograph but either way he wouldn't say anything. Why not? Because he wouldn't, that was all. He'd said all he had to say and that was it.

Importance is a relative concept. That's the trouble. For some while now it had seemed to Dobie *very* important to find out what Derya, and, for that matter, Seymour had been doing earlier that evening: Cem Arkin claimed to have seen them drive off together at around four o'clock and nobody seemed to have seen them since. Either of them. General opinion appeared to hold that Derya had been screwing around somewhere and Seymour's story confirmed that opinion. Yes, but only in the vaguest possible way. And what had *he* been doing meanwhile, anyway?

He'd come back later in a taxi. From the university, according to Zeynep. All right, maybe he'd been researching something, in the library or wherever. Nothing easier, in any case, than to ask him. If you didn't mind wasting a whole lot more time. Because he wouldn't tell you anything. Why not? He wouldn't. That was all. Unless in some way he could be forced. And it wasn't very easy to see how. But then, Dobie thought, that's what this is all about. All these papers on my desk. Everything. He stared down at the sheet of notepad paper upon which he had written, for some reason or other, 1974, then crumpled it up and threw it in the wastepaper-basket.

He felt tempted to do the same with all the rest of it. *The Mask of Zeus* by Adrian Seymour indeed. It meant about as much as 1974 scribbled on a telephone notepad. It was a story or it wasn't a story. It told the truth or it didn't tell the truth. And you could say the same of the confession transcript. 'Jacko gets 'em every day,' Kate had said. 'Or so he claims. By the dozen, whenever a case gets into the newspapers. They don't mean a thing.' Kate had a nice voice; soothing, somehow. Even on the telephone. Thinking about Kate's voice, Dobie felt the tightened corners of his lips relax.

'Well, the police are acting on this one. Although they don't seem to have very much else.'

'Are you *sure* it's a fake?'

175

'There are some very odd things about it,' Dobie said. 'But then he's a very odd person.'

'You think he didn't do it?'

'He may or may not have *done* it but either way I don't think he's telling the truth about what happened.'

'Well, I've just sent off the stuff you wanted but I had a glance through it on the train and I can't see that it'll be any help. Just a lot of semi-highbrow stuff about some kind of porn picture or other . . . Dobie, you got to behave yourself while you're out there, you hear?'

'Oh, I will. But—'

'What?'

'I wish you were here. As the postcards say.'

'Yes. So do I. If only to keep you out of . . . Dobie, do you really know what you're doing?'

'To be honest,' Dobie said, 'no.'

The office door was opening. Dobie removed the idiotic smile from his face, picked up his ballpoint and looked alert and intelligent.

'Oh, there you are,' Hillyer said.

'Yum.'

'I hear you've been doing the rounds with Kaya.'

'Yes, I have. Most illuminating.'

'And exhausting. Fancy a spot of lunch?'

'That sounds like a good idea,' Dobie admitted. He rubbed his eyes again as he stood up, then reached down for his briefcase. 'I've got something here you might care to take a look at. Afterwards.'

'Oh, right. Jolly good,' Hillyer said.

176

9

They went to the Aramis Hotel and the murl there was all
right but in no way better, Dobie thought, than the nosh
Zeynep served up in the little lokanta, though the atmosphere
of course was a good deal posher. I don't like posh nosh, he
said to himself, cuddling his tumbler of post-prandial five-star
cognac; let's go where the posh is nosher, let's go to the pub
next door. Bread from Evans's, tea from Thomas's, beer from
the Collier's Arms . . . The foggy Rhymney valleys far from
him now though never quite forgotten as he looked down on
to a strip of beach drenched in Mediterranean sunshine and
crowded with tourists, a strip of tourists (a good collective
noun, that), many of the girls near by being almost in the state
attributed by Kaya to their pagan forebears; one of them had
certainly entered the sea respectably attired in a cotton singlet
and tight red knickers but these didn't help matters much when
she emerged from it. Cardiff was never like *this*. Mindful
of Kate's prevention, Dobie manfully averted his eyes and
regarded instead the less rewarding spectacle of Hillyer with
his elbows planked firmly on the table, scrutinising with an air
of mistrust the final sheet of those spread out before him.

'Very strange,' Hillyer said. 'Very strange indeed. Very
puzzling.'

'It seemed so to me,' Dobie said. 'But then I don't read
much fiction, you see, in the ordinary way. And I'm not even
sure if you'd call that fiction or not. So I just don't know how
to approach it.'

'It's *literary* all right. Too much so, some would say. I

177

mean it's over-written, that's obvious, but Seymour tended to do that anyway. It reads rather as though he'd somehow managed to get through that block of his at last and then went on just writing and writing, getting it all down before it died on him. Or before the effects of the drug he was on to wore off. That's my first impression of it, anyway.'

The girl in the wet singlet had taken it off and was lying down now in the sun. Dobie repressed an anguished groan and tried to address himself to the matter in hand. 'It's as though he doesn't even know who he is. That's the trouble.'

'Yes. That's the change of persona. Shifting viewpoints. Moving from himself to this Zeus figure and back again. I don't see that as too much of a problem, though; it's a fashionable literary device these days, to the point of being overdone, perhaps. I don't think—'

'Viewpoints. That's all you get.'

'Sorry?' Hillyer looked up in mild surprise, struck no doubt by the hint of a bovine bellow in Dobie's voice. The girl on the beach had just sat up and was reaching across for a cigarette. 'I don't quite follow—'

'It's all about what he sees. Not about what he does. He never even says that he kills her, not in so many words.'

'The whole effect,' Hillyer said, 'is meant to be voyeuristic. Or *is* voyeuristic, irrespective of what he intended. But then voyeurism is so often to be associated with impotence . . . it's as though he's releasing himself from his mental block through this really rather intense visualisation of the scene—'

'Supposing,' Dobie said, 'he saw someone else.'

'Someone else?'

'Killing her.'

'But that's absurd.'

'I'm not really into this. I'm just supposing.'

'Coming from someone who lays no claim to a vivid imagination, that's about the most extraordinary theory I've ever come across.'

'Yes. That's what *I* thought. It's quite a relief for me to hear you say so.'

178

'But I'm not inclined to dismiss it out of hand. Not altogether.'

'You're not?'

'No. I mean . . . Coleridge springs to mind.'

'Not to mine he doesn't.'

'Well, it's now fairly generally believed that in writing *The Ancient Mariner* he sublimated the guilt complex he suffered from in consequence of his having in his childhood made an attempt upon the life of his brother. "With my cross-bow," if you remember, "I shot the albatross." And was made to suffer accordingly. Crime and punishment. And a kind of confession, if you like, expressed in symbolic terms. Is that the sort of thing you're hypothesising?'

'I don't quite know. Is it? I just thought he might have got to see her being killed, right? Being more than halfway stoned on drugs at the time, and then not being able to face up to the fact of it, sort of thing, maybe because it was something he'd wanted to do himself but couldn't . . . Yes, I suppose a guilt complex is what you'd call it. Because of course he didn't do anything to stop it. Just watched it happen. I can imagine anyone feeling bad afterwards, after a thing like that.' Dobie picked up the pages of typescript and leafed through them.

Hillyer watched him for a moment in silence. 'But if Seymour didn't kill her, then someone else did.'

'And you think that's impossible?'

'No. Not impossible, I suppose. But in that case Seymour must certainly know who that person was. He may for some reason be inhibited from explaining—'

'He mightn't if that person was wearing a mask.'

'A mask? Well, yes, of course. The mask of Zeus. How stupid of me not to . . . But it does seem a rather melodramatic touch. In fact almost farcical. Unless one could think of some practical reason why . . . And I suppose one could, without great difficulty. Such indeed as the one you've just given. To prevent recognition. In which case we have further to suppose that Zeus in his human guise, so to speak, would be known to Seymour or to Derya. Or to both.'

179

'I think I would have to assume that anyway.'

'Quite. It wouldn't have been a burglar or . . . a breaker-in . . . But that's a very *uncomfortable* assumption for us to make. In its implications.'

'Yes, it is. As you were all here and in the compound at that time.'

'And that's where we come up with a bump against reality. I mean, we're all academics here, aren't we? I'm an academic. That's why I find it, well . . . rather fun in a way to pursue these ideas of yours to an *O altitudo*. But no one of us could possibly have . . . To put it on the crudest level, we wouldn't have had the guts.'

'Sometimes it's more a matter of being pushed hard enough.'

'But who by? And why? Seymour was maybe being pushed. By Derya herself.' Hillyer sat back. 'When it comes down to brass tacks, you know, it so very obviously had to have been him that I don't think it occurred to any of us to suppose otherwise. Even before we'd heard about his confession.'

'The trouble is,' Dobie said, 'we're all living in such an intimate little enclave . . . and what's more it's virtually sealed off after midnight because that's when Ali closes the gates. Well, I know it's only a wooden barrier really—'

'And quite unnecessary. They put that up two years ago,' Hillyer said huffily, 'when we had some minor thefts. But that's Cyprus for you. Once something's there, it's there for ever.'

'The point is that cars can't drive in after midnight without Ali's knowing about it. And again, we've all got garages and there's no other place to park cars except the turning space at the end, and no one could leave a car there without everyone in the compound noticing – and probably complaining about it because it'd be in the way.'

Hillyer sighed. 'Yes. But that's—'

'There doesn't seem to be any possibility of any unauthorised person having entered the compound that night – not if Ali's to be believed. And we have to cross *him* off the

180

list at once because there's no way a one-armed man could avoid being recognised, mask or no mask, or could bump off a healthy young woman anyway. Shoot someone, yes, maybe – but not suffocate anyone with a pillow. For the rest, you can't bring a boat in to the beach behind the houses because of that line of rocks and you can't get in any other way because the bushes are too thick and scratchy and all wired off. So it looks as if—'

'She could have brought someone in with her.'

'How?'

'Hiding in the back of the car, maybe. It'd have been dark, after all. Ali very easily might not have noticed.'

'But why should she want to do that?'

'*I* don't know. We're just considering theoretical possibilities, after all, and everything you say goes to prove my point. It couldn't have been anyone else and it wasn't any of us. Therefore, it must have been Seymour. QED.'

Hillyer obviously wasn't a logician or he would at once have seen the flaw in the demonstration. *Wasn't* and *couldn't have been* are quite different concepts. But Dobie wasn't disposed to press the point, especially since the girl on the beach had now been joined by two other spectacularly topless young ladies and all three were giggling loudly and talking to each other in what sounded like German, and most probably was. Dobie made what sounded like a soft whinnying noise through his teeth and turned away to summon the waiter. Further supplies of brandy were now needed as a matter of urgency.

'Very stimulating,' Hillyer said. (Dobie nodded weakly.) 'On a purely intellectual level, all this speculation . . . But I can't see any need to interpret this stuff of Seymour's on a factual level. I mean, how *can* you? He's clearly giving the freest possible rein to his imagination . . . That's perfectly obvious.'

'But there are facts there as well.'

'What facts?'

'Well, he did burn his papers that evening. The dustbin was full of ashes. And all that about Derya and the play they did

181

in Cardiff: I know that's true because I saw the play myself. Although I grant you I don't remember very much about it.'

'Yes, but it all drifts away into unreality.' Hillyer tapped the sheaf of paper on the table impatiently, almost aggressively, Dobie thought. 'Into that ostentatious style of his, all those allusions and echoes . . . Tom o' Bedlam and Othello and DHL, it's all so affected and dated in a way.'

'Othello?'

'Oh, yes. He quotes Othello. At least twice.'

'That's interesting.'

'I see what you mean but it's the way in which he uses his quotations—'

'And who's Tom o' Bedlam?'

'It's a poem supposedly written by a lunatic. Yes, yes, but don't you see, my point is—'

'And DH what? The other one you said?'

'Yes, Lawrence, "Bavarian Gentians", that's one of the later poems in which he . . . But look, Dobie, if you want a proper literary analysis of the thing you'll have to give me a little more time. And I have to say that I doubt very much if it'll be a very profitable undertaking.'

'He seems to have been quite keen on that chap Lawrence.'

'He was. But that again, you see, isn't the point.'

'No,' Dobie said sadly. 'I'm sure it isn't.'

Dobie wasn't a man of letters but he wasn't an idiot, either. He could also be on occasion a tenacious sort of a beggar. The volume of *Collected Poems* was there on Seymour's bookshelf and, while 'Bavarian Gentians' seemed to be almost as impenetrable as Seymour's demented outpourings, Dobie found what Hillyer had called the *allusion* without much difficulty: the poem had at least the merit of being short. Although when he'd finished reading it and had read through it once again and still had no very clear idea of what the bloody thing was all about, he had none the less formed a general impression that accorded well enough with what he knew of Seymour's concerns and preoccupations. (And Kaya's, for that matter.)

182

There was no mention of Zeus in the poem but the flowers, the gentians – whatever they were – seemed to be obscurely connected with other strange gods and pagan deities, Pluto, Persephone, *et al.* being specifically mentioned. Apart from this and a generalised feeling that DHL (as Hillyer called him) was unlikely to have been a little ray of sunshine about the house, Dobie, overall, remained unenlightened. The naiads he had observed at play earlier that afternoon might have had some connection with Bavaria, where to the best of Dobie's knowledge they spoke German, but Persephone and the others – again to the best of his knowledge – certainly didn't, and other aspects of the effusion he found equally puzzling. He regretfully decided that Hillyer had been right.

Not a profitable undertaking at all.

Returning the volume to the shelf a little over-exasperatedly, he dislodged from its position its rather flimsy neighbour, which slid sideways and then down to the floor, not with a bang but a flutter. He stooped wearily to pick it up, glancing at the cover as he did so. *Cyprus: the Divided Island*, it was called. Political stuff, unquestionably. The fall unfortunately seemed to have detached two or more of the inside pages, and these Dobie guiltily endeavoured at once to return to their former pristine condition. But it seemed they weren't part of the book at all, but something else that had been pushed inside – possibly to act as a marker. It looked like a theatre programme.

The Cardiff University Players
present

AMPHITRYON

by John Dryden
produced by Adrian Seymour

. . . It *was* a theatre programme.

Dobie opened it. Inside, the usual advertisement panels; the cast list; the programme notes. *Similarly from this unlikely*

183

material does Dryden, in the footsteps of Molière, fashion a brilliantly amusing satirical comedy, not without profound political implications . . . There you are. There it was. *Another* fact. Another point on which Seymour could be proved to have been accurate. The theatre programme that he'd referred to really existed. OK, a fact; but again, not a fact that would *help* anyone very much. Any more than the photograph on the sitting-room wall did, or any more than the photograph that Dobie had discovered seemed to have done.

Political implications, though. That was curious. Still, almost anything might be given a political implication if you searched for it hard enough. Slipping the programme back into its place, Dobie saw that the page it might have been used to mark had indeed been marginated in pencil; or one of the paragraphs on that page, anyway. There were several paragraphs on the page, as most of them were very short.

. . . Also on the same tragic morning, a group of EOKA-B men entered the village of Tokhni and rounded up sixty-nine men between the ages of thirteen and seventy-four. On 15 August the intruders brought in fifteen more Turkish Cypriot men they had picked up in Mari and Zyyi. They then bussed fifty of their captives to a spot in the vicinity of Limassol, where a ditch had already been dug, and shot them. The remaining thirty-four men were never seen again, and are presumed dead.

In Paphos, the National Guard killed five men and a three-year-old boy. According to a United Nations observer, thirty to forty bullet holes were found in the child's body.

In the village of Ayios Ioannis, the National Guard and elements of EOKA-B killed five more men on 15 August.

In Alanici, near Famagusta, the entire population of the hamlet – twenty-six men, women and children – were forced on to trucks by the ZEUS geurrilla group; the trucks were then driven away towards the city. The villagers were never seen again, and are presumed dead . . .

184

It was this last paragraph that had been marked in pencil. Dobie read it again, rubbing his chin thoughtfully.

'Zeynep?'

The pummelling noises in the next room stopped and Zeynep, poking her head in through the door, came up with her usual catch-phrase. 'Ullo Derby.'

'Zeynep, what's the name of that village down the road? Where the army base is?'

'Scawl Alanici.'

'That's what I thought,' Dobie said.

He took the book over to the desk, sat down and read a few more paragraphs. The author, who appeared to be a Frenchman, expressed himself with far more clarity than D.H. Lawrence or than Seymour himself, and his subject matter was even more depressing. The whole chapter made out a seemingly interminable list of atrocities committed by Cypriot Greeks against Cypriot Turks in the summer months of 1974; the next chapter, which Dobie couldn't bring himself to read, catalogued the atrocities committed, over the same period, by Cypriot Turks against Cypriot Greeks. The only conclusion Dobie could draw was that, compared to this, Seymour's behaviour constituted the quintessence of sanity. He had been well enough aware that the year 1974 had marked a particularly troubled period in the island's history, but the depths of the lunacy – and infamy – hadn't as yet been really brought home to him. He had to suppose that they still hadn't. He was, after all, only reading words on a page. The reality would have been something else.

A nightmare. Far, far worse than anything of Seymour's imagining.

His car was in the garage. He got it out.

Alanici.

Most of the villages in Cyprus bore neat new blue and white plaques at their outskirts announcing their names. This one didn't. It didn't really exist. Not any more.

It couldn't ever have amounted to much of a village anyway.

185

Eight or ten single-storey buildings clustered to the right of the road behind the barbed-wire fencing. Blank windows, closed doors, splintered shutters, a few withered vine stalks obstinately clinging to collapsed pergolas. There *was* a sign at the village entrance but it was red-painted and said: DIKKAT ASKERI ARAC DUR.

Dobie didn't know what it meant but its purport was made sufficiently clear by the the white-helmeted Turkish soldier who stood, feet apart, beside it, clutching an AK47 and regarding Dobie incuriously. Dobie got out of the car and surveyed the scenery, a little self-consciously under the sentry's stare; he didn't want to be taken for some kind of a spy, although there didn't seem to be much to spy upon round here. Nothing. Absolutely nothing.

The flat bare fields of the Mesaoria, stretching out to the west and south. The backcloth of the Karpaz mountains behind, obscured by the afternoon heat haze. Blue sky and dry brown land; a hot, windless day. Total quietude. No movement anywhere. Dobie walked up the road a few paces, his hands in his pockets, his shoes scuffing up little puffs of dust from the powdery soil. This was yet another place embalmed in the stillness of past time. Another Salamis, broken not by earthquakes but by another kind of upheaval; death had come here and then had gone away again, frustrated perhaps by the calm indifference of the hills, the hot red earth, the overhanging sky. Life didn't think too much of the place, either.

Only ten minutes away, the Aramis Hotel: the cooling drinks, the beach umbrellas, the screams and splashes, all that enticing acreage of bare brown female flesh. But this was Alanici. A dead-end, Dobie thought, if ever there was one. Three or four lorries had come, had loaded up, had turned and gone back the way they'd come. No other choice. The road ended here. Maybe everything had been like that, in '74.

Maybe everything was *still* like that. Cyprus: smashed buildings, barbed wire and a motionless soldier, inactive as the headless statues of Salamis. The tourists and the

186

bikinis, somewhere else. The university, on another planet. Intellectual recognition? Cultural dynamism? Well, old Arkin was certainly trying hard, but you had to have a touch of fanaticism, surely, to believe it. And to put it over to so ultimately unreceptive an audience. Hillyer had put his finger on the spot. Academics . . . intelligent and cultured – oh, yes, extremely. Hard-working – yes, that too. Up to a point, Lord Boot. But *fanatical*? No way. It's true, Dobie thought, we don't have the guts. We couldn't kill anybody. Much less bring about an intellectual revolution in a place like this. If Tolga Arkin thinks that, he's expecting too much of us. We don't have the imagination. We don't have . . .

We don't have whatever it is that Seymour's got, when you think about it. That sharp little cutting edge of lunacy. Of course he'd killed Derya. Everyone was convinced of it.

A dead-end. Kaya, Ozzie, Cem Arkin, Berry Berry and (of course) Hillyer himself: a hopeless list of possible alternative suspects. Dobie looked at his wrist-watch; he'd be meeting most of them again soon: Mrs Berry Berry was having a barbecue. In the back garden, no doubt, in the shade of the trees, with blue smoke curling upwards from the grill and with neighbours strolling over to join in the conversation, then strolling as casually away again. The church clock standing at ten to three. The British way of life of sixty years back, effortlessly and thoroughly assimilated. Murder at the vicarage. Quite so.

He looked again at the empty buildings, at the long low army huts behind them, at the set of football posts sticking forlornly up out of nowhere. Then he clambered back into his car, executed a wobbly U-turn and drove away. Going straight back the way he'd come. He had to.

There was nowhere else to go.

Mrs Berry Berry showed every sign of being instantly bewitched by Professor Dobie. Not, it must be said, because of his impressive physique or charm of manner but (he guessed) because as a recent arrival he bore the aura of a visitant from

187

another and more exotic world . . . ET, perhaps, rather than Robert Redford. Mrs Berry Berry herself certainly carried no such aura, being blonde and fluffy and apple-dumplingish and rather too Kensington High Street. 'So here you are at *last*, Professor Dobie. I can't think why Berry didn't bring you round before. You really mustn't think us unfriendly or inhospitable, it's just that strictly between you and me the poor darling's getting a little absent-minded. Though I don't know why I say that. He always was. *You* know how it is.'

Than Dobie, none better. 'Well, Mrs Berry—'

'No, no. Doreen.'

'Well, Doreen, I'm afraid I'm inclined to be somewhat distrait myself. Or so I'm told. Although—'

'He was delighted when he learned you were coming to join us, I can tell you that.' She patted the plastic cushions spread out across the rustic wooden garden bench, relentlessly redolent of Derry and Toms, upon which she sat, and Dobie cautiously planted his bottom alongside. It occupied, he noted, perhaps one-third of the space that hers did. 'And so was I. It's so nice to know that from now on he'll have someone British, I mean, you know, someone really experienced and competent helping him out. Someone who knows his stuff.' Dobie nodded wisely. He knew his stuff all right when he saw it, which wasn't often. 'Because he's been taking far too much upon himself these past few years and I don't in the least mind saying so.'

Dobie didn't mind her saying so, either. 'Yes, I hope I can be of some use around the place, but of course it's a temporary appointment. I expect before long they'll find someone younger as a long-term prospect—'

'But that's what I'm *saying*,' Mrs Berry Berry wailed. 'It's people with experience we need here. People with experience and *balance*. Energy is fine when it's expended in the right direction but with young people it hardly ever is. Don't you agree? It's *guidance* this university needs. Not just enthusiasm.'

Dobie nodded, having by now caught and recognised the

general tenor of Mrs Berry Berry's argument and identified the tone in which it was being conducted. Not so much that of the Colonel's lady in British India; rather that of the Colonel of the Regiment himself. Mrs Berry didn't look the part but she played it extremely well, no doubt because she believed in it implicitly. 'I'm sure you're right, Doreen, we'd hardly be professors otherwise. I know that Ozzie's been brought in from a business background, but in his field that's not unusual. In fact—'

'It's not the Heads of Department I mean. It's the junior staff. And Berry's junior staff in particular. Do you know what the average age of the mathematics instructors was last year? Twenty-five. Berry's had no one to support him on faculty level since Ben Masefield left. Did you know Ben Masefield?'

'Er, no.'

'An American,' Mrs Berry Berry explained, with some distaste.

'Ah. But what about Derya?'

'What about Derya?'

'She was an Assistant Professor, wasn't she? Or did you feel that she was too young?'

'Of course she was. And a nasty little bitch. A real troublemaker, I knew that from the start.'

Diplomacy was needed here. 'Yes, I suppose her manner might have sometimes be considered a shade provocative—'

'Provocative? *Derya?* She'd fuck anything that moved and wore trousers. I know she's dead but that doesn't alter facts.'

It is, Dobie remembered, the prerogative of the Colonel of the Regiment to call a spade a spade, a wog a wog, et cetera, without exciting reproof, much less reprisal. Mrs Berry Berry, however, had gone slightly pink in the face, as if aware that she might have expressed herself over-forcibly. 'Perhaps,' he suggested tentatively, 'it's a form of reaction to the rigours of a severe intellectual discipline. There was a young lady in Lampeter . . . '

189

This suggestion, however promising as the opening line of a salacious limerick, was immediately and vigorously rejected by the Colonel. 'Intellectual discipline my arse. Jumping from bed to bed was what she was good at. All right – I know it isn't always politic to go round blurting out the truth but I don't see any point in beating about the bush. People have to take me as they find me. I don't care.'

'Well, you're expressing a personal viewpoint. And we've all got the right to do that.'

'I don't know that I am. *Personally*, I didn't give a shit what the little cow got up to. Promiscuity is none of my business, it was something for her and her husband to . . . Anyway I was never concerned about that. It was her *professional* conduct that I objected to. I considered it downright disgraceful.'

'In what way?'

'In the way she was always belittling my husband behind his back. Telling everyone he was past it. Just because he isn't fully acquainted with the latest developments in those computer things and information technology. Things that have got nothing to do with mathematics as *I* understand it. And spending all her time working at her own research instead of pulling her weight with the teaching and all the administrative chores. I don't know why Berry put up with it for so long, I really don't.'

'But why should she have behaved like that?'

'Because she was after the job for herself, of course. Why else?'

'You mean she wanted to head the department?'

'Of course. She'd have *got* the job, too, if Berry had retired as he was thinking of doing. And as he will do in a couple of years' time, if I have *my* way. That's why the bloody gel annoyed me so much. Getting up to all those dirty tricks when she'd have got what she wanted anyway, in no time at all.'

Two years can be a long time, though, when you're an Assistant Professor, as Dobie remembered only too well. 'Yes, I remember her as being very ambitious. But I never supposed—'

190

Mrs Berry Berry looked at him, seemingly a little startled. 'Oh, that's right. You knew her, didn't you? She was one of your students. Berry told me, but then it slipped my mind. She was good, was she? I mean as a student?'

'Brilliant.'

'That's exactly what Berry always said. I can never understand why it is that academics think brilliance excuses everything. God, I've been married to one for thirty-five years so I ought to understand it. But I don't.'

'Perhaps Derya thought that. About herself.'

'I'm sure she did.'

'But then,' Dobie said, 'so did her husband. Seymour. From all accounts. It's not just academics who think that, you know. It was all those writers and people who started it.'

'Yes. Oscar Wilde. He must have been really surprised when events caught up with him the way they did; he clearly thought of himself as being untouchable, somehow. But I adore Oscar Wilde. Don't you?'

'Not really.' It would, Dobie felt, be somewhat imprudent to admit any such an infatuation and, in any case, his knowledge of the works in question was of the sketchiest. 'And anyway, Derya wasn't like that. Surely?'

'She was always ready and willing to declare her talent,' Mrs Berry Berry said frostily. 'But there I suppose the resemblance ceases.'

It would be interesting for Dobie, in retrospect, to reflect that after so many excursions leading into dead-ends, after so much agonised beating – as she would have said – about the bush, it was Mrs Berry Berry who would eventually prove to have set him on the right track and that, as often happens, through a chance remark. Naturally, though, he wasn't aware of this at the time, his attention being at that moment elsewhere engaged by the arrival of a group of people with whom he wasn't yet acquainted but whom he recognised as other university colleagues; they had driven over, doubtless, from the other professorial compound located on the outskirts of Famagusta. Mrs Berry Berry had risen and gone across to greet them.

191

Dobie, thus left on his tod, allowed his gaze to wander over to where smoke was drifting upwards from the barbecue grill and where, under Berry Berry's supervision, the earnest student Ali was blackening numerous succulent chunks of chicken.

Ozzie, taking refuge from this expertly delivered form of chemical warfare, was moving away from the lee side of the grill and approaching Dobie's bench; these outdoor parties, Dobie reflected, indeed often resemble some obscure form of tactical military engagement, with battle lines being drawn up, alliances formed and discarded, and with any number of fiery sparks whizzing carelessly through the air. Undoubtedly it was through the exercise of command in innumerable back-garden skirmishes that Kensington High Street had acquired its Imperial General Staff incisiveness, not to mention its vocabulary. Ozzie, a neutral by temperament and by training, planked himself heavily down beside Dobie. 'When the goin' gets tough,' he observed, 'the tough get goin'.'

'Ah, so you're off, then?'

'Nah. Jus' that I'm not one for kebabs meself. Cookin's best done in the kitching is my opinion. What say you?'

'Well, for me at least it's got the charm of novelty. We don't get many opportunities for outdoor cooking in Cardiff.'

'True enough. Wet an' windy old Wales, right?' But Ozzie's eyes were clouded over with nostalgia. 'An' Lunnon's no better. Wun't mind bein' there right now, all the same. Trouble with this place, it's so dam' *boring*.' His eyes then jerked a little apprehensively across the tangled bushes towards Dobie's residence. 'At least, I didn't mean . . . Sorry. I meant in, like, the *ornery* way.'

Dobie tried to rescue his mind from the haze of mild befuddlement into which it was slipping. It often did that when he felt a trifle peckish. 'But you're a bachelor, aren't you, Ozzie? I'd have thought you'd welcome a chance to get out of the kitchen.'

'As for cookin',' Ozzie said, 'I never rightly got the 'ang of it, all them pots an' pans an' things an' I never know what to put in where. It's all got too scientifick these days. So I'll settle for a nice cheese sangwidge most of the time.'

That of course was one of the troubles with an all-male community. 'I know Hillyer's divorced. What about what's-his-name? Kaya?'

'Oh, he's got a wife an' fambly over in Turkey. Runs over to Ankara to see 'em every so often. An' old Hillyer, he's a special case, don't you think? Doesn't go in much for the social thing. Hasn't come today, as you've noticed.'

Dobie hadn't. 'He seems quite cordial to me. We had lunch together, as a matter of fact.'

'Oh. You'd get on all right with him, you're both Brits, I mean, aintcha? But he doesn't mix all that much as a general rule. Bit of a puritan I always think.'

Dobie looked round, puzzled. 'So he doesn't hold with all these lascivious garden parties?'

'What? Oh, see what you mean. Well, no, you got a point there. But of course it was different when Derya was around; we had a bit of colour about the place, or glammer, you might say. Bound to lead to trouble, though, one way or another.'

'Why do you say that?'

'Well, with all us blokes around, don't you see?' Ozzie waved a hand around his head, drawing Dobie's attention to the presence of all those ravening males currently cluttering up the garden. 'I expeck most universities are like that an' geezers like you an' Hillyer, you prob'ly got used to it. Bit different when you come in from outside, when you've been in the world of big bizness with sexy little secretaries an' such wigglin' their behinds at you. Miss out on it, you do. All right, you'll say we got sexy little students instead an' so we have, yis, but it ain't the *same* somehow, if you see what I mean.'

'But you've been teaching here for some time now.'

'Three years. An' it seems a bloody sight longer.'

'So you came here at the same time as Derya. And Seymour.'

'So I did. And Cem. We were all old Tolga Arkin's recruits,

193

like I told you. You met him the other day, didn't you? What did you make of him?'

'He's quite a . . . dynamic personality.'

'Oh, he's a top gun an' no mistake. He'll get to be President here I shouldn't wonder. Bit of a strain for old Cem, though, tryin' to live up to the image, as they say.' Ozzie jerked his chin towards where, through the clinging haze of smoke, Cem Arkin's bulky outline was vaguely discernible, stooped over a little as he chatted with Berry Berry. 'Gets him down a bit sometimes. He's quite honest about it, y'know. He'll tell you so.'

'I'll be seeing him tomorrow, as it happens. I have to make a formal call. But,' Dobie said, 'I don't think—'

'Not just his old man, neither. His uncle as well. Famous, I mean. My old man ran a shoe repair business in Wandsworth an' I'm just as glad. No one ever expected nothin' very much of me. You know Wandsworth?'

'No, I don't.'

'Pretty big place innit, Lunnon.'

Berry Berry was the next to approach, red-eyed, pink-nosed and with tiny fragments of grey charcoal ash clinging to his bristly moustache. This added, Dobie found, to the general effect of some other relic, or possibly refugee, from the Raj. 'Afraid I'm neglecting my duties as a host, Dobie. But I saw my wife had you in tow, so . . . Everything OK?'

'Yes indeed,' Dobie said. 'Pukka.'

'That's what *I'm* often tempted to say but . . . ' Holding a handkerchief to his streaming eyes Berry Berry sat down in the place only recently vacated by Ozzie. Dobie was beginning to feel there was something seriously wrong with his detective methods; if only he were a public nose or whatever these American characters called themselves, whizzing about from place to place in Cadillacs and pausing only to take in a snort of rye or to get themselves rather seriously stomped on by assorted evildoers, that would clearly be very much more interesting than sitting around in a cloud of smoke and being *talked* to by every casual passer-by. On the other hand, it seemed a bit too late to do anything about it now. 'So what have you been *up* to?' Berry Berry enquired, pressing the point home.

Nothing much. 'Well, I've been to see Salamis. And Alanici.'

'*Alanici?*' Berry Berry raised an eye towards him in some surprise, the other eye being temporarily out of service. 'Whatever for? Nobody goes *there*. Well, they won't let you in for a start. The army won't. Not unless you have a pass or know somebody there.'

'I just wanted to see if there was a stream or a river or anything like that. But no. There wasn't.'

'Of course not.' Berry Berry raised a hand in salutation and half rose from his seat as a very fat lady walked by, subsiding again with a little thump. 'No attractions whatsover. Quite the contrary. The locals never go near the place if they can help it. Rather a nasty incident there at the time of the troubles, you see. That's why the place is deserted.'

'I know,' Dobie said. 'I read about it.'

'Did you? Where?'

'In a book.'

Berry Berry treated him to another searching red-rimmed glance, obviously suggesting that a serious mathematician ought to have a mind above such frivolous diversions. Reading books, indeed. Whatever next? Better things had been expected of Professor D. 'Never been near the place myself. Nobody goes there.'

'I'm told that Derya did.'

'To the occasional hop, perhaps, at the army base. That was different.'

'What,' Dobie asked, 'exactly happened there?'

'I don't think anyone knows. No survivors. Apparently one of the local Greek murder gangs came along one night and put everyone in the village into trucks and drove off and that was it. All murdered out in the hills somewhere.'

'It's appalling.'

'Yes, but that sort of thing was happening all over Cyprus.

195

It was probably meant as a reprisal for some other killing somewhere. No one's ever been able to suggest any other reason for it. If you can call that a reason.'

'*They* would know what happened. The ones who did it.'

'Of course, but no one knows who they were. They'll be over Greek-side now, what's left of them, but the chances are high that most of them are dead. The EOKA lot had a high attrition rate, which isn't surprising when you consider the enemies they made. No one pretends that our lot behaved like angels, either, and all those Greek gangs were killing each other at one point. We don't like to talk about it much, but nobody's forgotten.'

'All the same,' Dobie said, 'it happened a long time ago. Derya was at school in England then. And so was Seymour.'

'And so was Cem Arkin. And I was teaching in the States. None of us was here then. Kaya was in Turkey . . . ' Right now he was, Dobie saw, over by the partition fencing, talking inscrutably with the very fat lady. 'But we all feel it, you know. A national disgrace and we have to recover from it. That's how Tolga Arkin feels, and very strongly.' Berry Berry stopped twisting his handkerchief between his hands, dabbed his left eye with it and put it away. 'I expect you'll cotton on to these things in time. By the way, you didn't go down to the village by yourself? You want to be careful about doing things like that. Perfectly safe as long as you stay on the road, but don't ever wander off into the woods or above all take a walk down any of the mountain valleys. It's very risky.'

'Because someone might take a shot at me?'

'Good heavens, no. Nothing like that. Except in the hunting season, and then by accident. No, but the stones and rocks are always shifting around and if you fall and break a leg you've probably had it. Tourist went missing two years ago and they only found what was left of him last summer – twenty yards away from a road at that. Trying to photograph the mountain scenery, obviously. There's some lovely views up there so it's a temptation. And even some of the locals have gone out

196

hunting by themselves and vanished for ever. I know you'll get a bit tired of being cooped up here with the rest of us for weeks on end – we all like to get away by ourselves sometimes for a bit. But be careful when you do. No solitary hikes.'

They seemed, Dobie thought, to be selecting exceptionally gloomy conversational topics even for a barbecue party. The chicken kebabs seemed, however, to be almost ready, which was just as well; his stomach was beginning to make plaintive creaky noises. Looking ravenously around him to see where the inevitable disposable plates had been stacked, he perceived Mrs Berry Berry approaching at a rate of knots. Arrived beside them, she at once addressed him in breathless and archly conspiratorial tones. 'A telephone call for you. A lady. *Extremely* urgent, she says.'

Dobie was pleased but also more than a little surprised. How could Kate have got Berry Berry's number? Was there no end to her resourcefulness? 'Dr Coyle, is it? Did she give a name?'

'She did. But not that one. Caroline Bartlett.'

Bartlett? *Bartlett?*

'You can take the call on the hallway extension, if you wish,' the Colonel said grandly.

Dobie barely had time to down a couple of finger-lickin' chicken joints before rushing off *chez lui* for a hasty shower and a change of clobber. He couldn't see the force of Ozzie's complaint that life in Cyprus was boring. *Boring?* Never a dull moment. Call me Twinkletoes. Even as he was hurling himself into a clean shirt Mahomet, in the not unpleasing shape of the nice lady, arrived at the mountain, this time in an important-looking grey Mercedes with a portly tight-blue-suited character at the wheel. Regretfully abandoning his claim to any further skewered and smouldering morsels, Dobie politely conducted his visitors into the sitting-room, where the nice lady seated herself primly on one of the armchairs and the portly gentleman prowled up and down with his hands interlaced behind his back, staring belligerently out of the window. Earlier at the

197

front door the p.g. had introduced himself as Mr Bilsel, the defence counsel; very possibly, Dobie thought, he had allowed his courtroom customs to affect his private life and was on the point of whipping round to address the members of the jury. Not that this was a private call. Far from it.

'I would like,' he said, not whipping round but continuing to gaze out of the window, 'to see where you found the document. *Exactly.*'

Dobie obediently escorted him to Derya's bedroom and showed him Derya's wardrobe and Derya's shoe.

'H'm,' Mr Bilsel said, poking at this latter object with his index finger much as Dobie had done. 'An ingenious hiding-place. No question, I would say, of the document having been placed there other than as of intention. The chance of it having arrived there by accident would seem to be remote.'

Dobie, the logician, having worked out more or less what Bilsel seemed to be saying, observed that one premise followed from the other and nodded a cautious agreement.

'So the further question may well arise of how you happened across the document in view of its, um, er, somewhat recondite situation.'

'You mean how I came to find it?'

'Just so. Perhaps you make a practice of examining the insides of ladies' shoes? You are, maybe, what I think is called a fetishist?'

'Oh, no. Nothing like that. I was really looking for something else.'

'Such as what? A lady's foot?'

'No. Mud.'

'What?'

'Mud.'

'Not blood?'

'No. Mud.'

Bilsel shook his head slowly; here, his manner suggested, was a witness who had at all costs to be kept out of the box. 'Certainly,' he said judiciously, anxious to be fair, 'I detect traces of mud on the shoe in question. But what were you intending to do with the mud when you'd found it?'

'*Do* with it? Nothing. I just wanted to make sure it was there.'

'I see. Yes. Of course. Silly of me. There was, I take it, no one else present when you made this discovery?'

'No.'

Bilsel sighed. 'A pity.' They returned to the sitting-room and Bilsel this time elected to seat himself. Dobie did the same.

There followed rather a lengthy silence, at the end of which Dobie cleared his throat. 'Er, well . . . '

'Yes. Yes.' Thus prompted, Bilsel sprang into action. He did this by placing the tips of his fingers together and initiating a strange bottom-waggling seesaw motion on the armchair cushions. 'It's a most interesting discovery you've made. And a perplexing one. I may say that we've managed to trace the person to whom the document was originally issued. And when I say *trace*, I mean that we have definitely established her identity. That may, in the rather peculiar circumstances, be all that we shall be able to do. I must ask you, by the way, to treat everything connected with this matter in the strictest confidence. Indeed, I'm only divulging such information as we have gained on Mrs Bartlett's insistence. The issues involved are very delicate, very delicate indeed.'

'You haven't divulged anything yet,' Dobie pointed out, 'I mean, we know who she is already. Someone called Sabiha something. Unless—'

'Sabiha Metti. But that wasn't her true name. Not exactly.'

'When you say it wasn't her name—'

'You grasp my implication quickly. Yes, she's dead, or at least has been presumed dead for these past sixteen years. In fact, virtually since the date on the document. August 1974.'

'In that case,' Dobie said, 'I suppose it can't be a very promising lead.'

'That depends. Sabiha Metti was the maiden name of the lady: her married name was Sabiha Arkin. She was then the wife of our present Minister of Education.' His eyes turned

199

again towards the window. 'And of course the mother of your colleague just across the road. You may possibly have heard something of the story. Which is deeply tragic.'

'I heard that she was killed in the war. Yes.'

Bilsel nodded. 'Though, legally, her death has always had to be presumed – as with many others. She disappeared. Her body was never found and so never formally identified. She left her house in Nicosia one morning and thereafter was never seen again. It was not a time that many of us now wish to recall, much less to reflect on. You'll appreciate that.'

'I think I can,' Dobie said. 'Though it seems to me to be the sort of thing you have to have lived through—'

'*Survived* might be a more exact term. Most of us did, but Mrs Arkin didn't – though she took the proper precautions, as that document witnesses. Precaution wasn't always enough, though. You sometimes needed good luck, as well.'

'When you say *precautions* . . . ?'

'The travel document is in her maiden name, as I explained.'

'Yes, but—'

'Let me explain further. Her brother-in-law, Uktu, as he then called himself . . . At that time he was one of the leaders of the Turkish-Cypriot resistance. Any of his relatives would have been prime targets for the EOKA and she'd have been in no little danger in Nicosia, where her place of residence, naturally, was widely known. So she'd have done her best to get to the Turkish-held area . . . in the event, to Famagusta. The document shows how she travelled – by car – and seems to prove that she got there. And that's something that wasn't previously known. According to the existent records, as I say, she left her house and that was the end of it. Vanished en route, it was generally thought.'

'Extraordinary,' Dobie said.

'Not at all. There were hundreds of Greeks moving south at that time, hundreds of Turks moving north, the whole country was in turmoil. And many people got killed while on the move, passing through villages held by the National Guard on the one hand or by Uktu's supporters on the other . . . Of course Uktu himself was killed a few days later, but the shooting went on all through August and way into September. You have to see it against that kind of an overall picture.'

Dobie couldn't. All that he could see, but for a few moments with a surprising clarity, was a pale oval dark-eyebrowed face framed in a mist of long black hair. A face like Derya's in one way, not at all like it in another.

'And if,' Bilsel said, 'in fact Uktu hadn't been killed, the smaller picture might have been clarified very much sooner, since the travel authorisation carries his signature. I've called it a travel pass but in effect it was a safe-conduct, as you'll realise. And the stamps on it show that, in effect, she reached Famagusta safely. What happened to her after that, well, that's what we still don't know. Uktu probably had some kind of a hideout arranged for her and Tolga, but the chances are high that she never got there. It's a quite perplexing business, and in view of Tolga Arkin's present eminent position . . . delicate. Delicate.'

'What I don't see,' Dobie said, 'is what all this has to do with Derya. Or with Seymour.'

'Nor do we. We don't know why Mrs Seymour had the document and we don't know how she came by it, *but*,' Bilsel said, raising one finger to emphasise the significance of the point, 'your evidence clearly establishes that she did have it and that she kept it in a place of concealment. And that's what matters. You can take it from me that the Attorney-General won't be pleased if that document gets introduced into the evidence; it'd be extremely embarrassing and painful – especially to Tolga Arkin himself. We could certainly call on him to testify if we chose, and that would be an unpleasant experience for him and for everybody. I'm convinced that the Legislative Assembly would go to considerable lengths to prevent that from happening. Therefore, if we hold back on it, the prosecuting counsel would almost certainly accept a plea of temporary insanity and a recommendation of immediate repatriation to the UK for psychiatric treatment. It'd be an unusual development – in fact, unprecedented – but it would be a highly satisfactory outcome from everybody's point of view. Most of all, of course, from my client's.' He smiled a tight, legalistic little smile and sat back in the armchair.

Lawyers, Dobie thought, like university professors, seem to be much the same everywhere, the marks of their profession seeming to outweigh even those of their nationality; lawyers and, for that matter, policemen. 'Surely,' he said, 'it's inadmissible evidence? You yourself said you couldn't see any connection—'

'Presumably there has to be one. And nobody wants to see that connection, whatever it is, established, as the defence would naturally be bound to try to do.'

'And will you try to do so, in fact?'

'That,' Bilsel said patiently, 'is what I am trying to explain to you, Professor Dobie. If I can indeed negotiate the terms I've suggested with the District Attorney and in effect secure my client's release to a recognised institution in the UK, then we must also keep to our part of the bargain. The document will remain on file and the whole matter will rest in abeyance. To all intents and purposes, you never found it and I myself will have no cognisance of it whatsoever. Nor will Mrs Bartlett here. That's why we have to have your assurance of your co-operation. A written assurance, of course, is quite unnecessary. Your verbal agreement will be perfectly satisfactory.'

This, Dobie told himself severely, is perfectly disgraceful. Under no circumstances would he consent. In any case, 'But in any case I won't be called on to give evidence. Not if—'

'True. It would be best, however, if you would undertake to make no mention of this matter to anybody, in private conversation or . . . through any other means, for as long as you remain in Cyprus. I can assure you that you'll be serving Mr Seymour's best interests by complying with my request, and Mrs Bartlett will confirm that, should you be in any doubt about it.'

'You said you'd be retaining the thingummy yourself? On file?'

202

'Certainly. Until such time as it may be conveniently destroyed.'

'So any comments I might make couldn't be very easily substantiated.'

'They couldn't. No.'

The nice lady, throughout this interesting exchange of views, had been fiddling with the strap of her handbag and gazing pensively at the toes of her sensible suede brogues. Now Dobie's air of deepening gloom provoked her, as it seemed, to utterance. 'You see, the Foreign Office is taking a hand in the matter now. That's another way of saying State Security. They have powers of deportation.'

'*Deportation?* I only just got here.'

'Oh, good heavens, it won't come to that. It's just that this . . . discovery of yours has rather put the cat among the pigeons. That's why Mr Bilsel insisted on seeing you. To convince you of the importance—'

'What cat? What pigeons?'

'It's the other way round, really,' Bilsel said. 'Any number of Greek cats. And a Turkish pigeon. We simply can't have Tolga Arkin involved, however indirectly, in a murder case at the present juncture. As a recent arrival here, Professor Dobie, you can have no idea how carefully they watch us, over on the Greek side, and make political capital out of the smallest slip-up. It makes things extremely difficult for us.'

'What you've told me,' Dobie said, 'is that Tolga Arkin's wife disappeared way back in 1974 and was very probably killed by terrorists. How can anyone make political capital out of that?'

Bilsel shook his head and sighed. 'It opens old wounds. That's what we don't want to do, not right now. Above all, Tolga Arkin's wounds. He's a figure of international status and an immense asset to us in our political negotiations, but he has personal and family feelings like everyone else. I doubt very much if you can imagine how a man feels when he knows his wife has been murdered. In cold blood.'

'Yes, I can,' Dobie said. 'Mine was.'

203

After rather a lengthy pause Bilsel said, 'I didn't know that. I must apologise.'

'In a way, that's why I'm here.'

'You felt you needed a change of scene.'

'Yes.'

'That's very much how Tolga Arkin reacted.' Bilsel, oddly enough, seemed now to be addressing his remarks to the nice lady; another courtroom tactic, perhaps, designed to cover up his temporary embarrassment. 'He left the country in September, I seem to recall. To undertake those researches in Europe and America that would lead him to his Nobel Prize. The workings of destiny are quite unfathomable, are they not? A change of scene, yes, as we think at the time, but who knows if Professor Dobie's stay with us may not prove in the end to be related to some as yet hidden but inevitable purpose?'

Dobie blinked, uncertain whether Bilsel had diverged into philosophical speculation or was rehearsing some future peroration before the Central Tribunal. 'It'd be nice to think so, certainly. But—'

'He's helped to get your client off the hook,' the nice lady said brightly. 'And that counts for something.'

'It does indeed. But he is, no doubt, a busy man. As I am myself.'

'So you'll be wanting to get back to your office.' The nice lady glanced down at her wrist-watch. 'I'm sure that now we've explained the situation to him, we can fully rely on Professor Dobie's discretion.'

'I have every confidence in him,' Bilsel said.

It had been a sobering, even a depressing interview. After his visitors had left, Dobie pulled on a lightweight sweater and went out for a stroll.

It was almost dark now but not all Berry Berry's guests had left: passing by his house, Dobie heard the sound of voices coming from the shadowed back garden. Some of his neighbours, however, had returned to their houses and in the

204

gathering dimness the windows showed little rectangles of radiance, curtained off yet glowing in the stillness, behind which other shadows seemed to move as the curtains were stirred by the evening breeze. Dobie walked on, taking once again the path down to the beach, where to the east the moon was slowly rising over a smooth dark sea. A long wavy line of glittering silver; everything else, dark blue and black. Dobie was reminded of something, but he couldn't think what.

For a while he watched the light sparkle on the incoming waves as they rippled gently against the rocks and broke, each one after the other, into a million shimmering facets. Dialectically speaking, the fate of each and every one of those slow-moving waves should be mechanically determinable; Dobie had better cause than most to know that it wasn't, since in 1974 he himself had formulated those variants of the Vernouli equations which were now held to demonstrate that it couldn't be, by virtue of the inherent strange attractors. Since those very calculations had two years later gained him his Chair in Mathematics at the age of thirty-four, arguably if he hadn't established those mathematical proofs he wouldn't be here in Cyprus now, watching those waves break or doing anything else. An interesting illustration, perhaps, of Bilsel's point.

Other things, it would appear, had happened in 1974, events he hadn't taken much notice of at the time, being otherwise occupied. Events of greater importance, perhaps, than the elaboration of Vernouli variants, at least to the people concerned in them. Dobie had always been a man of limited interests and had always been allowed – indeed encouraged – to cultivate them. In the past, he hadn't mixed very much with people of very different interests; literature, archaeology and the like. Because of Derya, Cyprus seemed to be offering him an unusual opportunity in that respect. For the first time, he was beginning to think that he might get to like the place, once he started work.

Work was the whetstone his mind invariably needed to retain its cutting edge. Holidays were what didn't suit him.

He'd been holidaying in the south of France when he'd first met his wife Jenny, and the mild distaste he now felt for all countries bordering on the Mediterranean was related, as he'd come to realise, to the sense of mingled dismay and alarm with which he'd subsequently observed the cock-up that between them they'd managed to make of their marriage. It was odd to think, in retrospect, that he had indeed observed it rather than participated in it – an attitude that couldn't have done much to help. Well, you do odd things when you're on holiday, that much was certain; but more importantly, now that the shock of her death was somewhat diminished Dobie was finding himself able to think of it not as an accident but at any rate of having come about *by* accident, and of their marriage itself in much the same way. He had also discovered that thinking in this way helped him to like Jenny again, as he had when he'd met her, and even in some ways to like her even more; and also to view his present intimate but vexed relationship with Kate Coyle as a bonus rather than as a betrayal of that earlier involvement, since it was Jenny's death that had chiefly brought it about, and in life one thing leads to another and you have to accept that fact if you want to go on living when someone else is dead. Which on the whole Dobie did. He didn't accept that conclusion as logically following upon this train of thought, which it didn't; it was something that, gazing at the moonstruck sea, he could only obscurely sense and yet felt quite sure about. Getting to like *himself* would be a different matter and might take a whole lot longer, but even that now seemed to rate as an eventual possibility. Feeling that he could now like what he remembered of Jenny was a pretty good start.

In at least one respect she had rather resembled Derya. *The elixir of youth*, Seymour had said. The eternal spring. 'I've been looking for it everywhere,' Dobie said. 'But I can't find it. Everything here's dry. Dry as a bone.'

Kate was reassuring. 'You found some fresh evidence, though. That was clever of you.'

'Only by chance. And all they've done with it is bury it. I thought people wanted to know the truth about what really

206

happened to Derya. In fact they only wanted to talk up a better deal.'

'They want a happy ending, Dobie, for everyone concerned. *You* want a solution to an imaginary problem all neatly worked out at the end of the theorem. *They* know that life goes on and on and there aren't any final answers. It's not like adding up a sum. It's like that,' Kate said, nodding towards the drifting waves. 'One wave and then another. And then another. One moment you see a ripple, the next you don't. And all the time it's just the sea, really.'

Kate herself was a bit like that because of course she wasn't really there at all, except in Dobie's imagination. Yes, he needed to start work very soon. 'I *do* know how it feels, Kate. That's the point.'

'You didn't go round writing fake confessions when Jenny was murdered. You fought back, in your own peculiar way. There was a problem. You solved it. But it was just a wave, that's all. Like this one. Only this wave is someone else's.'

'Mine, someone else's, it's all the same. It's all part of the sea. You said it yourself. Whether it breaks now or sixteen years ago, it's all the same. Or at any rate that's how I'm bound to see it.'

'You're not bound to see it in any way at all, Dobie. Try looking at it from their viewpoint for a change. It's someone else's wave and none of your business. Get back to *real* work. Do the job you came here to do and leave it at that.'

'It's not that simple.'

Anyway, he'd been sitting on the beach long enough. He got up and threw the cigarette he'd been smoking into the sea, where it vanished on the instant; then turned and walked at a methodical and pensive pace across the dry white sand. Its measure was marked out by imprints on the smooth surface, shallow but clearly discernible in the moonlight. Where might his shoes pick up mud? After or even during a rainless summer?

Not in the village, anyway, or in the army base. Not where, according to Seymour, she'd claimed to have been. Nothing

207

in the village but dust. Dust and desolation. And yet there'd been mud on Derya's shoes, traces of mud on the pedals of her car. She'd have cleaned her shoes, of course, if she'd had time. But she hadn't.

Time . . . That was what he and Kate had been talking about, really. An aspect of wave mechanics. Moving to regular or to irregular rhythms, but all the same . . . *time*. Quite so. And as such, all-embracing; like the sea. Jenny, Derya, Sabiha Arkin: their deaths could be thought of as being punctuation marks in a single long sentence, linking Seymour and Tolga Arkin and Dobie himself into some kind of complex syntactical structure. Complex, but not so complex as to defy analysis, if you were a mathematician and you knew your transformational grammar and you had a computer.

But then, Dobie thought, time isn't only measured by people, by their lives and deaths; there's more to it than that. Time is this beach, those rocks and those pine trees, and behind the pine trees the walls and the high windows of the university buildings, and behind those buildings the tall grey columns of Salamis, and further away still, behind and beneath the dark star-laden sky of the Mesaoria and at the centre of it all, Dobie himself standing alone, a puzzled stranger on a foreign shore. Analyst, analyse thyself. Because that was what it came down to, really.

Dobie sighed, and lit another cigarette.

'You're smoking too much, Dobie.'

'Oh, stop *nagging*,' Dobie said.

All the same, this conversation with Kate had cheered him slightly. When he got back to the house, he'd give her a ring.

10

Two a.m. A light rain falling.

The body lay to one side of the road, under a grey plastic sheet in the puddle of light cast by a regulation police lamp. Not a strong illumination, but strong enough. The ambulance was also drawn up to one side of the road, well clear of the turning, its roof hazard light flashing in the darkness. Kate, who for the past five minutes had been stooped over the cadaver, straightened up and turned and walked away towards the other car and the two men who stood beside it. Jackson offered her a cigarette and then the flame of his lighter, stifling a yawn as he did so.

'Nothing much for you here, Jacko. Classic hit-and-run, I'd say. Fractured skull, shattered pelvis, contusions on legs, a right mess. Hit him at high speed, obviously. Death near enough to instantaneous, that's why there's so little blood. They can take him away now.'

'Nothing in it for me, you say? That's what *you* think, Doctor. Real swine, these hit-and-run bastards can be. Poor old geezer had taken a few aboard, hadn't he?'

'A few beers, yes. Oates'll tell you about how many when he's done the PM.'

Jackson signalled to the ambulance crew, who advanced at their usual bent-kneed lope with body bag and stretcher. Detective Constable Box turned to look up the road, down the road, and finally up at the sky; droplets of rain splashed against his face. 'Missed the last bus, like as not. Walking

209

home. Probably none too straight and in the road anyway, to judge by the skid marks.'

'ET call home,' Jackson said. 'Tell them the body's on the way. No ID as yet. Check with the mortuary as usual.' But Box had already ducked back into the police car; he knew the form as well as Jacko did and he welcomed the chance to get in there out of the rain. Jackson escorted Kate across the road, where her own unassuming 1978 Escort waited in the shadows. 'Sorry to get you out of bed, Doctor, on a night like this. Thanks for coming.'

'I hadn't gone to bed. I was reading.'

'Reading, eh? There's nice. Any news of Mr Dobie?'

'Rang me up last night.'

'Did he now.'

'At considerable length. Must've cost him a bomb,' Kate said with some satisfaction.

'Don't suppose it's raining like this in Cyprus. Nice place, from what I've heard.'

'Yes. And quiet and peaceful. Until *he* got there.'

'Oh,' Jackson said. 'Like that, is it?' In the act of suppressing another yawn, he sneezed instead.

'Like that. I don't understand it.'

'Amazing, the trouble he goes and gets himself into. But then he's not such a fool as he makes himself out to be. He's quite a hirsute character, when push comes to shove.'

Kate shook her head tiredly. *Hirsute?* Jacko had her beat this time. 'Now he wants me to find out something about someone called Amphitryiton. Well, I *ask* you.'

'No good doing that. I wouldn't know. Sounds like some kind of a foreigner.' Jackson considered the matter. 'I expect there's a lot of 'em running about, over there.'

'I suppose there would be,' Kate said. 'Funny. I never thought of that.'

Dobie wasn't at all in a philosophical mood the next morning. Work was what he felt he needed, none the less essential for being largely routine. In a week's time he'd be facing his

210

first seminar groups and he still had to familiarise himself with the detailed requirements of the syllabus. Seated in his office, he went through the relevant departmental memos and course descriptions and checked them out with Derya's lecture notes. Not a few of them were based on material covered in his own supervisory tutorials and it was strange to be reading once again her small, neat, careful handwriting; it brought her very much closer to him than had that photograph on the sitting-room wall which reflected, after all, another aspect of her personality and one that he hadn't known so well, indeed hardly known at all. She'd been an exceptionally gifted student and that for him, as always, had been enough. But she seemed also to have been, whatever her other defects, a competent and conscientious teacher; his future students, again as always, would be of varying abilities but all would appear to have been sufficiently well prepared for third- and fourth-year courses.

He spent most of the rest of the morning running her programs through the computer and they seemed to be straight-forward, though one of the discs in the file puzzled him a little. He searched the records cabinet for the corresponding print-outs, but they weren't there. In the end he set the disc aside and did a little work in the old-fashioned way, using pen and paper. When he'd finished these calculations he ran the disc again and still couldn't make head nor tail of it. He ran a new set of print-outs and took the sheets round to Berry Berry's office.

'What's all this then?' Berry Berry said.

'I don't know. I thought at first she'd been working on some vector analyses but the outlines aren't right and anyway that doesn't come into the course she was supposed to be teaching. I thought you might know something about it.'

'Maybe some private work she was undertaking. Or some research project.' Berry Berry studied the sheets for a while, his eyebrows raised and forehead theatrically furrowed. 'Have you tried expressing these ratios graphically?'

'Yes. I can't make anything of them that way, either.'

211

'Address is given as K4. That tell you anything?'

'No such designation in the filing system.'

'Forgot to enter it, perhaps.'

'Very likely,' Dobie said. He didn't, in fact, think it was.

'Could be it's K for Kaya. She was working out some programs for him, I seem to remember. That might account for it.'

Indeed it might. 'Indeed it might. Because if the symbols express an orientation function, then the references are simple co-ordinates. That's what was puzzling me.'

'I should ask him about it,' Berry Berry said.

Dobie did no such thing. He had put in a full morning's work and it was now one o'clock. He went round to the staff cafeteria and ate a shish kebab and afterwards drank Turkish coffee. While he was drinking it two of the maths instructors he hadn't met before came over to introduce themselves and to talk about this and that and after a while Dobie, who was unused to maths instructors with honey-blonde hair and cornflower-blue eyes, ordered another coffee and began to wax quite eloquent on the topic of the concept of the integer. Towards the end of this impromptu tutorial the solution of the problem of the K4 mini-disc came to him quite naturally but he dismissed it at once from his mind as a matter of relatively little importance. It was in any case nearly two o'clock and time for his interview with the Vice-Rector.

Cem Arkin's office, as befitted its owner's status and overall bulk, was considerably more palatial than Dobie's or Berry Berry's and very much more elaborately accoutred; on the wall directly behind the desk hung black and white portraits of Kemal Ataturk, of the President of the Assembly, of Tolga and Uktu Arkin and of various other unrecognised dignitaries whose penetrating gazes transfixed Dobie as he sat down in the armchair opposite. He was a little relieved to find that the armchair cushion emitted the same wheezing sound as that in the office of his own much-loved rector; it enabled him to feel rather more comfortably at home, though the crossed flags of

Turkey and of the North Cyprus Republic angled over Cem's own chair might have dissipated any such impression.

'Oh, I know, I know,' Cem Arkin said, waving one hand disparagingly. 'But one has to put on a show, of course, of patriotism and whatnot.' His own chair didn't wheeze when he seated himself upon it but instead sent forth admonitory creaks. 'Well, now. This is where you tell me about the problems you've encountered and I explain why I can't do anything about them. Or, more probably, don't intend to. The usual thing. My secretary should be bringing us in some coffee in a moment and that will be the high point of my day. How about yours?'

Dobie said that his day had passed very pleasantly so far and that only routine problems had presented themselves. 'I'm having no difficulties at all, really. Everyone's being most co-operative.'

'I know,' Cem Arkin said. 'I saw you getting some excellent co-operation just now in the cafeteria. Good-looking girls, those two. I hope you formed a favourable opinion of their abilities.'

'Oh, yes, I did.'

'Maths is compulsory here for the first year, as you know. It isn't a very popular subject, to be frank. But we get pretty good attendance figures with those two around.'

'And Derya, too. I'm afraid I'm not a very effective substitute from that point of view.'

'Nobody's perfect,' Cem said.

'True.'

'And *she* had a very high opinion of you. As a supervisor.'

'Really?' Dobie was flattered. 'That's nice to know.'

'She thought you were one of the best theoretical mathematicians in the UK and that your seminar expositions were absolutely brilliant. I mention this because I'm afraid your fourth-year students will be coming to your classes with very high expectations. Not that I suppose for a moment they'll be defrauded.'

213

'They may well be. Most teaching in my particular field is nine-tenths bluff. The students do the work and you take the credit.'

'Yes, she said that, too. But put it rather differently. She said your mind operated on such a level of abstraction you were always worried that the students might think you completely inhuman, so you tried to convince them and people in general of the contrary by showing off your inadequacies in other directions and bumbling round about the place like an academic Bertie Wooster. She thought in fact you were a very lonely person, intellectually speaking. Ah. Here's the coffee.'

Its arrival was opportune in that it obviated any immediate need for Dobie to reply to this absurd attempt at amateur psychoanalysis. He? Dobie? *Inadequate?* Perish the thought. 'Derya,' he said, spilling a dollop of coffee over his trousers in his pardonable agitation, 'had enormous potential as a mathematician, certainly. A natural gift. But she had no qualifications that I'm aware of as a psychiatrist. Any remarks she may have made of that nature,' he said, smearing spilt coffee over his jacket with a handkerchief, 'I would most certainly take with a pinch of salt.'

'But talking about psychiatrists,' Cem Arkin said, frowning thoughtfully, 'I gather you've been to see Adrian Seymour.'

'Yes, I have.'

'You know, I've made several efforts in that direction myself. But I was told he was refusing to see all visitors and that in any case they might have had a disturbing effect upon him. So I'm a little puzzled—'

'I was told he wanted to see me, but I was never told why and he didn't tell me why, either. He may have been feeling intellectually lonely, too.'

'What was your impression?'

'He certainly seemed to be in some . . . distress. He talked to me fluently enough, but what he said didn't seem to make an awful lot of sense. However, I don't know anything about psychology, either.'

214

'But you knew him quite well in Cardiff?'

'Hardly at all. Perhaps he felt he could talk to me just because I wasn't in any way involved with . . . what had happened here. A neutral, so to speak. I suppose that's possible.'

'Very possible.' Cem heaved himself upright and turned to stare out of the window. As always, the admin boys had copped themselves the best location: Cem's fourth-floor window offered a magnificent view of the long curve of Salamis Bay, of the marble columns of Salamis itself and of the maquis scrub surrounding them, and finally of the upreared peaks of the Karpaz Mountains, blue-grey in the distant heat haze. 'You know,' Cem said, 'I went to school and university in England, I've worked up to now in the UK. I'm a Cypriot but I've got to say that when I came back here it seemed like a very strange place. Even the mainland Turks, the students, the girls you were chatting up just now . . . they often get a kind of culture shock when they arrive. Ozzie's wife went back to England. She didn't like it here. And though you've always been very polite, I'm quite sure that you yourself must feel it. The atmosphere. The tension. Whatever it is. You'll feel it even more strongly after a while. It's a very small island, after all. Maybe claustrophobia comes into it. I don't know.'

'It's certainly very hot,' Dobie admitted.

'Yes. In the summer. Maybe the climate, too. Anyway,' Cem said, turning back again, 'people seem to react to the overall situation in one of two ways. Either they think of their stint here as a kind of working holiday and see themselves as what you might call academic tourists; or they try to assimilate the place, to come to terms with it, and find themselves being dragged in. Sucked down, as it were, by the undertow. Two thousand years of history makes for quite a maelstrom, you know, and it's a very violent history. Perhaps Seymour was a little over-sensitive, a little too easily . . . or perhaps he simply brought too many problems with him. As Horace says, what exile ever fled his own mind? But I think you told me that you weren't a very imaginative man. So *you* should be all

215

right. Unless of course that's just a part of what Derya called your bluff, as I rather suspect . . . '

'I suppose,' Dobie said, 'you could say that I'm fleeing my own mind. And to that extent I can sympathise with Seymour. Though he's doing it in rather a different way.'

'Yes. That's obvious. He dramatised things, you see. I think he saw himself as a kind of T. E. Lawrence amongst the Arabs, and the trouble is we're not Arabs. And we're not Turks and we're not Westerners, either. We're not *anything*. Except maybe mongrels. A bit of everything. So Seymour was like a chameleon sitting on a tartan kilt, if you see what I mean. It was all a bit too much for him, really.'

'Mrs Berry's English but she seems to manage all right. Of course, she may not be very imaginative, either.'

Cem smiled. 'No, I don't think she is.'

'Though she seems to have got the idea into her head that Derya was after her husband's job. As Head of Department. Is there anything in that? It really seems very—'

'Oh, no. I don't think so. I'd have said Derya's ambitions lay in other directions. In the States, maybe, or the UK. I never thought she'd stay with us very long.' His coffee was still on his desk, untouched. He sat down again and sipped at it pensively. If it had grown cold, he didn't seem to notice.

'And you?'

'What?'

'What are *your* ambitions, Cem?'

'Well, I suppose I have ambitions, yes, but they tend to be outweighed by responsibilities. I expect everyone's told you that I'll be the next Rector when old Ibrahim goes back to Turkey. And that's very likely. I don't want the job. But I can do it. And it won't be easy for me to refuse.'

'Because you're expected to take over the family business.'

Cem didn't laugh. 'In a way. And the catch is that it won't be just my father's business. It'll be my uncle's business as well. *Every* damned business in Cyprus leads you into politics sooner or later. My father's been drawn

216

into it already. Ten years from now, it'll be my turn. No, I don't look forward to it.'

'But you really can't avoid it?'

'I don't see how. As a Moslem, I have to be persuaded that it's my destiny. Well, I don't mind that so much . . . It's fulfilling other people's destinies that I object to. When I was a boy, I thought my Uncle Uktu's destiny was to be President of a united Cyprus. My admiration for him was quite unbounded. But all it took was a few machine-gun bullets to change all that. Then suddenly he was nothing but a dead body lying at the side of a road just outside Nicosia. As for my father, he was a schoolteacher. Did you know that? With his nose always buried in a book. No one ever thought of him as a national hero. I certainly didn't. But now it seems very probable that *he*'ll be our next President and whether he is or isn't, he'll still be an *international* hero, which is something that Uktu could never have hoped to be. I've always thought it strange,' Cem said, 'that twin brothers could be so different, and yet somehow have interchanged roles in such an unexpected way. You can only suppose that destiny does indeed have something to do with it.'

'Or genes, perhaps.'

'I hope not. I like to think I'm different again, or at least have been shaped by events in a different way.' Cem was leaning forwards now over his desk, staring down into the depths of his coffee-cup as into the embers of a sinking fire. 'One can't attribute everything to the workings of DNA molecules, the double helix or whatever it's called. No, I'm not a materialist. Not in that sense.'

Dobie's own gaze was now directed towards the sepia-toned portraits on the wall: Tolga Arkin, Uktu, looking down at him with similar expressions of stern impassivity. 'And besides, your mother . . . '

'What about my mother?' As though conscious of having spoken more sharply than he had intended, Cem sat back again with an abrupt shifting of his weight that made the chair beneath him again squeak plaintively. 'Sorry. It's just

217

that we never speak of her, my father and I. She was killed too, you know, at the time of the intervention.'

'Yes. But she'd have had some influence upon you before that. I mean, when you were a child. All mothers do.'

'Of course, and I remember her very well. That's not why we . . . I can't really explain it. But when my father came to England after she and Uktu were killed and visited me at Oxford, I was shocked. More than that. I was terrified. He was in a state of complete mental collapse . . . much as I imagine Seymour to be today, but in all probability worse, much worse. It took him many months, perhaps years, to recover. Indeed I sometimes wonder if he ever has.'

'It's understandable.'

'Of course. And I was greatly shaken myself. She was only thirty-four when she died, my mother, and over the last four years of her life, I never got to see her. Not once. Working for my Oxford scholarship and then . . . I regret it deeply now. Of course I do. And she never wanted me to go to school in England, it was my father who insisted. Arguably, if I'd stayed the chances are high that I'd have been killed as well. But if I'd known what was going to happen, I'd certainly have taken the risk. And then I'd probably have been killed with her, because I'd have been with her if I could.'

'To protect her?'

'I like to think I'd have tried. But in any case it wasn't to be.' For a few moments the deep-set eyes under the heavy eyebrows looked at Dobie searchingly. 'Shall I tell you something else? It's good to be able to talk to you about these things. I can only do it because you're a stranger. In Cyprus, we never talk about such matters amongst ourselves. Again, you'll say that's understandable. But it isn't good.'

'Did you talk about these things to Seymour?'

'Oh, no. I don't think he'd have . . . You're an older man, after all. Or . . . I don't know what it is but I'm sure people *do* talk to you, don't they? As you say, you're not a psychiatrist and yet people confide in you. I've noticed it. Seymour wasn't like that at all. He argued too much.

218

Maybe in England we could have talked about those things. But not here.'

'That seems illogical.'

'Life isn't logical. In fact, it's full of ironies. Tragic ironies, sometimes. You know, my mother was travelling to the Turkish-occupied zone when she was killed. Nicosia was dangerous for her, so they moved her to a place of safety. As they thought. See what I mean?'

'They told me that in fact she disappeared. No one knew where she'd gone.'

'Uktu knew. He sent her there. He arranged it. But he was killed himself, three or four days later. And of course my father must have known, but after it happened he wasn't in any condition to answer questions. Anyway, what would have been the point of asking questions? It happened somehow. And that was that.'

What, indeed, was the point? And how much, Dobie wondered, do any of us know about our parents? With the first twenty-five or thirty years of their lives inevitably and impenetrably sealed off for us, known to us only through hearsay and mostly *their* hearsay at that? Years that presumably made them whatever it was that they were, to us and to themselves? We think we know them well. But we don't. It's like unravelling a length of twine: seemingly a single piece, but the more you unwind it, the more the two ends go off in different directions. And neither of them, in the present case, pointing towards Seymour or even Derya. Ah, but the piece of twine itself had to have another end and that was where he should have started from, if only he'd been able to find it.

Or maybe he should have thought in terms of searching for a pattern. An overall design. Something with a mathematical form, something a sensibly programmed computer could effectively deal with. The pattern formed, say, by six houses grouped almost in a circle, the light from their uncurtained windows uncertainly illuminating the roundabout at their centre, the light from his own sitting-room window contributing to the general glow that after all didn't really do much more than emphasise the surrounding all-pervasive darkness. A hot, still night, the sea-haze obscuring all but a few of the clustered stars. Dobie sat at the window, staring out at it.

Cem Arkin's house, directly opposite. Then Ozzie Ozturk's, its porch light striking reflections from the roof and bonnet of Ozzie's black BMW drawn up just outside. In Kaya's house the curtains were half drawn across and a shadow moved to and fro behind them; Kaya pacing up and down, maybe doing some fetching and carrying. Only the Berrys' house was hidden from view by the silhouetted bulk of Hillyer's, where the nearest window showed a faint glow, that of the reading-lamp in the corner of the sitting-room; Hillyer was probably also preparing his notes for next term's lecture courses. Shakespeare, maybe. *Othello*. Put out the light, and then . . . put out the light . . .

A play on words, of course. Dobie sighed. Seymour did that, too; that was the trouble. Unless you were a literary person yourself you couldn't see . . . the hole for the trees or whatever it was he'd said. Not that Shakespeare was all that difficult. No. He thought he could make sense of the death scene all right. Jealousy came into it, of course, as Hillyer had said, but mostly it was pride. Pride turned to self-hatred and from thence to ashes. She's like a liar gone to burning hell. It was me. I did it. Else, he could have pushed her out of the window – again, as Hillyer had said. Or down the stairs. A terrible accident. And she *had* lied, about going to the village; to Alanici. Or Seymour had lied on her behalf, so to speak. The words he'd written didn't have to be the words she'd spoken, as was obvious. And it was crazy, anyway, the way he'd gone about it. He could have got away with it easily, but for his pride. But then he was jealous, wasn't he? Not thinking straight.

Any more than I am now . . .

But Seymour hadn't been *writing* straight, either. And not because of jealousy, not because of any young Turkish officer, Cassio or whoever. I'm hot-tempered, he'd said, but not a jealous person. OK, maybe one didn't have to believe that,

220

either. He was a literary person, that was for sure. He liked to play with words. Or perhaps he didn't like to. Perhaps he just couldn't help it.

Perhaps what he'd had to say couldn't have been said in any other way. It had to be put obliquely because seen through a glass, darkly. Put out the light. Reach me a torch. Not Desdemona, then. Alcmena. Yes, you could understand that part of it, once you'd grasped the part in the puzzle that jealousy played or didn't play. But that didn't help. Because where was the connection?

Maybe Seymour hadn't got it right. '"Reach me a gentian, give me a torch." A poem of Lawrence's,' Hillyer had said. 'One of his best-known. "Bavarian Gentians". Seymour was a great admirer of DHL. Sad to say, I could never share his enthusiasm . . . ' Dobie didn't think that he could, either, but he thought that he might as well make sure. He put *Othello* down on the table and went to fetch the other book from the shelf. Opening it, he found the poem every bit as incomprehensible as it had seemed before.

A *black* lamp? Burning *blue*? No kind of illumination might be expected from such a source. Surely it was bilge, pure and simple? Dobie flipped the book shut with an irritated gesture and looked once more out of the window, staring at those other lights, those *real* lights, as perhaps Seymour had done while waiting waiting waiting for Derya's return . . . and seeing the pattern made by those lights against the dark crouching shapes of those other houses he had . . . yes, another. Another extraordinary idea. Or maybe just a wild guess, a brief and fleeting version of the other end of that coiled and knotted length of twine. Not a guess as to where it was, but a guess as to where he ought to look for it. Not the same thing, of course. No, not the same thing at all. And while he was still pondering on the implications of this intuition, the call that he had been waiting for came through and he went to answer it.

'At least I think I know now how this Amphitryon character comes in on the scene.'

'I'm sure that's a giant step forward,' Kate said.

'Er, no. Not really. But it's all to do with Seymour having made heavy use of similarity. Which is basically quite a simple mathematical concept, I mean I can understand *that*. What would you say, for instance, to a twin brother?'

'I haven't got a twin brother. Neither has Seymour. Has he?'

'Not as far as I know.'

'Dobie, you're being difficult. Again.'

'So how are things back at the ranch?'

'Oh, just the usual cholera epidemic. Nothing out of the ordinary. Got called out on a patho, though. Hit-and-run case by the look of it. Jacko's doing his nut.'

'He can't find the culprit?'

'He hasn't as yet.'

'Nor have I.'

'I gathered as much,' Kate said.

'Mind you, I've broken the case.'

'You have?'

'But it's the wrong one.'

'I see. For a moment there, you had me worried.'

Dobie, of course, was showing off. A flicker of enlightenment isn't a solution, not by a long chalk. Just because he now thought he knew what he was looking for didn't mean it was going to be easy. The elixir of life? Gilgamesh had found it, according to Kaya, but hadn't been able to keep it. It might be easier, Dobie thought, if I could question Kaya directly about it, but I don't want to do that. I've a feeling I may have asked too many questions already. The only thing I can safely interrogate now is sitting there in my office and it isn't human. Therefore, it doesn't tell lies. Though that isn't the only reason why it's safe. Derya's computer is running fine, but Derya is dead.

Professor Dobie reached his office punctually the following day and spent the whole of the morning with K4 in the slot, questioning away, letting the print-out sheets pile up in the

222

reception tray on his desk. They made an imposing heap but that part of the program didn't take very long. Going through them and making his first selection took much longer. By the time he had printed out that selection again, this time on graph paper, and re-checked the results, it was time for lunch. He felt he could take his lunch break with a clear conscience. There were indications that he was on the track of something. Maybe, indeed probably, not the *right* something. But it was something that there should be something there at all, where it shouldn't be.

Before heading for the cafeteria he took his metal wastepaper-basket out on to the balcony and lit a nice little fire inside it, committing his entire morning's labours piece by piece to the flames. When the last charred edges had smouldered into darkness he churned up the ashes and surveyed the residue thoughtfully. Rather a futile gesture, he thought, that of Seymour's. Symbolic, maybe. Burning papers instead of his boats. But (as he now felt sure) Derya's papers also. Futile, because the disc was what mattered, not the print-outs, but Seymour probably didn't know much about computers; he wouldn't have been able to find the disc very easily, tucked away in the office filing cabinet, or to distinguish it from the eighteen other discs where Derya's lecture programs had been filed. And naturally he couldn't have interpreted the print-outs. Only the computer could do that – if Dobie could persuade it to do so, with due perseverance and loving kindness. But he must have known what the print-outs *represented* or why else would he have destroyed them? That had to count as another indication that the something Dobie was searching for was the *right* something. He'd known what they represented because Derya had told him.

Or, just possibly, someone else.

Dobie chewed methodically away at his fried chicken, the K4 disc securely stashed away in his inside jacket pocket. Today the blonde instructresses with the long brown legs weren't in evidence and he ate alone. He wasn't disappointed. On the contrary, he was beginning, just beginning to feel

223

excited. Thinking not about the instructresses but about the near-naked German girls on the beach, the Bavarian gentians, and about other girls, totally unclothed, splashing about and giggling in the shallow sparkling waters of the swimming-pool. The elixir. It had to be there *somewhere*. That was obvious.

He vaguely recalled an Egyptian parable of time he'd read about somewhere. The goddess endlessly plaiting a rope of straw, the donkey walking along behind her eating it up. No doubt as to Dobie's role in that little picture. But this wasn't like the other nonsense, unravelling a length of bifurcated twine; this was a completely familiar challenge, a mathematical problem pure and simple, set not (as it turned out) by Derya but by some forgotten geometrician long ago. Some of the greatest mathematical intellects known to history had been operating around about that time, but this had to be a comparatively straightforward problem and some advances, after all, had been made since the days of Pythagoras and Euclid. Derya's computer was one of them. Nevertheless a straight line was still the shortest distance between two points and Dobie was still as ready as any Greek to shift the world on its axis, once provided with a fulcrum. 'Direct in her methods,' Kaya had said. '*And* her approach.' Oh yes, Derya had always favoured the straight line, that was for sure.

Not so her husband.

That's the advantage of a mathematical as opposed to a literary intelligence. You see what you want and you go for it. But of course you can have that kind of intelligence without being a mathematician, as such. You might be an electrical engineer, like Ozzie. Or have been trained as an architect, like Kaya. Or even be into IT, like Cem Arkin. In almost any university you'd find plenty of people capable of working out a set of multiple co-ordinates and three-dimensional ratios, such as K4 appeared to specify. Given, that is, a starting-point. A fulcrum. Such as Derya might have indicated, or inadvertently let slip, to someone else. Dobie, lone Archimedes, would have to discover the entry key for himself.

Because the print-outs didn't tell the true story, any more than Seymour had done. There were closed-access files (which Dobie had singled out) and naturally an encrypting algorithm (which Dobie had established) which meant that Derya had committed the researcher's cardinal sin of holding information back. She'd have had her reasons, or a reason. Which didn't matter. What Dobie had to do now was uncover the encrypting key and option that she had used to secure the data, which wasn't something you could hit upon by stretching yourself out in a bathtub. You had to go at it through a process of elimination. You'd have to run a hundred and sixty-odd print-out pages again and again to find out which two or three or maybe four of those pages contained the material upon which the computer, agile dialectician, could base the required metathesis. It all took time . . .

Go and eat more straw, Dobie.

Throughout the long hot afternoon Dobie sat at the computer keyboard, sweating profusely and conjuring up image after image after image on the monitor screen. Sometimes messages appeared, not all of them very enlightening. ERYSIP HDNIRM PFFYWE NYNCOC KFYWQN . . . *That* sort of thing. But mostly the images were graphic. Endless patterns of intersecting lines. Squares. Rectangles. Cubes. Boxes. Dobie moved them about the screen, superimposing one image on another, re-COPYing, re-PRINTing, frequently CANcelling. The sense of mild excitement he'd felt while gulping down his lunch had of course long since disappeared; within ten minutes of setting himself down at the keyboard he himself had become something like a machine, impervious to all external noise and movement, incapable of tiredness, eyes that watched and fingers that tapped in conditioned response to the visual messages coming through while querying the source of every stimulus, perhaps as a hunter moving through a dark wood queries every movement in the swaying branches . . . or perhaps adopting the status of a common-or-garden moron, making his mind a near-total blank so that the disturbing static of normal thought shouldn't blur the reception of that tiny flicker of

225

communication which might come and be gone in a millisecond – if it came at all.

Because this is how mathematicians *work*, damn it. In a kind of miasma of self-imposed stupidity. Dobie could well see why some people imagined it to be dull and he himself to be . . . let's say a shade distrait . . . and indeed the idea that his was in some ways an *odd* occupation was one that often occurred to him. If he was a hunter at all, he was a hunter of a most peculiar kind. More like the army recruit who, according to the legend, wandered round and round the barrack square picking up bits of paper and then throwing them away again, sadly muttering, 'No . . . *that's* not it . . . ' Summoned before a medical tribunal and duly dismissed the service as a congenital imbecile, he seized upon his demobilisation order and began to caper round the room with it, shouting, '*That's* it! *That's* it! *That's* it! . . . ''*That's* it,' Dobie said out loud, staring at the monitor screen.

Eureka . . .

He didn't start capering round the room, however. He'd found his fulcrum but he didn't altogether believe it. What he couldn't believe was the size of it. And the depth. If the figures were correct, the leverage was going to be colossal. He checked the figures for several minutes before running off his final page print. Then he ejected K4, sleeved it and slid it into his pocket; folded the print-out and put it into his briefcase. 'That's it,' he said again, and pushed his chair back.

Now he could feel tired. And did. The task was completed.

But he couldn't go home. Not just yet . . .

11

> . . . Pluto's dark-blue daze,
> black lamps from the hall of Dis, burning dark blue,
> giving off darkness, blue darkness, as Demeter's pale lamps
> give off light,
> lead me then, lead me the way.
> Reach me a gentian, give me a torch
> let me guide myself with the blue, forked torch of this
> flower
> down the darker and darker stairs, where blue is darkened
> on blueness,
> even where Persephone goes, just now, from the frosted
> September
> to the sightless realm where darkness is awake upon the
> dark
> and Persephone herself is but a voice
> or a darkness invisible enfolded in the deeper dark
> of the arms Plutonic, and pierced with the passion of dense
> gloom,
> among the splendour of torches of darkness, shedding
> darkness on the lost bride and her groom . . .

Maybe, Dobie said to himself, that's the secret of serendipity.
To make of one's mind not a thoroughfare for alien thoughts,
other men's flowers, but a cul-de-sac, a *huis clos*, a darkened
cave where all the tracks go in and none come out. A sort of
prison, in fact. Because a prison can also be a refuge and
it had been stupid of him not to have seen that at once.
A prison cell, yes, you might well feel safe in a prison

227

cell when someone wants to kill you, provided of course that person stayed outside. And a suitably vaguely phrased confession might well be your quickest and easiest way of getting there. No visitors would be admitted, as a matter of simple and sensible precaution, except for poor old Dobie – no reason to be afraid of Dobie who hadn't been around at the time and knew nothing about anything, anyway. Seymour had maybe asked too many questions and been vouchsafed too many answers. Asking questions . . . That's dangerous, or can be. Dobie had been asking questions, too, but luckily he'd been able to put his most pertinent questions to a computer; Seymour hadn't done that and couldn't have. He'd asked people, instead. Derya, naturally.

Where've you been?

Just down to the village.

So what's the latest gossip?

You may not be a jealous husband, but you can still ask awkward questions. And invent them, sometimes. He had to have known where Derya had been because they'd left together. And he'd come back in one of the university taxis. Down to the village, bollocks. A false scent, if ever there was one. They'd taken the other road, a different direction completely.

A set of co-ordinates was what Seymour had lacked. He'd probably seen Derya's print-out and had known what it represented – if he hadn't, why should he have destroyed it? – but he couldn't have interpreted it because a set of tridimensional co-ordinates isn't a map. There's a *similarity*, of course; you might even call it a map translated into another language and Dobie did in fact have a map tucked into his pocket alongside his copy of the print-out, a map with nice clearly drawn lines and neatly marked rectangles showing the salient features of Kaya's Salamis, the lines of the access roads and crumbled aqueducts, the rectangles of the gymnasium and the temple of Zeus and the baths and the pumping stations.

But it wasn't Kaya's Salamis through which he was now walking or even the Salamis of the shady woods and sunny

228

clearings where the picnickers parked their cars and set up their barbecue grills. Dobie, too, had parked his car some little way back where the sand track ended, only to have it vanish from his view before he had taken ten paces down the overgrown footpath that led him in an instant into a tangled wilderness of thorn bushes and spiny burnet, into the garigue that filled the two-mile-wide space between Salamis and the university buildings. Even here, great lumps of roughly dressed stone showed through the twisted branches of the scrub as the pathway he was following twisted this way and that, pursuing the tortuous line of what two thousand years ago might have been a narrow city street. Now the relics of stone foundations and of shattered paving lay under hard-packed sand, mixed in with the humus of centuries and riddled through with tree-roots. The soil was so slippery that Dobie found it difficult to keep his footing and when, some four or five minutes later, he reached what appeared to be the end of the trail he paused for a while and looked about him. He didn't attempt to get his bearings (since nothing was visible from where he stood except for the encroaching mass of thorny scrub and a pale stretch of evening sky overhead) but waited to give himself time to come to terms with his surroundings and with his own sense of bewilderment. This wasn't at all what he had expected.

Apart from anything else, it was stiflingly hot. The density of the thick-leaved vegetation choked off any breath of sea breeze and the stored-up heat of the day seemed to be rising from underfoot, where the splintered building-blocks of a vanished city lay tumbled amongst softer layers of native sandstone, sinking deeper and deeper into the earth. Dobie could see a few traces of a later civilisation, where two or three of these fragmented shards of granite had been pushed together to provide a backing for the ashes of a recent camp-fire and where a couple of used Pepsi cans had been tossed aside into the undergrowth. Otherwise, the site had been left abandoned to the darting sand lizards and the drifting winged insects. Dobie, sweating, wiped his hands carefully with his handkerchief before taking the print-out from his pocket and unfolding it again.

He could just make out the line of the collapsed pediments that had once supported some kind of aquifer, commencing just to the left of the camp-fire ashes and running southwards to be engulfed almost at once by an advancing wave of spiky-leaved bushes that had smothered the scattered blocks completely before surging over them like a breaking roller. Circumnavigating the bushes clumsily, Dobie found further half-buried traces some thirty paces further on, where the broken stones emerged briefly before sinking irrevocably out of sight into the sand. Crouched down like a playful puppy he edged his way further round the circle, pushing his way at times under the clinging twigs until he had returned to his starting-point. The effort involved cost him a certain amount of muscular strain, some of his convolutions having moved him into positions he had imagined only to be attainable by limbo dancers at the peak of form; he eventually crawled out, perspiring more freely than ever and with his arms and shoulders aching from innumerable nasty prickles. 'Oh, bother it,' Dobie said. Or words to that effect. He sat down and lit a cigarette and when he had finished it, he tried again.

Casting this time a wider circle he did himself more damage with the same result. Wriggling through thickets, he decided, just wasn't his scene; this was completely different, as was obvious, to a computer search and he wasn't cut out for it. His body was the wrong shape, for a start. Ideally, to explore this kind of terrain you'd need to be a snake. And there was a self-defeating element inherent in going round in circles, returning each time to the place you'd started from; you began to feel that in pursuing some hypothetical Wizzle you might indeed be chasing yourself, or (worse) that the Wizzle (or possibly Woozle) might not inconceivably be chasing you. Unable to shake off the suspicion that he, the hunter, had somewhere in this twisted wilderness become the hunted, Dobie plodded back to the convenient marker of the camp-fire and surveyed the said wilderness with extreme disfavour. A measuring-tape would have been useful. He didn't have one. He walked back towards the bushes, counting his paces. Five of them were sufficient to bring him up against a particularly inhospitable patch of needle-pointed briars; a chainsaw, or maybe a flame-thrower, would have been even more useful, but he didn't have either. Either. The prickly pear or whatever it was at least afforded him shade from the angled sun; Dobie sighed, and sat down heavily on the hard and dusty ground.

He hadn't expected what he was looking for to be easy to find – 'You can't see the hole for the trees,' Seymour had warned him, if perhaps inadvertently – but he had certainly expected it to be easier of access. The bloody bushes grew so quickly in this climate. And there again, he didn't know exactly what he was looking for. A White Rabbit, maybe, with a large watch clasped in one paw. There *were* rabbits here, certainly; he had encountered evidence of their activities under those bushes and now carried some of that evidence adhering to his trousers. There were birds. You couldn't see them but you could hear them. There were lizards and my goodness, yes, very probably there were snakes . . . A nasty thought which fortunately hadn't occurred to him earlier. And there were flowers, late summer flowers of one kind or another scattered here and there. *Carpeted with flowers*, Kaya had said, but these were the survivors of the long hot summer. Mostly very small yellow ones. But there were quite large clusters of dark blue ones over where the line of stones sank into the sun and where the lowering sun now cast dark shadows. Snakes and Snarks, Dobie thought tiredly. Maybe the Snark would turn out to be a Boojum after all. Annoying, though, to have got so far and . . . no further . . .

Dark blue flowers with long woody stems and tapering leaves. Dobie stared at them for quite a while. He knew bugger-all about flowers but he could tell a dark blue flower when he saw one. Blue, darkening to black where the shadows touched them. Surely they wouldn't be . . . ?

No.

231

But they were blue all right.

He got up and walked over to them. Some were actually growing from crevices in the broken stonework. Some had driven their roots down into the pebble-laden sand. Others had discovered a convenient ditch where the stone foundations of the aqueduct had formed a bulwark against the drifting soil, a ditch some three or four feet deep, matted with decaying humus and with thickly sprouting vegetation, a ditch at one point almost deep and dark enough to be called a crack or anyway a crevice, some kind of natural fault where the night humidity and the spring rains might collect to refresh the deep roots of those dark blue flowers that otherwise had no business to be growing there at all.

Yes.

Dobie went back to the car and took the torch from the glove compartment. He no longer needed to ask himself what it was doing there; Derya had clearly been better prepared than Alice when she'd gone down the White Rabbit's hole. Though in fact, as Dobie discovered when he returned, it wasn't a hole so much as . . . a crack, exactly that, a chink in the layer of stonework where the foundation blocks had been pulled a little apart by some earth movement or subsidence, leaving just enough space for him to push inside his head and shoulders. You had to lie down full length in the ditch even to see the crack; entering it was going to be . . . Dobie sat up again and took off his jacket, rolled it up and thrust it out of sight under the flower stalks. When he switched on the torch, all he could see inside the crack was a mixture of sand and rubble; he guessed that the fault would continue to run along the line of the pediments and so would involve him in a sharp right-hand turn, or more exactly wriggle, but of course he'd have to insert most of his body in order to be sure of that. It wouldn't be very nice, of course, if the three or four feet of sand above his head then decided to come down on top of him. *Another* nasty thought. Dobie, by no means an adventurous spirit, vacillated. It was borne in upon him that he was putting himself in very much the kind of situation that

Berry Berry had warned him against: alone in the maquis with no chance of summoning help if by any mischance . . . Better, perhaps, to come back with a spade and open the entrance a little further; a little judicious nibbling at the edges here and there might . . .

'Come *on*, Dobie. What are you? A man or a mouse?'

'Eeeek eeeek,' Dobie said, scrabbling his way forwards into the tunnel. Of course it was easy for Kate to talk. If I were a mouse, he thought, I'd have no trouble at all, I'd be used to this sort of thing. Or even if I were a rabbit. White or otherwise. The crack seemed to get narrower, if anything, as he advanced, leaving him barely elbow-room to move the torch beam round to his right.

Yes. It was as he'd suspected. Not exactly a tunnel. Just more and deeper darkness. Open space, then. The tricky bit was getting himself round the corner without getting his knees . . . There. His groping fingers encountered a sudden unexpected coolness, a hard smoothness; not sand underneath them, but stone. A stone slab. Beyond it, emptiness again. But . . .

Aha.

Lower down, another slab, gritty with dust. Dobie pushed himself yet further forwards and, redirecting the torch beam to a steeper angle, found himself peering over the edge of the topmost tread of what appeared to be a flight of stone steps. Turning the torch beam upwards and levering his head back to neck-crick point, he saw stone slabs above him as well with twisted tree-roots thrusting through the interstices. Stairs, then, and some kind of a roof, and the dim shape of a keystone arch. Extraordinary. And also a little reassuring. Not *very* reassuring. But a little.

He had room now, it seemed, to shuffle himself forwards on hands and knees. He did so, manoeuvring his long limbs awkwardly down the first few steps and then finding that he could rise comfortably upright . . . well, upright, anyway, and continue down the steps in a rather more dignified manner. He counted them as he descended. Anyone would have.

233

Eighteen steepish treads, and more of them dimly shown in the torchlight on the far side of the archway. That put him at some fifteen feet underground. Deeper than he liked. He'd do best, perhaps, to stop counting. The co-ordinates given by the print-out indicated an eventual depth of forty feet, something more like a bloody coal mine, at any rate to a man of nervous disposition with a tendency to claustrophobia. Still, the walls to either side of him now felt completely solid – rock solid, in fact, since that was what they were. This passage, or whatever it was, had been dug down into the native island rock, going deeper and deeper into . . .

Ugh.

He continued the descent into Avernus, counting the steps again because he couldn't help it. Eighteen more, with the passage seeming to turn slightly as he made his way cautiously down it. Why? *That* wasn't indicated in the print-out. Probably an illusion, then. You get easily disorientated when you're deep underground. Easily scared, too. He trailed the palm of his free hand against the left-hand wall as he moved down the final steps, not so much to keep his balance as to gain confidence from that feeling of cool solidity. Not only cool, but moist as well. Wet, in fact. He paused to examine his fingers in the torchlight. They were wet, all right. Water leaking through, then, from the subterranean spring that had to be near at hand, the source that through some primitive but probably effective pumping system had supplied the now bone-dry baths and swimming pools of the Salamis gymnasium. He had reached the foot of the flight of steps anyway. He turned the torch beam this way and that. Not more steps, surely?

Yes. But much wider ones. Enormous ones, leading to another archway. Incredible. Dobie cast the torch beam upwards again. The roof seemed to be really high above him now, unless that too was an illusion. Thirty feet or so, at a guess. And he was no longer standing in a passageway but in an open space. Beyond the archway, the floor seemed to be flat and to extend beyond the range of the torch beam.

He was entering some kind of a room. Or chamber. A burial chamber, maybe? Or a Temple of Doom? Hopelessly miscast as Indiana Jones, Dobie went on swinging the torch beam to and fro. Dithering, as usual.

'For God's sake, Dobie, don't just *stand* there.'

'All right, all right,' Dobie muttered crossly. 'I know. Pass down the car, please.' He stumped forwards and on through the archway, still swinging the torch beam about, however, more than was strictly necessary. The walls were a darker colour now, a deeper shade of grey, with an occasional silvery glitter of quartz. And he was no longer moving through a total silence. He could detect a very, very faint trickling sound coming from somewhere. He went through another archway and turned the torch beam downwards and there it was. Right in front of him.

The Zeus mosaic.

Blue of the Mediterranean, black of the Cyprian night, other recurrent colours worked into the design, all fresh and glowing brightly in the torchlight. In the centre, the two great naked figures, outstretched, grappling. It wasn't the sheer size of the thing that Dobie found amazing but the *trompe l'oeil* effect that, strangely enough, none of the earlier observers had mentioned and which therefore Dobie hadn't been prepared for: the angling and ingenious perspectiving of the brilliant facets so that what lay, in reality, flat on the floor seemed to be lifted upright like a cinema screen and rendered almost tridimensional while remaining none the less unrealistic, abstract, the mystic figures converted into flesh and blood through a paradox as staggering as Dobie had ever struggled with in the course of his professional career. Those interlocked shapes conveyed a sense of the total intensity of some mental or psychological struggle rather than of physical effort – the struggle perhaps of sanity with lunacy, of the rational human mind with the inconsequence of destiny. That, at least, was how Dobie – an eminently rational being – immediately saw it.

Though it could, he realised, settling the beam of the

235

torch on the masked face of the uppermost figure, be seen differently. The upshot of this conflict wasn't after all as obvious as it appeared. The woman, violated, still seemed to be somehow inviolate, as though the mind thus briefly and brutally subjected to the will of a mindless god remained, though totally possessed and willingly surrendered, none the less intact – and even perhaps in some way enhanced by the mutual fury of the embrace. But another person – Seymour, for instance – might have created an alternative picture, have seen the human mind ravished and defeated, dragged down like Persephone deeper and deeper into the Stygian shades. Neither of these images had any special appeal to Dobie, though it seemed obvious to him that only a fool would consider the depiction to be shocking . . . unless that was the word with which you described the snake-head of the Medusa or the spaces between the whirling galaxies. It was marvellous; for all he could tell, a masterpiece; but it wasn't what he was really looking for. He moved away with a certain reluctance to run the torch beam again around the grey rock walls. He saw other, narrower archways opening into other and smaller rooms, other chambers. In the second of those chambers, he found them.

Twenty-six of them, it had to be supposed. Naturally, he didn't count them. Stone steps are one thing, human bodies are another, espccially when in a stage of advanced decomposition. They lay along one bullet-hole-pitted wall in a confused tangle of yellowing bones and dark strips of rotten clothing, more or less (no doubt) as they had fallen. The torch beam began to waver wildly as Dobie swung it to and fro; he felt a taut hot pressure inside his stomach and stepped back to press his forehead for a moment against the rock wall and to close his eyes. 'It's all right, Dobie. They're bones, that's all. Fossils. Like the ones you see in the museums. There are bones like those in tombs all over Europe. People were living and dying in Salamis for two thousand years. Every step you take, you're treading on their dust. That's all they are, Dobie. Dust. It all happened a long, long time ago.'

'I know,' Dobie said. 'I know. I know. I know.'

All very well for a police pathologist. But death, he thought, is like that bloody mosaic. Different people see it in different ways.

There was another fossil in the next chamber. A mouldering blanket on the floor and the skeleton stretched out upon it, its angled bones resting on scraps of what had once been a red flannel-like fabric – probably a dressing-gown, since the remnants of what had once been its sash seemed to be still identifiable. And so of course was the necklace with the V-shaped pendant that was still looped around what had once, no doubt, been a white and delicate throat. A woman's leather handbag lay half open by the far wall. It was a minute or two before Dobie felt able to stoop to pick it up: when he did so, his sense of giddiness, of nausea, was even worse than he had expected.

Something had caught his eye, though, as he had bent over: a small metal object, lying just clear of the disintegrating blanket. A used cartridge case, Dobie thought; there had been dozens of them lying scattered on the floor in the other room. But this one seemed to be longer, much bigger, a different calibre altogether. Instead of stooping to pick it up, he lowered himself carefully down on to his knees, keeping his head stiffly upright. Turning the cartridge case over in his fingers, he saw that it was in fact a lipstick holder, almost emptied. The lipstick that remained inside had turned to a thick black grease, but he could see that it had been used roughly, violently; its tip was flattened out instead of rounded and the thin metal casing itself had buckled to some kind of a jerky pressure. From where he knelt, he had only to raise his eyes a little to see what the lipstick had been used for: uneven streaks, black in the torchlight, ran in a long unbroken line across the far wall just behind the blanket and low down, only some six inches above floor level, a smeared scribbling that was still easily legible although the writer had had to work lying awkwardly on the floor and probably in the dark and quite certainly in frantic haste:

237

Of course the writer herself was still there. In a manner of speaking.

Tolga söyledi Tolga Tolga Tolga Tolga Tolga

It was writing that somehow had the quality of a scream and that, Dobie thought, was in effect what it was. ' *"They're killing them."* That's what it says. And then, *"Tolga told them."* Then—'

'*Tolga Tolga Tolga Tolga Tolga.*'

'Yes. I expect it was all she could think of. Or all she had time for. The others were being killed in the other room while she, I imagine, was being raped. She'd have been in a state of shock. Physical and mental. But it's clear enough what she was trying to say. Clear even to you, I suppose . . . '

'Oh, yes,' Dobie said. He kept the torch beam directed towards the wall, although it had once again become a little unsteady. Enough light was reflected from the rock surface to show a pair of booted feet standing close beside him and the long dull gleam of what could only be the barrel of a rifle or a shotgun, held pointing downwards but otherwise, he had to assume, ready for use. The tautness of the muscles in his stomach and thighs had come back and had become almost unbearable. 'You're not going to need a *gun*, are you? I'd have thought there'd been enough killing done down here already.'

'That depends on how you look at it. But, after all, you're a reasonable man. We both are, I hope.' The booted feet stepped back and the dark shape of the blued-steel barrel receded into the shades. Dobie took a deep breath, feeling the taste of vomit at the back of his throat. 'Let's just step out of this . . . room, shall we? I find the atmosphere in here much too oppressive.'

That was understandable. 'So do I.' Dobie got slowly to his feet.

'You go first, then. Mind your head when you . . . Good.

238

That's it.' The boots made no sound as they followed Dobie's hesitant steps through the archway. Crêpe soles, obviously. But Dobie could hear the sound of the other's heavy breathing coming after him; both reasonable men, yes, and both scared stiff. Of each other. 'You've realised what this place was used for, of course.'

'Some kind of a meeting-place, it must have been. Or hide-out. For those Greek . . . That's why they called themselves that. The Mask of Zeus.'

He had crossed the floor and was standing on the edge of it now, looking down at it. Alcmena, a giantess, her huge thighs straddled, lifted. Procreating a hero. Dobie wasn't a hero. Just an ordinary chap, really, who was feeling the pressures build up too high for his liking. He stared down at the writhing interlocked figures and didn't turn round. Was that how it had been in the other room? *While she was being raped?* . . . The shapes and colours were swimming now before his eyes, were melting together. He wished that he could see a little more clearly. The sweat was running into his eyes, that was the trouble.

A reasonable man, yes. But a murderer. With a gun. That made it reasonable, in turn, for Dobie to feel scared. Being scared didn't prevent him from thinking, but as what he was thinking was that he should maybe have done a bit more thinking before getting himself into his present position of being alone with a murderer, with a gun, that didn't help very much. His thoughts seemed to be running round in circles. *That* wasn't reasonable. In fact it was crazy.

'They must have been all completely mad. Looking back on it. And yet, in another way quite logical. They brought everyone in the village down here at gunpoint and then they shot them. Everyone except the man they really wanted.'

'Uktu,' Dobie said. He found he was nodding his head in approval. Not of the action, of course. But of the logic.

'Uktu. Oh, he was *there*, of course. The Greeks knew he was there. They caught him with his pants down, as the saying goes. They caught him and they drove him back to Nicosia and they shot him and left him by the side of the road and it was just one of those things, you know? Bad luck. Or bad judgement. Or anyway . . . not a betrayal. No connection with this massacre here. All these people here, they just disappeared. But they didn't want Uktu to disappear. They wanted to show us all that Uktu was dead. They wanted to score a propaganda victory over us. And they did. They did.'

The voice was normal enough but seemed to be pitched several semitones higher than usual, so that it sounded almost like a woman's. That might be an acoustic effect, but there was something else rather strange about the intonation that couldn't have been caused by local conditions and which Dobie really didn't like at all. 'But the villagers knew that they'd caught him here.'

'Some of them did, anyway. So they all had to die. Because if we ever found out that Uktu had been taken in Alanici, we'd naturally have wondered how the Greeks knew that he was there. Somebody told them, of course. And there was only one person who could have done that.'

'*Tolga söyledi*,' Dobie said.

That was one Turkish phrase he was sure he would never forget.

'*Tolga söyledi*. Tolga told them. Yes.'

The voice seemed to have moved away, to have edged over towards Dobie's left, and there was a short pause before it spoke again. 'There should be a gas lamp here somewhere. Derya had a . . . Ah, yes. Here it is. I've only been down here once before, you know, and quite frankly I hoped never to have to come down here again.' Dobie heard the sharp scratch of a match, ludicrously loud in the water-dripping silence, the hiss of a gas jet and a moment later a brittle and golden light struck off the dark walls at his eyeballs, the stones of the mosaic instantly echoing its sudden brilliance. 'This place has a . . . I don't know . . . an aura . . . I haven't felt completely myself ever since. But then I'm *not* myself. I'm not the person I believed myself to be. No one is. It's just that this place makes you realise it.'

Dobie rubbed his stinging eyelids with his fingers. It only made them worse. 'It's hotter than you'd think,' he said foolishly. And dark, and deeper than any sea-dingle. But then this was Hades. It was supposed to be just like this.

'You see, the moment Derya showed me that room . . . and that writing . . . in one way I couldn't believe it, it was totally incredible . . . and in another way it was as though I'd always known it. Can you understand that? I can't. I mean, when I was a boy there may well have been things that I couldn't have understood, things that I may have noticed without ever really making anything of them, and then of course they sent me to England and that may have been why or at any rate one of the reasons so I never got to know him well; that's Uktu I'm talking about . . . ' Dobie turned at last and watched Cem Arkin lower the gas lamp to the floor and adjust the control lever, the hissing light shining full on the pale, abstracted face. 'I'm rambling a bit, aren't I? I suppose it's an idea I still haven't managed to come to terms with. Uktu and . . . ' His head turned slowly on its heavy neck till he was staring back towards the other room. 'And me not being who I thought I was. It's all so *bizarre*. You know what I mean?'

A wooden bench ran along the wall behind him. Dobie hadn't noticed it before. Cem sat down on it, propping the shotgun against his knee, his right hand gently caressing the barrel. Dobie kept his eyes fixed on that hand as he approached and seated himself alongside. He welcomed the chance to sit down. His legs, too, were tired and aching.

'They must have looked very alike. Being twin brothers.' He was aware that he was still talking foolishly, but that couldn't be helped. It seemed important that he should go on saying things, somehow, to keep that hand where it was, stroking the gun barrel. And away from the trigger.

'Oh, they did. Yes. They did. But they were very different, really. I mean, my father was, well . . . a schoolmaster. An academic. With all that the word implies. Very like me, in fact. The marriage was arranged, of course, so my mother's people must've thought he was due for a prosperous career

241

– though I'll bet they'd be staggered to see where he's got to today, if they were alive to see it. Which they're not. But Uktu, he was more a man of action, he was . . . glamorous, I suppose you'd have to say. Or what's that . . . Charisma. That's the word I was thinking of. He had *charisma*. In fact it got up my nose a bit, all that hero-worship. But at the same time, yes, it was exciting or *he* was and I felt that even then, so if my mother felt . . . or if she . . . Yes, but I can't bring myself to understand it. I keep telling myself I don't blame her. Or them. But I do.' He raised his eyes, fixing Dobie with a dispassionate level-eyed stare that seemed to be completely at odds with the undertone of desperation, or of something else, apparent in his voice. '*You* understand it, though. Or at least you guessed it. And yet you didn't know either of them. That's just not possible. Is it? *How* is it possible?'

Yes, Dobie thought, he'd need to know that. To prevent anyone else from making guesses in the future. In the future that it seems pretty obvious I haven't got. Yes, he'd want to know that. 'I suppose it was the necklace,' Dobie said.

'What necklace?'

'The one he must have given her. With the letter V as a pendant. V for Victory. Uktu. And for the rest, I'd have to say that Seymour told me about it. Or tried to. Amphitryon and Zeus . . . The same, but different. The human being and the god. He couldn't put it more directly than that. Either he didn't want to or he couldn't. Or a bit of each.'

'He couldn't. He still can't. Ever. Ever.'

'And Derya certainly can't. You were having an affair with her, I suppose? Off and on?'

'An affair? What a very *English* expression that is. But off and on . . . Yes. Yes. That describes it very adequately. In fact, that sums it up. Do we really have to talk about that as well?'

It was a shotgun all right. Single-barrelled. He had both hands on it now; the hands were large and capable and perfectly steady and looked to be well practised in the use of deadly weapons. If Cem reckoned that one barrel would

242

prove to be enough, he was almost certainly right. Dobie looked down at the torch still gripped a little too tightly in his own right hand and switched it off. It wasn't needed now.

Fiat lux. Cem would need light, of course, to do what he was going to do, but the lamp was on the far side of the bench, way out of Dobie's reach. 'You don't have to talk about anything,' Dobie said, 'if you don't want to.'

'Because you know it all already, right? You're rather a maddening fellow, Dobie. But you have to know that, too. You seem to be such a harmless chap and in reality you're about as harmless as a king cobra in a lucky dip. That's why I'm going to have to deal with you accordingly.'

'As with the female of the species?'

'Oh, no. No nice soft pillows for Professor Dobie. No, I'm going to blow your fucking head off. And,' Cem Arkin said, 'if you nod your head wisely and say, "I *know*," just once more, then I'm going to get really angry.'

'There's no need for that, I hope,' Dobie said.

Outside, the sun was setting behind the Karpaz mountains. It was difficult to see what could stop it, or why anyone should want to. Professor Berry pressed Cem Arkin's doorbell for a third time before turning sadly away.

Professor Berry was a reasonable man. He could, in other words, draw logical inferences from established facts. If nobody answered Cem Arkin's doorbell when somebody rang it, the inference might be drawn that Cem Arkin was out. The next step would naturally be to seek further confirmation of this hypothesis. Standing at the gate, Berry Berry saw that Hillyer was approaching, walking-stick in hand, returning no doubt from his evening constitutional. 'Have you seem Cem anywhere?'

Hillyer halted, blinking uncertainly in the fading light. 'I saw him go out a couple of hours ago. In his car.'

'Oh,' Berry Berry said. 'Indeed.'

'Maybe gone to shoot a pigeon or two. He had his gun with him, anyway.'

243

Berry Berry found this puzzling. 'That's very strange. I'd arranged to call on him at this hour. It's not like Cem to forget an appointment.'

'Well, he should be getting back any moment now.'

'What makes you think so?'

'It's getting dark,' Hillyer explained patiently. 'You can't shoot pigeons in the dark. Or anything else, for that matter.'

'Ah. Quite so. That's true. Well,' Berry Berry said, turning away, 'in that case I'll try to catch him later.'

Hillyer watched him march away. Berry Berry, he thought, was a strange fellow, but then he'd long since come to the conclusion that all these Cyps were loopy. It was nice to think that he had a Britisher as a next-door neighbour. But then he wasn't altogether sure about Dobie, either.

Who, to add to his other troubles, now had a headache.

'There's no need for that, I hope,' he heard himself saying. Curiously, his own voice seemed to have risen a pitch or two, though he wasn't speaking loudly. 'After all, there are things that *you* still want to know. Or so I imagine.'

'Yes. There was some kind of a map, I suppose. It'll have to be destroyed. Where is it?'

'Not a map. A set of computations. On a mini-disc.'

'I looked everywhere. I couldn't find anything. Then later I thought that Seymour might have burnt it with the rest of his stuff. A mini-disc . . . where is it?'

'In my jacket pocket. Up there.'

'That's all right then.' Cem, too, was speaking softly now, almost gently. 'Except . . . You worry me, Dobie.'

'Why?'

'Because there are times when it's politic to lie and this is one of them. And yet you're telling me the truth. I know you are.'

'Of course it's all in that book that Seymour wrote.'

'What is?'

'About the mosaic. He got most of it from Kaya, apparently. And some of it from Derya. She was running the computations for Kaya, but when something came up that she thought was *really* interesting . . . she held it back. It's on the disc all right, but it's encoded. So you see—'

'Yes, that's what she was looking for in the first place. The mosaic. Or so she told me. Of course it must always have been underground, this . . . temple or whatever it is. They celebrated things here. Mysteries and I don't know what. Fertility rites and all that. He had it on the brain, all that mythology stuff, Seymour did. But we take it all for granted, here on the island. It's no big deal.'

'A massacre is,' Dobie said.

'Well, the Greeks have made progress, I suppose. Like everyone else.'

'What did Derya do, exactly?'

'You mean, when she found . . . *that*?' He didn't mean the mosaic.

'Yes.'

Cem shrugged. He seemed to have very few un-British gestures, but this was one of them. 'She read the message. She knew what it meant. They came to my office and she told me about it. That handbag you saw in there, my mother's handbag . . . There was a paper in it, a document. She showed it to me as proof. I couldn't . . . It wasn't enough. I wanted to see for myself. So they brought me down here. Yes. I saw.'

The wooden bench was becoming uncomfortably hard and Dobie's headache was getting worse and worse. Yet he had to keep on talking, and to keep Cem talking. Easily and affably. It hardly seemed worth the effort involved, but he had to because he had to. No other reason. He said, 'There would have been something that she wanted, I expect.'

'She had what she wanted from that moment on. Power.'

'Then she'd want a way in which to exercise it.'

'Let's say,' Cem said glumly, 'she made of it a future threat. Not against me. Against my father. Or you could even say against the whole bloody republic. Because it'd be nothing short of a national disaster if my father were to be discredited at this stage. He's done so much for us the people here would

245

forgive him almost anything. But not *that*. Betraying Uktu to
the Greeks. Informing on his brother. It'd take us all back to
1974 again and this time we wouldn't even feel able to trust
each other. Derya knew all that. Of course she knew it.'

'And Seymour? Did *he* know it?'

'Seymour? Look, we were sitting here on this bench just
as you and I are sitting here now. And he was listening to
us talking. But like he *wasn't* listening. Like he couldn't
understand Turkish – which in fact he can, well enough.
Then he walked out. He knew what she was up to but he
couldn't do anything to stop it, was the way I saw it.'

'So *you* had to stop it.'

'Yes.'

'Did he know that you meant to?'

'I think so. Yes. But he couldn't do anything to stop *that*,
either. Or maybe he didn't want to. She had him blocked
every which way, you know. Blocked in his work. Blocked
in his sex life. I don't know how she did it. She had the
power, that was all. So she exercised it. Kept him on those
drugs he used, poor sod. She had him riddled right through
with guilt, like with . . . machine-gun bullets. It's crazy, *she*
never felt any guilt, not at having it off with me or those soldier
boyfriends of hers or anyone else or for anything at all; if she
had she might have realised what it was I had to do, but no,
it didn't ever *occur* to her . . . But Seymour . . . Yes, well,
Seymour . . . '

It was starting to happen, whatever it was that Dobie had
been waiting for – and perhaps Cem Arkin, too. Dobie looked
away from the gun and down at Cem's booted feet, at the thick
smears of grey mud coating the heels and insteps. Dobie's
own shoes were also bedaubed with it. Here in Hades there
was always moisture, the water seeping down from the walls
and into the earth, forming here and there a dark film of
gluey mud.

'He came here with us but he didn't know, the way, he
didn't have the map, otherwise, don't you see? I'd have had
to kill him, too. But I didn't, I couldn't. He was so high on

his goddam drugs that night, I didn't think he'd be in touch
with reality until the morning. Derya didn't think he would.
He wasn't supposed to. He never had the times before, when
I'd spent the night in her room. Shit,' Cem said, 'I had to
do it, I *had* to. There wasn't any choice. Any other way out.
None at all.'

'What was it she wanted?'

'I've told you. She wanted . . . Oh, she wanted Berry Berry's job for a start. She wanted money. Prestige. Everything.
But chiefly she wanted me . . . where she'd got Seymour. She
wanted to use my father's guilt the way she'd used Seymour's.
Maybe I saved Seymour, too – had you thought of that? He
may be able to get back on top with . . . proper medical
attention. That's what he *needs*, you know. What Seymour
needs. He's a junkie all right but he's crazy like a coot on
top of it. I mean it's *genuine*. His mind gave way. His mind
is . . . You know how it happened? You think you know it all,
don't you, Dobie? Well, he came back. That's what happened.
He listened like he wasn't listening and walked away and then
he came back – when I was having her. You're going to say
I'm crazy, too, but when she . . . when she . . . After I'd seen
what I had to see and we talked about it, look, it was so damned
hot and we were sweating and she took her clothes off and I had
her right down there on that . . . on that . . . And you know
what he *said*? Standing over by that archway, looking down at
us? "Why don't you take that mask off?" he said. And then
he went away again. Mask, what mask? I wasn't wearing any
mask, I wasn't wearing . . . But later on, I thought, perhaps
there was something that . . . something that made me look
different to the kind of person I really am because I'm not the
kind of person who does things like that, so OK . . . A mask,
if you like . . . And perhaps the men who raped my mother
and killed her, shot Uktu and all those other people, perhaps
they weren't really that kind of person either, you know what
I mean? Like something that comes down and hides your real
face, the mask, you see? . . . of Zeus . . . '

It had happened all right. Dobie sat very still. It was very

247

hot and they were both sweating, too, but Dobie could feel something very cold in the pit of his stomach and he wondered what it was. 'It's as good an explanation as any other. Except that it raises another question.'

'What question?'

'*Did* you take it off? Or are you wearing it now?'

Once again that level-eyed gaze, disconcertingly like that of the woman in the photograph, took him in, enveloped him, discarded him. 'A *maddening* fellow,' Cem said. 'He just sits there and lets me talk and talk. And then asks me what I'm going to . . . What do you want, Dobie? I mean, what are *your* terms? You want me to confess or something, like Seymour did? And how the hell can I do that without explaining everything that happened? All this? Or do you want me to say it was a crime of passion? That I climbed into her room and . . . Who's about to believe a story like *that*?'

'I think I might,' Dobie said.

The telephone in Dobie's house went on ringing.

It was dark in the house and nobody answered the call. Dobie was out.

The telephone rang a few more times and then stopped. In Cardiff, Kate put down the receiver and stared for a while at the circle of numbers on the dial. No. She was sure that she'd dialled the right number.

Dobie had to be out. That was all.

'Fuck you, Dobie.'

'You're rationalising it a bit too bloody much. You loved her all right. You must have done. Being a god's next door to being a machine, and you're not like that. You're Cem Arkin.'

'I'm Tolga Arkin's son.'

'But—'

'And I'm all Tolga Arkin's got. I'm his only son. His brother's dead and his wife's dead and he killed them both and *that* was a crime of passion if ever there was one, a crime of . . . jealousy . . . hatred . . . I don't know. But if anything

248

happened to me now, it'd destroy him. No, I'm not Zeus, I've
got no power at all but I've got responsibility and I'm sick
and tired of it. Confessing? What good would that do? Me
or anyone? You're just not thinking straight, Dobie, you're
thinking in terms of all those . . . British things, fair play and
justice and all that codswallop. The criminal being brought to
book and paying the penalty. That's fiction, Dobie – the sort
of thing that Seymour writes. This is Cyprus, this is real life,
it just doesn't work out like that.'

'So you have to put the mask on again, after all.'

'If I have to,' Cem said, 'I have to.'

'Because of Derya. Because she has you where she wanted
you. Shot through with guilt, just like Seymour. *That's* what
you really have to hide.'

After a while, Cem Arkin said, 'I suppose that's true.'

'Only you can see that clearly and he couldn't.'

A drop of sweat fell from Cem's forehead. It splashed on
the floor. The sound it made was audible. Dobie tried to ease
the pain in his stomach by leaning forwards a little on the
bench. It didn't help.

Cem said, 'All right. I'm not a god. And you're not a drug
addict or a blackmailer. We're both human beings and I'm
prepared to trust you.'

'You can't do that.'

'Why not?'

'Let's say that I don't see how you can possibly *know* that
you can.'

'Ah,' Cem said. 'I trust the human being. Not the logician.'

'The trouble is you're up against what mathematicians call
the tontine.'

'What's that?'

'In the present case, you can take it to mean that a secret is
safe when it's known to one person and one person only.'

'In the present case, to the person who walks out of this
dump alive.'

'Yes,' Dobie said.

'And I'm the one with the gun.'

'Which makes it all very simple.'

'But *will* it be safe?'

'Yes,' Dobie said.

The eyes turned towards Dobie once again and this time didn't discard him.

'I shouldn't have put my hand in, should I?'

'Put your hand where?'

'Into the lucky dip.'

Dobie switched his torch on. 'I'll be going now,' he said.

His knees cracked noisily as he stood up and started to walk away. Or not so much to walk away as to move one foot and then the other, each in turn; something that required immense, indeed total concentration. He couldn't think about anything else. Because he knew that if he paused for so much as a moment, the gun now pointed at his retreating back would make a very loud noise and after that he wouldn't be hearing any others.

It's remarkably hard, he thought, to keep your balance when walking steadily forwards. To hold yourself upright as one muddied shoe swings past the other and the rearward ankle starts to flex. The ankle and then the toes. Moving out of sharp white light and into darkness. Keeping the torch beam pointing straight ahead. A great black shadow dancing up and down on the wall in front; why dancing? *He* wasn't dancing. He was walking, very slowly. And as steadily as he could. Breathing very slowly and very deeply, as there didn't seem to be much air about the place right now. The noise when it came was very loud indeed, seeming to pulverise both the air and the quivering darkess and to hammer at his eardrums, and when it came he *did* lose his balance, his right knee jerking uncontrollably and throwing his body sideways against the wall of the archway . . . He pressed his hands against the cold damp stone surface, holding himself stiffly erect as the echoes of the shotgun blast reverberated round and round the chamber. Nasty things at close range, shotguns. He didn't want to turn round.

250

But he knew that he'd have to.

When he did, he saw the body sprawled out with the shotgun lying beside it and with its face turned away towards the inner room. Rather luckily, Dobie thought, since Cem did indeed seem to have very nearly blown his fucking head off. His shoulders rested on the edge of the mosaic where the subtle blues and blacks of the faceted stones were splashed with stains of a glistening red. The great masked figure, poised to thrust, stared towards Dobie inimically, its empty face spattered with other drops of blood. Dobie turned again and went on through the archway, moving more quickly now, the torch beam leaping wildly up and down; not only his hand but his whole body was shaking. All logical, he told himself. The only remaining alternative. Though mathematical, mathematical . . . mathematical . . .

He knew that he was going to be sick.

He was.

He collected his jacket and went back to his car. A fine warm starry night, with plenty of fresh air coming in from the sea. Dobie gulped in lots of it.

The torchlight showed him Cem's car, half hidden in the bushes some ten yards behind his own.

Tomorrow, perhaps, the search parties would go out. They'd find Cem's car, sooner or later. But of course they wouldn't find Cem.

Not ever.

'Kate,' Dobie said. 'You're a doctor.'

'I know.'

'No, listen. Did you ever . . . Did you ever talk anyone out of committing suicide?'

A pause. 'I like to think I may have done. Once or twice. Why?'

'Because I've just done exactly the opposite.'

'Oh.'

Silence. Over a thousand miles of space.

251

'You can't feel too good about it.'

'I don't. Kate?'

'Yes?'

'Can you come?'

'Yes,' Kate said. 'If you need me.'

'I do.'

'Then I'll get the next plane out.'

'I don't think,' Dobie said, 'I'm going to be scared of flying any more. And everything else is going to be all right, too. You know . . . You and me. Jenny. Everything. Whatever it is I had, I'm cured of it.'

'Cyprus must suit you.'

'It's a fine warm starry night,' Dobie said. 'You'll like it when you get here.'

'Meantime . . . '

'Yes?'

'Those pills I put in your travel bag. Take a couple of them. *Now*.'

'What'll they do?'

'You'll get some sleep.'

'Yes,' Dobie said. 'That'd be nice.'

Cem wouldn't need any pills. Cem would be sleeping soundly, sleeping there below, sleeping the big sleep – hadn't they called it that in the days when such acts of violence had been allowed a comfortingly rhetorical conclusion? – resting with Sabiha and all the others, sharing in a dark seclusion that might last for centuries or even for ever, since Dobie of course intended to keep his part of the unspoken bargain and to take a share, also, in their silence, if in nothing else. Recalling now that final macabre conversation in which so much had been said and so very much more had been left unsaid, Dobie realised that he'd never be able even to guess what the odds against him had truly been when in the end he'd stood up and walked away, nor what had finally tilted the balance away from the logical fifty-fifty when Cem had

252

raised the gun. So he couldn't decide if he had been brave, or very stupid, or neither.

He was getting tired, anyway, of sitting there in the dark. He leaned forwards in his armchair and turned on the table lamp. On the wall directly in front of him the photograph of a dead girl glowed into life again, though of course it didn't really. It was a photograph. That was all.

Guilt, Dobie thought. So many people find it hard to live with. Perhaps he should have learnt from Derya way back, when he'd had the chance. No morals, no sense of guilt, a selfishness that bordered on self-adoration; it was easy for Derya. There'd always been others around to pick up the tab for her. Seymour, perhaps, had wanted to learn from her, had tried to learn and had failed. Even for the Greeks and the Romans, the worship of beauty and of youthful vitality hadn't been quite enough. Because in the long run, it isn't.

Derya was sleeping too now, sleeping with but apart from the others in a tree-shaded cemetery somewhere in Famagusta. And other people had picked up the tab again and done all the wheeler-dealing and Seymour would be given at least as good a chance of returning to life as Dobie had given himself, down there in those other depths. Probably better. In England there'd be other people, again, who'd help him to kick the habit. Not the drug habit, though that no doubt was bad. But the guilt habit. *L'honte d'être homme.* Which was worse.

As Dobie knew.

Looking at the photograph, he suddenly recollected his old blue towelling wrap, long since discarded. Derya had had it around her bare shoulders when she'd come in from the bathroom that night was it five? six? years ago, entering the horrible airport hotel bedroom where he'd had to stay before catching the early morning redeye to the States. Then she'd let it fall. Fifty-fifty? Nothing like that. Not one chance in a hundred for poor old Dobie. Though, again, he'd tried.

'Derya, I, I, I . . . I don't go to bed with my students, I mean not as a rule . . . '

253

'Well, you're going to bed with *this* one. Move over.'

Calm. Self-assured. Full of confidence. Of course, she'd had every reason to be so.

'But it's, don't you see I . . . '

'Don't be silly, Dobie. I've done a bloody good thesis an' you know it. That's got nothin' to do with it. I *like* you.'

'I like you too, Derya. Very much.'

'That's OK then. Isn't it? *There* . . . You see? . . . Mmmmmmm . . . '

Voices in the memory. Fading into silence, into darkness.

Dobie wondered if Cem had ever heard those two quiet voices. Derya wouldn't have told him about them . . . but yes, he'd have heard them. He'd have known. And maybe that knowledge had tipped the scale the tiniest fraction as he'd come to his last decision. Cem had known. And Seymour, too. All along, an unadmitted bond between the three of them that explained some things you couldn't explain otherwise.

While other things still seemed very strange. All those people, for example, the villagers of Alanici now lying underground, and Cem's mother . . . they'd have had countless mourners. Hundreds had wept for them, and no doubt still did on occasion. And there'd be many on the island who'd mourn for Cem Arkin, for his sudden and inexplicable passing. But nobody, as it seemed, had been prepared to shed a tear for Derya, any more than they had for Jenny. For Derya, the bitch goddess, with her devouring ambitions. For Derya, that other pagan deity. For Aphrodite. Dobie stood up and took down the photograph. He placed it face downwards on the table and then took off his glasses.

There was still something the matter with his eyes. They seemed to be wet.